HIGH TIDE

HAL ALPIAR

©2013
Nightengale Press
A Nightengale Media LLC Company

HIGH TIDE

For information about Nightengale Press,
please visit nightengalepublishing.com.
Email: publisher@nightengalepress.com
or send a letter to:
Nightengale Press
370 S. Lowe Avenue, Suite A-122
Cookeville, Tennessee

Library of Congress Cataloging-in-Publication Data

Alpiar, Hal,
HIGH TIDE/ Hal Alpiar
ISBN 13: 978-1-935993-47-6
Fiction, Mystery Thriller

Copyright Registered: 2013
First Published by Nightengale Press in the USA

May 2013

10 9 8 7 6 5 4 3 2 1

Printed in the USA and the UK

For Kathy

*It is with deep love, gratefulness,
and the embedded images of
her laughing eyes, that I dedicate
this writing to Kathy (Marshall) Alpiar.*

*My loving wife, my best friend,
and my daily business partner
for twenty-five years.*

*After a courageous health battle,
wielding humor as her sword, Kathy
passed away quietly on March 9, 2012.*

*Without her help and encouragement
—and the good graces of God—
this book would not have been possible.*

HIGH TIDE

Chapter 1

STORMTREK

Mobster-muscled into the muck of Jersey Shore wetlands in the middle of the night, Professor Rick Maddigan treks headlong into approaching storm gusts and freezing drizzle.

He searches.

JP's words keep creeping in. "I wish you wouldn't be doing this, Rick. It scares me that something worse will come of it. They're just *using* you! I mean, you really think they'd follow through on their threats? And you think the College would believe them?"

He remembers her eyes welling with tears. The ticking of the kitchen clock filled the room. She stood motionless.

"I know," he said.

She wrapped her arms across her chest and spun defiantly sideways to stare out the window, her boyish figure silhouetted against the reflection. He inched toward the door.

"You're right about what you said, Green Eyes, but I have to do this," he begged, hands outstretched, raising one eyebrow. "Don't you get that?"

Almost imperceptibly, she nodded.

Slam ordered him to find and deliver a quarter-size computer chip embedded in a dead, plastic-bagged, hundred-pound Loggerhead turtle. The corpse, Slam said, is cinderblock-anchored in the mud, somewhere in the vast outreaches of the freezing low-tide coastal swamp.

Look at this mess I'm in. I did it to myself! Am I ever going to learn to keep my big mouth shut?

He thumps his gloves together.

Stress. He visualizes the dazed, Cheshire-cat-smiling delivery guys leaning down into a sample line of coke, examining the ounce of dope for seeds and twigs, eyes scanning the parking lot, folded cash fanned and pocketed in a blink, smoked car windows slithering closed, departing slowly while checking rearview mirrors...exhaling.

By the time Maddigan finally figured out that the little zip-locs of marijuana were coming from a mob member who knew the buyer was Seaport College Professor of the Year—it was too late. He had already said too much.

Near blinded by the heavy drizzle and no-chance-of-stars night, Maddigan stops to rest.

To locate the creature's body, Slam told him, he had to align himself with some vaguely calibrated point across the bay, opposite the distant fog-enwreathed Atlantic City skyline (which he can now scarcely see), and to count steps.

He has been counting.

He starts up again. Ocean-driven bayfront waves slap the shoreline to his left.

He slogs his way through the easternmost sprawl of this desolate expanse of gook, his tracks flooding with sucking sounds almost as fast as he lifts each foot.

Eleven hundred and eight steps, eleven hundred nine...

Marshlands choke off the jutting, pot-holed, dirt and blacktop patchwork that locals call 7-Bridges Road. It spans the full length of the narrow seven-mile-long peninsula.

He remembers her fine, straight, shoulder-length black hair tucked securely behind her elfish ears, her trademark dimple fully dissolved.

Clamped, clenched jaw. It was a look he'd seen before: just a gasping breath or two from streaming tears. It was clear that his failure to follow her intuition created, for her, a sense of betrayal. He hated this. Why wouldn't she just accept that he was doing this for her?

"That's why they've—well, you know—they, they've got me trapped with this blackmail thing, and, and I—I can't risk them drawing you into it now too."

He gestured dismissively, his voice trailing off, "Look, I...I *love you*, dammit!"

He stepped out, and closed the door quietly behind him. The doorjamb click followed him to the driveway.

Biting blustery drizzle. His eyes asquint. Dizzy. Cold sweat. His pulse a drumbeat. He surges on across blankets of ice-slick reeds, scruffy clumps of seaweed and crackling wafer thin slivers of frozen tidewater leavings.

The cold dark silence rings in his ears like some distant alarm ... a shrill steady buzz that swallows whole the shoreline sounds and far-away roar of ocean waves. Muck slithers through the last unclogged treads of his mud-caked boots.

His breath, a diminishing trail of puffs above and behind his head, is absorbed into the billowing wall of fog.

From far across the bay, muffled blurs of light brushstroke the visual cacophony of a rooftop skyline—the size of a book of spent match heads from this distance.

Somewhere ahead, somewhere in the ebb tide mud, lays the heavily-shelled object of his mission.

Eleven hundred thirty-five, eleven hundred thirty-six, eleven hun...

The young professor is beginning to feel frantic. He aches to be over and done with delivering the goods and putting this mission behind him.

"Either locate and lug back the bagged corpse of the giant Loggerhead turtle—shell it, dismember it, and find the embedded microchip—or else!" he was warned convincingly by Solamente's thugs.

Slam and the other henchmen of reputed mob boss "Apple" Solamente gave Maddigan little choice when they threatened to end his career by exposing his marijuana habit (the professor's face pushed to the wall, knife blade to his neck) unless he obliged their demands to accept what they called the *Turtle Orders*.

Maddigan stops to clear his glasses with swipes of his wool glove cuff, but streaks the lenses instead like a bad windshield wiper. His watch face glows: 2:37AM 2·26·81. Again, he remembers her words: "It scares me something worse will come of it."

Eleven hundred fifty...and two-freakin'-thirty-seven in the morning—Shit!

He is forced to rely on muted moonglow—a flashlight would risk drawing attention. Such precaution though would probably not matter much in this fog, or godforsaken time and place. Even if by some remote chance he might be seen, an observer, watching a blackened silhouette of his five-foot-ten frame drag itself forward in this ominous setting, would surely think him a zombie mirage.

Maddigan's ears attune themselves to the squish-squash sounds and snapping crackles of ice that rise abruptly beneath him. Like a snake slithering from its skin, he starts to shed the trancelike state gradually enveloping him in the monotony of counting his steps.

He is still frazzled, but begins to feel more alert. The drizzle turning rapidly to rain hasn't helped his awakening. *Another stupid move,* he chastises himself, *whatever made me think weather wouldn't be a factor at this time of year? Winter weather is always a factor here.*

Eleven hundred and sixty-one...

"Welcome to the Jersey Shore!"

The tourism jingle bippity-bops through his mind. He pictures JP singing it as she dances seductively above him on the bed. A smile pokes its way through his frost-tipped beard, but quickly dissolves as he pushes the image aside or, as he likes to say, changes the station...

sixty-three, -four, sixty-five...

He has no idea what he'll do when he finally gets the turtle, he realizes. Yes, cut the cinder block connecting rope, but how thick is the bag it's in? What if it's covered with blood or some kind of turtle goop? What if it's not where he was told, or heavier than they said? He felt stupid for not even asking, but that knife against his neck, and the slurred threats that were spit into his ear, overwhelmed his ability to think clearly.

Eleven hundred and sixty-six steps, sixty-seven...

He recalls his last two telephone questions about Solamente's Turtle Orders, and the jarring answers he got from Slam, the gangster boss's go-between:

"And what do you expect me to do with the leftover parts?" Maddigan asked.

"Eat 'em, Teach! Have a freakin' barbeque! Use 'em fer fish bait! Make soup! Stick 'em in yer ear! What the hell do I care? Just don't get anything traced back, an' keep yer mouth shut, or —remember— Mr. College President finds out dat yer a pothead, got it?"

Whispering weakly into the phone, he answers the question with a question: "What's so important on this embedded microchip you guys want?"

"Curiosity kilt da cat! Stop askin' stupid questions and just do the damn job!" Click.

Chapter 2

BODY BAG

Eleven hundred sixty eight steps...

And cutting the thing up to find this microchip? I'm a damn business professor, for crying out loud, not some biology geek! He sets his right foot down, lifting his left foot from the grasping slop beneath him.

Energy in! he says to himself as he inhales. *Tension out!* he says as he exhales. With the disorientation of feeling like he's going through an ice-water-and-scrub-brush carwash without a car, the *Energy/Tension* chanting caters to his consciousness.

Raising his head to the wind, he scans what the fog lets him see of the far-off buildings—vague specks, corona-cloaked blurs of dusted orange and gold. Angry low-tide waves collide with wetland bulwarks of mud to sling stinging salt spray high into the wind and whipping across his face. Icy blasts drive the rain sideways into his back.

Eleven hundred...

To survive the career he loves, he has resigned himself to the fact that this ordeal is simply the price he must pay for being a loudmouth when he should have just shut up. Do the turtle thing or lose the job. So "turtle" it is. Losing his job would be catastrophic. His two "Professor-of-the-Year" awards plus any chance of teaching again would be flushed away with one jerk of the handle.

Eleven hundred seventy-one... Fatigue barber-polls its way up his legs.

Having traded his double-barrel-powered, fat-salaried New York advertising career, and his long-term friendships and dream home for an $11,000 faculty appointment, the stakes were already inflated.

None of his friends or associates could believe he'd given it all up to teach at a Podunk little tourist town college with the academic reputation of a snail. But none of them knew what Maddigan stood to gain by escaping the existence he detested, and by finding a life where he could thrive.

Being able to combine his business training and on-the-job experience with his independent studies in psychotherapy, represented a challenging opportunity. He would pioneer teaching a unique blend of self-esteem and communication skill development to Seaport's unworldly business students. That struck him as having real redeeming value. It trumped all the acclaim bestowed upon him for the high-profile advertising campaigns that his conscience resented having ever created for guns, butter, hair dye...hot dogs.

None of his New York cronies could appreciate his surrender of such a successful Madison Avenue career. His decisions, to them, were enigmatic to say the least. Of course those people had no way of knowing how his focus now on teaching, counseling, campus impact and human development—instead of on money—could be so fulfilling. And the whole student girlfriend deal—well, that was another matter altogether.

They would never understand his needs to override the mind-consuming distractions of a spiteful failed marriage. On top of that, and that alone is a lot, Maddigan's newfound career commitments also eased his parental heartaches. His preoccupation with excelling as a teacher had a way of distracting his frantic feelings over his ex-wife's ongoing efforts to abort his communications efforts with his children. How devastating to him her vindictiveness became, misguiding the children from six states away.

Eleven hundred and seventy-nine...

But getting out of the fast lane has been worth it all. Lifelong teaching dreams stand fulfilled. He feels embraced by the campus every time he sets foot on the mall walkway, and is rewarded daily with the "Aha's" he provokes in his classes. Sure, a handful of his tenured and entrenched fellow teachers resent his New York brashness. They call him a "rumbling freight train"—intruding into their sluggish, provincial existences. Yet his unabashed enthusiasm, commitment, and entrepreneurial zeal have been mostly contagious, especially with his students.

Eleven hundred eighty-three, four...

Even if he could get back behind a desk, Maddigan knows he'd have to do some serious tap-dancing to avoid New York City drug charges and a prison visit. The thought shivers through him. He knows now he should never have stirred the pot to begin with.

The rain picks up. *Energy in! Tension out!* He continues counting out loud, each planted step pulling the next forward. He remembers Slam's instructions: "It's in a black plastic bag our boat dumped at high tide. You hafta cut the cinderblock ropes, then get the body to yer car and take it home. Do the autopsy gut job and find the implanted chip..."

Maddigan stares hard at the ground, trying to find his way, gain some perspective.

Find the implanted chip...

But there is only the ground. Steadily worsening weather has left him no horizon, no shoreline, no marina, no scrub pines, no anything. Just black. And the ground. Just wet. And the cold. And the wind...

hundred and ninety-five, eleven...

He pictures his loathsome colleagues being able to see him here suck-stepping through sludge. Wouldn't they just love to have a bizarre scene like this to reinforce their animosities toward him? Accusations would whiz across campus. He could see them gathering "facts" then running off to the board, the deans, and President Stafford.

He steps in a slop hole. His knees buckle. Stumbling forward, he catches himself.

Even with his wool knit hat pulled down tight, his face and ears still sting. He tugs his collar. The freezing rain has now become a downpour.

...hundred and ninety-six steps...

If the weather controls his brain, he knows he'll never survive. But thoughts of his career convictions make it, as he liked to say, to his mind's "front burner."

Coming from the business world as he has, instead of academia as his colleagues have, sets up clashing visions of what students should and shouldn't learn, how teachers should and shouldn't behave. Maddigan knows his views of coursework as a means to the end are not widely shared in faculty ranks. He believes most "career professors" to be pompous asses, more concerned with tenure than with teaching. The gap widens at every turn, every semester.

Twelve hundred. Twelve hundred and one, twelve hun... Find the implanted chip...

How close is he getting?

Imagining that coven of English faculty witches for the nth time, he wonders again how much they would revel in unearthing some grounds to condemn him.

He coughs into the weeds. Aware his focus is once more beginning to fade, he slugs his glove to the side of his head: *Shut up, Maddigan! Energy in! Tension out! You teach students not to be judgmental! Stop wasting time and energy. Damn wind, rain—mud!*

He presses on, reconstructing events that led him to this point of no return. It started in his first class. No, it was after class. But that was just the call that got him here now. There was more. So much more. And fear alone is what seems to be fueling the internal engine that keeps him lurching onward.

Twelve hundred six…

Every second or third raindrop, it seems, is an ice pellet. His trail bike, with its attached wheeled storage box is stashed a mile back under a sprawling stubble of scrub pines alongside the road. Another deep breath. He sneezes.

Energy in! Tension out!

He checks over his shoulder for any sign of light, but gets just dark outlines of gray shadows against black sky. He grits his teeth, tugs his collar, blows in his gloves and drags himself on through the mud, which is now sputtering its way above his ankles and almost into his boots.

Twelve hundred and fifteen steps, sixteen…no, wait! Is it seventeen? Shit! It's twelve hundred and SIXteen…

Six miles back past where he left the trail bike, hidden in the pitch dark labyrinth of winter-dry-docked boats scattered around the

Gwyneth Bay Marina parking lot, his canvas-top Jeep is tucked into the shadow of his pedestal-propped-up thirty-eight-foot cabin cruiser, the *Here & Now*. The boat is his and JP's three-season live-aboard.

He'll have to haul the turtle body, that he's yet to discover, to the bike and trailer, and then peddle it all the way back to his Jeep. Maddigan knows his plans to not be seen are overkill, but now, facing the enormity of the actual physical task, and compounded by the storm, he wishes he hadn't parked so far away.

Except for the Jeep, his boat, meager monthly paychecks, divorce and custody decrees, piles of attorney bills, and a bunch of advertising awards, many would be startled to learn that he has little to show for his before-Seaport and before-JP life.

Waves race frantically along the low tide shoreline fifty feet to his left.

Find the implanted chip...

He starts counting again.

Dear Jesus, what a mess I'm in!

His face and fingertips feel numb. His back muscles are beginning to burn, and twitch sporadically. His eyes tear up at the corners.

"Listen, Green Eyes," he had said to JP the night before, "I'm going to need you once I get the bag back here and start slicing that baby up. It won't be pretty. Can you do it?" He sat, watched, and waited.

She picked up a joint off the dresser, lighted it, inhaled, and handed it to him as she pulled her t-shirt over her head. Except to work, she never wore a bra, which pleased him immensely. She exhaled and smiled her eyes into devious-looking slits.

"Professor, I can do just about anything except maybe shoulder a body and carry it through the swamp. Anyway, your wish is, you know. So..." She slithered around the foot of the bed and spilled into his lap, kissing his neck as he inhaled.

Again he slips but catches himself. *Where the hell is the damn thing? I thought he said twelve hundred and twenty-five; maybe it was twelve hundred and thirty-five...or was it fifty-three...?* He struggles to stay focused. *Energy in! Tension out! Twelve hundred and thirty-two, twelve hundred and thirty-three...twelve hun...* He kicks a rock. *No, it's not a rock. Oh, my God! Finally!* He stumbles and nearly trips in the mud puddle. He squats and surveys the dull black bundle, shivering at the thought of what's to come.

Cold blasts of wind and heavy rain snap him to attention. Like a wet dog, he shakes. He grunts as he stoops and bear-hugs the bagged corpse. He wobbles and nearly passes out from the exertion of pulling it from the mud. Then, in one final burst of what little energy remains in his arms and legs and lungs, he hefts it up and over his shoulder. His feet stutter and slide. Eyes half shut, clothes plastered to his skin, the now relentless rain and unforgiving onshore winds force his face to the cold wet bag.

Flying ice crystals rattle off the plastic like fistfuls of pebbles being hurled one after the other. No rhythm. No grace periods. Steady but erratic layers of *tat-tat-tat-tat-tat-tat-tat-tat-tat-tat*, like so many apostrophes, follow each panting groan.

Between blinks, he can make out just enough of his backward footprints. The dark vacuum of space has swallowed up even the smothering outline of the scrub pines. A fog-swaddled moon floated eerily by somewhere above the horizontal sheets of rain.

The acid climbs inside his throat. He gags and fights off the choking and a new wave of nausea. He doesn't stop to wipe his eyes and shake the mud from his gloves for fear of losing his glasses, or never being able to pick the body back up again, or both. A leg, it seems to him, is somehow flopping loose inside the bag. It hangs limply over his right shoulder where it thunks against his chest and rib cage.

Oh dear Lord! What next?

Chapter 3

CHALKBOARD

"Okay, people, let's settle down. My name is..." he chalks it on the board in rapid, assertive, near-perfect lettering, "...Rick Maddigan." Tiny flakes of chalk fly off as he dots each "i" and implants the final "n" onto the center section of green slate board that wraps around the room. He turns to face the class. Yellow and white chalk dust blotch his hands, elbow patches, and the right front pocket of his jeans. A shock of white to the right of his bearded chin looks like his jaw was hit by a tennis ball that had just bounced off the foul line.

"I'm a professor of management and business psychology," he says, almost apologetically, as he removes his Greek fisherman's cap and tosses it against the grainy dark leather mailbag he uses for a briefcase. A watermelon seed-sized marijuana leaf that's pinned to the cap brim blinks a silver glint in the process. He gives a little backwards hop up onto his desk and slides himself back, facing the class, legs dangling. "But Rick is my name, so please just call me Rick." Some murmurs and raised eyebrows. He leans forward and strokes his beard.

"I don't like brownnosers, by the way, so calling me 'Rick' doesn't entitle you to cozy up to me or think we're going to be partying together. It simply means we can dispense with the bullshit titles and get on with the coursework." He says it good-naturedly enough to prompt a smattering of chuckles.

Three students, though, seem to snap their heads back at the word "bullshit." Two are goody-two-shoes-looking females with parted pageboy haircuts. Their starched white man-tailored shirts are tucked neatly into unflatteringly long drab skirts. They sport matching black patent leather flats with gold buckles. In the fashion statement sea of denim, velour, paisley, tie-dye, sunflowers, loafers, high-tech sneakers, short skirts, Afro and layered curl haircuts, the two are missing only their Girl Scout merit badge sashes. Both sit flagpole straight with hands folded on their laps.

The third case of "curse word whiplash" is a pale, pimply-faced, blonde male. The skinny nineteen-year-old, arms-crossed, sports a welcome-mat haircut and bulging blue eyes that project a permanent state of shock. His astonished pupils are framed by pink plastic eyeglass rims. A dusty-rose pink starched shirt pokes out from under his pale pink crewneck collar and cuffs. Ironed khaki pants and spit-shined, tasseled loafers complete the look.

Maddigan mulls over the trio's appearances and the severity of their reactions to what he considered a fairly innocent narrative.

Each had jumped at hearing one of society's "Top 7" taboo words...utterances banned from churches, schools, and FCC airwaves. And here on campus, it was Maddigan's trademark, part of the daily student buzz.

He used a rubber "BULLSHIT" stamp to attack homework assignments and quiz answers. At some point every semester, the students realized that coursework grades were not always a direct reflection of rubber stampings. From that moment forward, insulted egos would give way to humorous bragging. "I got eleven BULLSHIT's stamped on my paper," became a peculiar reverse psychology emblem of honor.

Other teachers were aghast at his indiscretions. Administrators muffled their laughter. But as each semester progressed, the real bragging rights fell to those who saw fewer and fewer stamp-pad pronouncements. These were the emerging "A" students, the ones Maddigan affectionately referred to as *The Communicators!*

To the shock and dismay of his fine arts colleagues, those "A" students inevitably ended up writing more clearly than their English major counterparts. This accomplishment alone justified the faculty wrath associated with his rubber stamp. But it gave the Dean of Instruction more than enough reason to "clear out uppity cobwebs" from the English Department. Maddigan laughed off the secondhand news about being the object of spiteful faculty lounge harangues. He seemed to enjoy rattling the literary know-it-alls who pretended to have a lock on how to communicate because they studied and wrote what Maddigan privately called inane poetry and empty-headed essays.

"Stop with the Shakespeare crap," the Dean's words jolted Department Chairperson K.B. Ozzly. As Dean Oliviero launched into his bombast-the-English-Department lecture, he knew he would be perceived as buying into Maddigan's assertions. The truth though was that Maddigan was right: communication skills improvement needed to be Seaport's academic priority, and the English Faculty was busy delivering dangling participles, Lady MacBeth, and "th" speech enunciations ("Theophylus Thistle, the successful thistle sifter was sifting a sieve full of unsifted thistles and thrust three thousand thistles through the thick of his thumb...").

"Our students," the dean started, thinking he was being gracious by not saying *your* students, "don't know how to write a letter for crying out loud! They can't read a goddamn newspaper! Most of them haven't even a clue about how to express their own ideas or carry on an intelligent discussion. These are things they should have learned from their flaky high school teachers, but didn't. So you, Dr. Ozzly, have got to make up the difference! That's all there is to it."

"B...B...Bu...But, D...De...Dean Oliviero," protested the denigrated apostle of fine literature with outstretched palms, elbows glued to her six inches of rib-cage-protective fat, "With all due respect to you, and to Professor Maddigan's thinking about this, it's important for us to understand that our students need to..."

"This AIN'T Harvard, dammit!" shouted the dean, clutching the bowl of his unlit pipe. Three sharp pokes of the pipe stem punctuated the two feet of space between them. "Seaport County is not some hotbed of intellectual activity. Maybe, doctor, you are forgetting that the Royal Academy of Dramatic Arts is in London? This is the Jersey Shore! This is a two-year community college here. We're in a summer tourist town that's dedicated to bed and breakfasts, beaches, boats, burgers, bait, and boardwalks!" A feint smile followed his alliteration.

"And most academics," the Dean looked around, then lowered his voice to a near-whisper, "think we're a brain dead institution—just a notch up from an old age home. Remember, Dr. Ozzly, nine out of ten of our students survive on seasonal tourist business employment. We're not talking rocket science here. Need I remind you that the majority of our students aren't seventeen? The average age here is thirty...*thirty!*"

"But, Dean Oliviero, we can't..."

"Don't give me any more of that *we can't* crap, Dr. Ozzly! You can! And you're going to have to! That's all there is to it! Our students need to make a living for themselves. What? You want to see them be lifeguards, bait and tackle guys, hot dog vendors and cotton candy twirlers reciting Shakespeare and earning minimum wage all their lives?"

He stepped back and poked his pipe once more, "And the sooner you realize that they have to fend for themselves before they can be worried about who wrote what damn sonnets, the better!"

Not waiting for Ozzly's answers, the dean turned and strode off, feeling satisfied at having represented the right point of view. Certainly this is the kind of thinking SCC needs to foster at every level. It's not just because Maddigan champions the cause. It's right academically, he thinks. It's also the most financially justifiable path.

It's no secret that improved student communications and inspired internship job performances attract increased government grants. And even putting government grant issues aside, this is the stuff—as Maddigan has already begun to prove by rallying area business support for campus programs—that heightened community relations is made of, that prompts private building fund donations. And of course secures deanship tenure.

Ozzly's people, the Dean mumbles to himself as he leaves the room, will just have to shape up, and start teaching what's important, that's all.

Maddigan pulls a stack of semester schedules from his mailbag and, moves quietly up and down the rows, beginning to pass out the pages.

Acceptability of Maddigan's ways had been a festering rank and file issue for more than just the contentious Mrs. Ozzly and the rest of the disgruntled English teachers. A barrage of Psych and Counseling Department complaints fingered Maddigan for overstepping business curricula bounds with his focus on self-awareness and self-esteem development, and for doing more student counseling than they were, which was after all what they were trained for and paid for.

The gripes, he was told in confidence by Dean of Students, Ted Brown, centered on charges that Maddigan, the business professor, lacked appropriate psych credentials.

"But what else is business," countered Maddigan, "if it isn't self-control, self-esteem, self-development, communicating clearly, and dealing effectively with others? And," he added with wrinkled forehead and an outward twist of the wrist, "these characteristics, which all evolve from more fully-developed self-awareness, are heavily rooted in business success."

Dean Brown nodded agreement, "Yes, and by the way, how's your boat?".

Maddigan now watches his students skim the schedules and comment to one another. A number of small discussions start. He nods approvingly toward each of the groupings. The students look to him as if for parental approval, to make sure this classroom conduct of talking without professorial guidance—clearly not the norm on this provincial campus—is acceptable.

The accumulating registry of complaints prompted SCC President Andrew Stafford to intervene. Dr. Stafford, who shared the dean's admiration of Maddigan, suggested it might be useful to have the upstart business professor run an in-service training session with adversarial colleagues role-playing as students (a "Shrinkout" Maddigan called it).

"Let's have them experience your classroom approaches first-hand," Stafford explained, "so they're not so threatened. It might even win you some converts!" The accompanying clap on Maddigan's shoulder made him think Stafford had once been a football coach.

Seizing the opportunity to win support from his detractors, Maddigan naïvely agreed on the spot.

The President and Dean Oliviero hastily arranged the session, which started under a cloud of skepticism, annoyance, and no small amount of hidden hostility, but ended with Maddigan enjoying colleague appreciation. His resource documentation, presentation skills, and flair for the dramatic overwhelmed the Ph.D.-laden audience.

He diffused their opening flurry of hand-grenade questions that challenged his psychology-enriched approach and credentials. His response was to pull back sheets that covered mounds of materials he'd placed end-to-end, on six-foot long tables. The unveiling revealed a display of classroom game resources, posters, and 178 business textbooks. Each book was page-marked with references to psychology-based functions as the mainstay of business success.

He backed that up with overhead slides documenting 2,000 study credit hours he had racked up over three years of intensive training weekends in Gestalt counseling and personal growth psychology—surprising news to his detractors. The credits he accumulated from Princeton, NYU, Rutgers, Columbia, and UCLA earned him the equivalent of a second master's degree, this one in human development.

The list of personal instructors he had worked with was a "Who's Who" of the psychology and human behavior world. It included first-generation protégés of renowned Canadian psychiatrist Eric Berne ("Father of Transactional Analysis") and German psychiatrist/psychotherapist Fritz Perls ("Father of Gestalt Therapy"). Half a dozen others, prominent educators and authors all, included Carl Rogers, Andrew Weil, Barry Stevens, Ken Dychtwald, Ilana Rubenfeld, Elisabeth Kübler-Ross, and Virginia Satir.

Dropped jaws and raised eyebrows brush-stroked the rows of faces in the room. It was immediately evident to Maddigan that the authorities he matter-of-factly cited were no doubt considered super-stars by many of his colleagues.

Awestruck with what he had learned from the simplicity of these prominent educators, from their diverse-yet-parallel teachings, he never thought much about their notoriety. He knew that many of his colleagues often referred to the names, credentials, teachings and philosophies of the luminaries on his list, but it was transparently clear that none of his colleagues had ever shared room space with any of them, never mind having enjoyed the opportunity for one-on-one guidance and instruction.

Chapter 4

SHRINKOUT

Maddigan treated his colleagues as students by introducing his cognitive teaching style with actual classroom exercises. He disengaged their "closed" body language by having two arm-crossers stand face-to-face and explain how they felt about what each was communicating to the other: defensiveness, superiority.

He asked those who sprawled back in their seats to sit up straight, and those who were sitting erect to slouch back. He asked what changes in feelings each experienced: positive and negative attentiveness, involvement and disengagement.

He questioned if those peering over the tops of their glasses were parents, and if they felt more parental than when they looked *through* their glasses. Laughter filled the room, followed by an eager barrage of questioning and feverish note taking.

Maddigan talked about how he dealt with both problem students, and student problems. He demonstrated how he used empty chair role-play dialogue to help students project their feelings and dissolve on-the-job (and at-home) anger. He explained why he promoted the objective of having students learn what makes them "tick" as an important criteria to both personal and professional career growth.

He ended the session to applause, thank you's, even some handshakes. He was genuine and gracious throughout, and thanked them all for the opportunity to share his methods and experiences. He provided resources for those interested to find out more about the methodologies he used.

The session boosted his peer ratings, but his ever-rising star among the student population continued to stoke resentment and jealousy among some fellow teachers. Of course those who did dare to admire his style let caution prevail. After all, a few acknowledged, imagine the professional teaching career consequences of being associated with using words like "bullshit" in the classroom.

He strides quietly now across the Planetarium stage. His enrollments have been too high for standard classroom space. This session has sixty-one names signed in. His next class had 110. The campus average is twenty-five to thirty. Turning slowly to take in snippets of hushed conversation, he moves a few steps into the center aisle. The chatter subsides. Sixty-one faces look eager, attentive.

"Since we're here to learn about how to survive and succeed in business, you'll find that my focus is more on reality and less on traditional textbook approaches."

He stops, opens the second floor window, leans out, takes a deep breath and looks around, then turns back to the class.

"In fact," he continues, "how many of you have purchased the recommended text for this course? It's this book." He holds it shoulder high. A folded index card tumbles out; he stoops to pick it up, and opens it to familiar handwriting: "See you later Professor! Prepare for some physical exercise! – Green Eyes."

He smiles to himself as he visualizes JP grinning, then folds and pockets the card. He hoists the book back to his shoulder:

MANAGEMENT by Peter Drucker. How many of you have already bought it?" Forty-five hands proudly oblige the request.

"Well, Drucker is considered The Father of Management and there's probably a lot you could learn from him, but I was just informed yesterday that I'd be teaching this course. Drucker's book was originally prescribed by Professor Melanie Adair, who—I understand—left this esteemed institution last week with Professor Jameson Duffy to conduct some grant research on retail display preferences among pigmy tribes in the Australian Outback, or some such thing. And, unfortunately, I'm not a big Drucker fan.

"So I must tell you that as far as having this book for our guide," he takes another quick lean out the window as he tucks the book under his left arm, "the first rule of business, my friends, is that there are no rules," which he writes across the board under his name.

"I suggest, therefore, that we start with the agreement that if we're really going to learn about business, we'll have to learn it firsthand, by doing, and not by reading about it." Puzzled looks surround him.

"Soooo, Mr. D r u c k e r," and, with this, he pulls the book out from under his arm and heaves the 840-page tome over his shoulder and out the window. Two seconds of rapid page fluttering follow, then a nerve-racking thud on the walkway below. The text trashing is accented by a roomful of startled looks, gasps and assorted nervous laughs.

He peeks quickly over the ledge at the dead book, then leans forward over the teacher's desk to face his students with the pronouncement: "Mr. Drucker, my friends, with apologies to Professors Adair and Duffy, can take a hike! Or," he adds, "as the case may be here, a skydive!"

He waits for the groans, murmurs and spattering of giggles to die down.

"Okay, people, I'm sorry if you ended up having to spend all your hard earned beer money on that book, but maybe the bookstore will buy it back. Next time, you should probably wait until you actually attend the first class to confirm a text before coughing up the big bucks!"

He lifts his glasses and rubs his tired eyes, smiling as he thinks about the folded note in his pocket.

"Now let me ask one other question before we get going. How many of you came straight here to Seaport County College this semester and straight into this course from high school? You are seventeen or eighteen-years-old. You are eager to please. You have no work experience beyond babysitting and newspaper delivery. Let's see the hands!"

Four arms go up, including one of the goody-two-shoes and the wimp in pink. "Uhuh, okay, well, in order to save the four of you a lot of hassle down the road, I'm going to ask you all to go to the dean's office, and withdraw from this course."

The shock of this request causes the four to hesitate.

"No, right now," he prompts politely. Two heads tilt sideways in disbelief. "I love you all," he adds, "but I am serious,"

They stir, stand, fumble and gather their belongings, looking confused, red-faced and scolded.

"Thank you. I'll welcome each of you back with open arms after you have some real-world work experience behind you, which you'll positively need in order to understand this course. Oh, and thank you for giving me a try. I'll hope to see each of you next year!"

The four leave in a mixture of huffiness, shock and tears. He waits for quiet.

"Right. Now, as I was saying, we're here to learn how to succeed and survive. So the first step in that process is that I'm going to ask you to pull your seats out to the walls and let's make a big circle so that we are all facing the middle of the room. The reason for this is to remove divider lines and barriers."

The ensuing ruckus—chairs and desks scraping across the floor, things dropping, whispers—finally ends.

"Divider lines and barriers need only exist in big companies. This is a small business county in the biggest small business state in America. In small business, we don't need divider lines and barriers. We need open and direct lines of communication." He pauses. "The other reason of course," he smiles, "is to make sure none of you falls asleep without having everybody else in the room notice. Ha!

"Next, I'm going to walk around the room and shake hands with each of you, and try to learn to put your names together with your radiant beaming faces. When I get to you, I want you to tell me your name, where you live and where you've worked. Tell me what you've done; don't give me titles unless you were in top management. And tell me what you want most to get out of this course, besides a grade."

Chapter 5

FLOUNDERINGFLUKE

He works his way around the room.

"Hi, I'm Rick, and you are...?" he says to each with a smile and a handshake.

He prods students to speak up, smile, look him in the eye. He tells them to stand up straight and not lean on desks, walls and windowsills, to put all their weight on one foot so they aren't swaying, and to shake hands firmly. He's never critical about it. Always with a friendly smile, he repeats names two or three times each.

"Did I miss anyone?" No hands.

He starts talking as he strolls nonchalantly around the circular space, "We'll soon be discussing management as in managing people, but first I'd like to have us spend some energy on the idea of managing functions and tasks. Let's begin our management journey by, for example, talking about the critical role of marketing.

"Marketing should be the first, though too often it's the last place to make a judgment about the value, skills, and direction of a company's management.

"Consider the notion that everything we do everyday is marketing...we market ourselves to our friends because we want them to like us. We market ourselves to our parents to get money or use the family car. And of course we market ourselves extra hard to any police officer who pulls us over. Ah, and don't we also market ourselves with extra gusto to anyone from whom we're seeking romance?

"THERE IS NO SUCH THING AS A SECOND FIRST IMPRESSION." He writes the statement on the board next to "THERE ARE NO RULES" and laughingly comments that since there are always exceptions to rules, there are also exceptions to NO RULES!

"So what we're saying here is that HOW we come across is at least AS important as WHAT we have to say. The great cultural historian, critic, and oracle Marshall McLuhan says, 'the medium is the message.' Think about that! The medium is the message!

"People judge you by how tall you stand, by how attentive you are, by your eye contact, by how clearly you speak and if you speak up loudly enough or not. They judge you by your handshake and your smile."

Always in motion, he speaks as he strides around the room, "How many of you want to do business with someone who looks over your shoulder while you're talking to her or him, who mumbles like he or she has a mouth full of peanut butter, who smirks instead of smiles, and who has a handshake that feels like a dead flounder?"

"Fluke!" says Rocket, a bright young man named for his Fourth of July birthday.

"What's that, Rocket? Why would you think that what I said is a fluke? It's true!"

"No. You're from New York. You haven't been living in these parts long enough. Fluke is what we mostly catch around here when we go fishing, not flounder!" The room explodes in laughter.

"Right," grins Maddigan, realizing the unintended pun, "so...'a handshake that feels like a dead fluke,' yes? And how do we know the difference, Rocket, between fluke and flounder?"

"One has both eyes on one side and the other has one eye on each side."

"Great! So which one's which?"

"Well, they're both fish," he says with utmost sincerity, "but whichever one's not a flounder is a fluke!" Now the class is in an uproar.

Grinning as much at the student's earnestness as his response, Maddigan continues to meander around the chair-bordered inner circle, waiting for the laughter to die down.

"Okay, thank you Rocket. I'll remember that distinction. Now if we can get back to the subject of HOW we come across, and I'm not talking about being ramrod straight like a West Pointer, or staring at someone like you have x-ray vision, or being too loud or overbearing, or giving bone-crusher handshakes. I'm talking about coming across to others the way you want others to come across to you. Good business practices require good judgment and good communication skills, which—in my business life—have often proved to be even more important than the actual words you say.

"We can deduce a great deal about the management of a company by examining the kinds of marketing its management creates... that is: what do their market messages say? We also need to look at what? The ways that those messages are communicated...that is: what media are used, how and when are they used, and who uses them?

"I want you to explore how you market yourselves—how you come across to others. Based just on how you present yourself to others, ask them to tell you what musical instrument you remind them of and what type of animal or reptile they equate you with. Are you a flute? (Aah, that's fluTe, not fluKe!) Or are you a tuba? A harp? A bass drum? A wolf? A bull? A snake? A pussy cat? A weasel? Are you coming across to others the way you want to, or do the musical instrument and creature comparisons you get back surprise you? Stop yourself every time you engage another person, and ask yourself what you're learning about yourself, at that moment. Write it down."

He works his way to center stage. Crouching slightly, he wheels deliberately around with his right arm outstretched and his forefinger pointing in a slow sweep toward each attentive face.

"What are you learning about your SELF *right this minute?* Write it down! Right this minute, I am learning about myself that I ... Go ahead and finish the sentence. Put it down on paper! There's no right or wrong. You're not going to turn these in. The first thought you have is fine. I'll wait."

He pauses, then resumes circling the circle, watching the surge of nervous scribbling. He asks some to share their "learnings" and thanks each one who does—even the two or three with wiseguy responses.

"The reason we want to learn more about what makes each of us tick, is that it will help us get to know and understand others better. It is having that knowledge and understanding that is the blanket under all of marketing and management and, in fact, all of life! So the more you know about yourself, the further you will go in both life and business.

"Practice this *Right-this-minute-I-am-learning-about-myself-that-I...* written exercise, tonight at home. Practice it tomorrow at work and everyday you're here. Do that, and you'll find self-learning will become habit by the time you move on."

He looks at his watch. "Now, speaking of time to move on, it looks like we're done for today. If someone would be kind enough to pick up my crash-landed textbook from the courtyard below and run it back upstairs, or over to my office, I will be very appreciative. Accommodating my request isn't worth a grade, but it's a good way to start out the semester, and," he grins while adding good-naturedly, "it might justify a point or two down the home stretch when final exams are looming and the heat is on."

Students start to stand and pack up. He summarizes, "Anyway, as you leave this room, go market yourselves, and start keeping track of how you do that! I'll remind you once more about only getting one chance at a first impression, as I urge you to make the most of every exchange you have, with every new face, as well as with those who are familiar to you! You'll be quizzed on it tomorrow, either before or after I teach you all," he smiles and winks, "how to *b r e a t h e !* See you then—same time—same station." He begins gathering his papers, bag, and hat.

"Er, Profes…ah, Rick, how will you quiz us on this tomorrow?"

"Thanks for asking, Dave. Subjective observation and subjective judgment: the way most consumers buy most products and services."

As the room empties, the professor wiggles his fingers around inside his pipe tobacco pouch, stirring the de-seeded and ground-up pot he had tossed in with the aromatic mask of cherry tobacco, removes a couple of pinches and tamps them into his walnut special, which he lights as he follows the last two students out of the building.

The chatter of all the events that took place in Maddigan's class would reach every corner of the campus before lunchtime ends.

After a few puffs under the portico outside the planetarium, Maddigan takes a brisk walk to the student center and cafeteria, which he prefers over the stuffy, pedantic environment of the fancier faculty lunchroom.

Chapter 6

SWAMPCALL

Lunch tray in left hand, seemingly balanced by his right shoulder bagful of books and papers, Maddigan wiggles sideways to the rhythm of Kool & The Gang singing *Celebration* over the hollow PA system speakers. He steps quickly over some spilled ice cubes to avoid being launched into a slide and somersault spectacle.

Some jokester's airborne straw wrapper whizzes by the professor's left ear. He smiles at the near-miss and works his way through the rowdy center-stage table area to join a cluster of second-year students seated in the relative quiet of a far corner. He sees that most of the corner occupants are students he once had in class, or presently has in advanced subjects.

"¿Que passé, Hombres? Mind if I sit in?" he asks no one in particular as he pulls out a salmon-orange, plastic form-fitted chair and brushes the crumbs off the seat. In one sweeping motion, he grabs his cup, clacks his tray to the tabletop and shifts his mailbag to the back of the chair before sitting.

"Hey Rick, heard you tossed some rookies out today, along with the book?" comes a familiar female voice from the far end of the sixteen-foot-long table.

He leans forward to see the source, smiles and answers, "Hey,

Suzanne. Yeah, well, 'rooks 'n books,' y'know? How's that waitress job of yours?"

"Foodservice Manager, now!" she says, beaming, as she reaches to hand him a badly mangled copy of MANAGEMENT. "I found this on the walkway. Figured it was yours." Her grin told him that she indeed had his number.

"Hey! Muchas gracias! See how smart you get after you have me for two semesters? And now it's MANAGER Suzanne? No kidding! That's great!" He gives her a thumbs-up and takes a sip of coffee.

"Hey, Rick, howcum I got five 'bullshits' stamped on my final paper last semester?" a voice shoots across the table.

"Whadda-tcha-have on your first paper last semester?" he responds with a mouthful of cheesesteak sub.

"Nine."

"Ha! See that!" He chews and swallows. "You ended up four 'bullshits' better than you started, Jeffrey...congratulations!"

A tap on his shoulder. He turns to a defeated-looking face. "Hi, Darcy, what's up?"

Her doe-like eyes peek at him from behind an eighteen-inch stack of books she is hugging to her ample chest, "I need to see you," her breathy voice approaching desperation, "do you have a minute after lunch we can talk?"

"Sure. How about my office? I have to stop there before my next class. Twenty minutes?"

She nods.

He takes another bite. His mind drifts to the puzzling observation that females always hug their books to their chests and males always carry books tucked to one hipbone or the other.

"Hiiiiiii, Riiick," a flirty voice floated from one of two books-to-chests girls who wave as they pass by across the table from him.

"Are you going to play in the faculty charity soooooftball game next week?" The silent girl smiles and nods in agreement with her friend's question.

"I signed up for it, Rene, so I hope so. You two will both be there?"

"Yeah, we're cheerleading, and collecting money for the waaaaaalldlife preserve. See you then." Still grinning, the silent girl nods again.

He nods back, takes another bite, and washes it down with more coffee.

A throaty feminine *pssssst!* floats from two chairs to his left. Carole is leaning back trying to catch his attention behind the college's star linebacker who is sitting between them. Boomer is leaning forward, sinking his teeth into a dripping cheeseburger, "Professor Maddi...I mean, Rick. Can I see you after my three o'clock? Will you be in your office?"

Maddigan leans back and returns the whisper, "Sure." He checks his watch. "Four-fifteen okay?"

She smiles and bobs her head up and down. The linebacker wipes his chin with a napkin, "Hey, old weird Rick, wass happenin'? You still chasin' the little honeys around campus?"

"Aaah, hi Boomer! Nice to see you too."

A static-surrounded crackle followed by a quivery voice barges in over the student center loudspeakers, interrupting Kim Carnes' number one song, *Bette Davis Eyes*: "Attention please. Professor Maddigan? There's a call for you at the front desk."

"Hey, Rick, there y'go — another romantic mystery phone caller's lookin' for you, even follows you to lunch!" Boomer delivers a forced laugh. Carole kicks his leg.

Maddigan disregards the comment, takes a final slug of coffee, stands, pushes his chair in, and takes the last bite of his sub while grabbing his tray and hoisting his mailbag shoulder strap over his head. *Bette Davis Eyes* segues to "John Lennon's number four hit," *Starting Over.*

"See you guys later. Gotta run. Have a great day, and keep studying!" He turns and rushes off to the tray return counter, then heads for the entrance alcove. A student assistant at the front desk hands him the phone. He drops his bag to the floor between his feet and hugs it with his ankles, a growing-up-in-New-York habit.

"Hi! This is Rick Maddigan. Who's calling?"

"Listen up, Teach, here's the instructions..."

"What?" He recognizes the voice immediately as Slam's, the thug who held the knife and whispered threats while two others held his arms. He glances around, slaps the mouthpiece angrily against his leg and kicks at his leather bag. He moves sideways to the end of the counter. No one else is nearby. He lifts the mouthpiece back to his face, and cups it with his free hand to contain his voice.

"Damn!" He grimaced. "I told you not to call me here. This is totally unacceptable. I can't..."

"Shuddup and listen!"

Maddigan drops his hand again and shoots stabbing glances around the lobby to see if anyone is watching or listening to him. He pulls out a pen and turns over a countertop advertising leaflet featuring eight-track cassette tape players. He starts to write on the back.

"Go on."

"About twelve hundred and thirty or forty or fifty steps east northeast from the dirt road two-mile marker by the scrub pines on the way out to the University Marine Field Station on 7-Bridges Road at the end of Great Bay Boulevard. Stay in a straight line with the Resorts Casino building."

Hunching the phone with his left shoulder, Maddigan scribbles furiously across the leaflet blank back panel.

"You will go there at night and find the subject in a heavy black plastic bag that we dumped there at high tide. You hafta cut the cinderblock ropes that are tied to the bag. Then you get the body to yer car and take it home with you. You will do an autopsy gut job and find the implanted chip I told you about. The next day you will signal yer success to Billy in your class with some kind of clue that you tell him about ahead of time with a call to him that you message onto his machine, and we'll pick up the chip after dark. We'll call you to meet someplace near. Got it?"

"Twelve hundred and thirty or forty or fifty. Gut it. Billy. Signal. Yeah."

"Right! Give or take a few steps. Got it?"

"Yeah, but what do you expect me to do with the leftover parts?"

Eat em, Teach! Have a barbeque! Use em fer fish bait! Make soup! Stick 'em..."

Hours later, classes over, quizzes graded, counselees counseled, Maddigan makes a quick call from his desk as he packs up his books and papers.

"JP?"

"Hi, Professor! Did you get my note?"

"I absolutely did get your note, Green Eyes. Yup! Pretty smart of you to figure it'd fall out of that book."

"Well, I know you told me how you love to throw books out of windows, or did you say, 'throw looks out at bimbo's?'"

Feigning annoyance, "Ha! Ha! Very funny! Listen, I know I told you I was going to toss the book, but what if the card had fallen out when...?"

"I l o v e you."

"I love you too, JP." He laughs. "Hey, you know tonight's the night?"

"Oh, Rick, I'm so glad because I'm hot for your sweet little body t o o o o."

A big laugh this time. "Psssh. I wish. No, you know what I'm talking about."

"Rick, you know I'd do anything for you, but the boss just called. He has me scheduled in tonight, and I was planning to stay at my parent's so I can drive my Dad to the doctor's for an early morning appointment."

"Oh, yeah, I almost forgot: Saturday morning doctor. Hey, I hope he's okay. (Pause) So do what you gotta do."

"I'll see you first chance."

"Yeah, I didn't forget the physical exercise you mentioned. Maybe tomorrow, huh? Love you, Babe."

Chapter 7

GREEN EYES

After Maddigan's agonizing trek through the muck, wind, and freezing rain, dismantling and hoisting the trail bike, trailer, and bodybag up and onto the tailgate, and into the space where he'd pulled out the back seat, nearly collapses him. It's all he can do to muscle-up the strength to close the back end, climb into the driver's seat, towel off his face and hands, and catch his breath. He leans, exhausted, over the steering wheel. Stress "floaters" in the configuration of fuzzy white stars hover and drift past his closed eyes. His mind races to the drive ahead, the shortest route, driving slow, staying alert. Acid is still crawling up his throat.

Keeping as low a profile as possible in the blanket of night, he starts the Jeep and works it into second gear with just the parking lights at first. Then, edging slowly to a more drivable surface, he turns on the fog lights and cranks the gearshift into third. His head is raised enough to see, but his shoulders still slump, and his aching arms encircle the steering wheel.

Wishing now, for the first time in his life that he could trade clutching and shifting for an automatic transmission, he downshifts into second as he slows to turn onto the main road. He flips on his high beams. His legs are weak and rubbery. The muscles burn. Jell-O knees. His back feels like it's been whacked with a pizza oven paddle, and his neck aches when he shrugs.

He's over the thirty-three-year-old hill but the athletic body he woke up with this morning is now reduced to sopping wet rubble.

Heading home, the Jeep a hundred pounds heavier, he barely sees another vehicle. But not wanting to leave anything to chance, he locks his brain on maintaining the twenty-five mile an hour limit. His failing windshield wipers clatter like a poked basket of blueclaw crabs.

Pulling up to a red light, he spots two police cars head-to-tail in the diner parking lot forty feet away. Conscious of the need to appear relaxed and preoccupied, he sits back and stares straight ahead. But his sweat glands erupt. Waves of spinal shivers accompany the perspiration that runs down his forehead onto his nose and cheeks and weaves its way through his whiskers. One drop rolls along inside the bottom edge of his left eyeglass lens frame. Thankfully, the rain and shadows obscure his face. But knowing the police sit only the length of his classroom away, his thawing fingers begin to cramp from gripping the wheel so tightly. The light takes forever.

Three rigged fishing poles standing erect in his front bumper holders with two white plastic buckets hanging by their handles seem to him to have successfully undercut any suspicion. Rain or not, it's a common winter sight to see fisherman-rigged four-wheel drive vehicles rumbling in slow motion along oceanfront roads during early morning hours. Only a very savvy, extremely alert fellow Jeep-owner might notice the extra weight load taxing his suspension system.

But wait! Flashing red lights behind him. It's one of the patrol cars from the diner lot. *Crap! How the hell do I explain this? And the damn turtle? Oh, yeah, officer, I was just sittin' around my house earlier, all warm and dry and cozy, and started thinking about how great it would be to have some fresh turtle soup, an' it'd be no problem gettin' a little wet and muddy tryin' to catch one. Well, would you believe? This huge motha shell-dweller jumped right out of the shadows at me and I was able to grab it and stuff all hundred pounds of it in this big bag and now I'm headin' for my kitchen, y'know what I mean?*

Shit! Where's my license and registration? Please dear God, don't let him ask me what's in the bag. The sweat, like a row of leaky faucets, is now dripping frantically from his forehead. He swipes at it with a towel he yanks out from between the seats. He pulls the Jeep to the side of the road and stops as the blinking swirls of red light swarm over his glistening face and rain-streaked windshield. The police car pulls alongside.

Maddigan unzips the see-through plastic window from the canvas door and lets it flop in on him along with a few tossed ladles' worth of rain. The patrol car window is already open and the officer is leaning across his front seat.

"Hey, Professor, is that you? It's me! Mel. Mel Lane?" He removes his hat. "From your career development workshops? Class of '79! Remember? I was gonna be an accountant? Well, this job paid better, Ha! Ha! So here I am!"

"Oh, s u r e, Offic-e-ah-ah, Mel. Mel Lane. R i i i g h t! Mel. Mel the accountant; I thought I recognized you!" *I hope he can't tell I'm lying through my teeth. Who IS this guy?* "Looks like your career has developed just fine!" Maddigan gestures through the unzipped canvas with an open hand, something like a little wrist flip that a stage emcee would use to introduce someone off to the side.

"How are you, Mel? I'm not like under arrest or anything?" A nervous chuckle and best wedding/graduation picture smile followed the question.

Mel smiles back. "Nah, nothin' like that, Professor. Sorry to bother you but I get off work in about four hours and seen you been fishin' and I was wonderin' how the blues are runnin'?"

"Aaah, yeah, the blues. Not too great, Mel. I heard they were hittin' them pretty good last week. Word is the schools were so thick, you could throw a teaspoon out on the end of your line and reel in a pair of four-pounders fighting each other for a bite, but I didn't see much of anything this morning. A couple a small founders . . . er, *fluke* that is. That's about it."

"Oh, well, thought I'd ask. Thanks! You'd better get home and get dried off. Oh, and by the way Professor? You know your brights are on, right? And you might want to have your rear end suspension checked. You seem to be riding a little low."

"Right. Brights. Yeah, it was pretty dark at the beach. Forgot 'em. Thanks. And the suspension system. Glad you noticed. I'll check it out. Thanks again, Mel. Ah, Officer Lane."

"Hey, Rick, it's Mel, just Mel. Be safe gettin' home."

"Right. Thanks Mel. I'll be sure to do that. Stop over the campus some time. See you around. And good luck in that job of yours!"

Maddigan gives a half salute, zips the window closed, pulls gently away from the curb, and exhales a gazillion cubic yards of CO_2.

The rest of his drive home is a blank. He remembers fumbling to clean his glasses with the only remaining dry corner of his towel, and taking two thermos swigs of blackberry brandy when he reached his driveway. Exhaustion has otherwise shut down his awareness of how he ever made it back to the deserted summer tourist blip he occupies on Fort Avenue, a drafty three-room bungalow, half a sandy block from the ocean.

The first blush of winter daylight is still an hour or two away as he backs in alongside the cottage. In what has now become torrential rain, he drags the bodybag across his tailgate, and lets it thud to the ground, spraying the tan and white driveway pebbles like buckshot. He pulls out the bike and cart, and tosses them to the side. Then, he drags the heavy plastic-wrapped treasure through the dark, over his crackling driveway stones, now hop-scotched with puddles.

He shoves the dead weight into an outside shower stall that consumes a dark corner of the six foot high stockade-fenced-in back-yard of sand and weeds. Wayward scatterings of pebbles glimmer in nearby streetlight reflections that accent rainy rivulets. *Three more weeks 'til St. Patrick's Day and the boat goes in the water. Three more weeks and we're outta here,* consumes his mind as he stumbles to his door, the bed.

The winter rental is one of two occupied cottages on the block, the only two with insulation and heat. The other, four doors closer to the beach, houses an attractive, trim, mystical looking, twenty-some-thing. She's apparently a single mother with a three or four year-old daughter. He'd exchanged glances and barely perceptible smiles and head nods with them a few times on his walks up to the surf, but they hadn't spoken.

Completely exhausted, he thunks his muddy boots into the sun porch corner, and splats his dripping wet clothes onto the planked floor. Guided by random beams of light flying through window blind slats, he gropes for table and chair support as he staggers across the front room and stumbles into a sprawling body-bounce fall onto his bed. The illuminated digital clock atop the dresser clicks to 4:40AM SAT. He's asleep before it clicks to 4:41AM SAT.

Chapter 8

Yo-Yo ALERT

Four hours later, he awakes momentarily to the dull squeak and muffled thwack of his plastic-covered screen door slamming shut, but is too tired to lift his head or even open his eyes. He thinks he hears someone whisper his name. He sleeps.

At 10:30AM SAT, with a stroke of his forehead, and soft skin pressing against his arm and chest, he slowly opens his eyes. He aches everywhere except the places soothed by JP's warm hands and legs. She nibbles softly at his ear. He stretches with effort, then yawns.

"Hey, Green Eyes," he mumbles, "Y'know, if I could wake up to this every morning, I would do swamp work stuff for a living."

"Well, if I could wake you up like this every morning, I wouldn't let you get so swamped with work." Her smile pushes his favorite dimple to the corner of her mouth. She shakes her wispy black hair out of her face.

"Deal," he answers like he'd just closed a corporate merger. "How's your Dad?"

"He's okay. I see you got it." She brushes a sleep-erupted clump of hair from his forehead.

"Huh?"

"The body. I followed the drag path through the pebbles from the driveway to the shower."

"WHAT?" He jerks himself up onto one elbow with a panicked look on his face.

"Don't worry, Babe. I covered your trail. Just like always." She raises her chin and eyebrows in mock superiority, then laughs. He falls back to the pillow and moans.

"Jesus, JP, my aches have pains!"

"Yeah, well from the look of your boots and clothes, which I cleaned, you could have been down at Sinn's Bar applying for a mud-wrestling position. How about some Uncle Phil's Horse Liniment on those shoulders?"

"Thanks. Thanks. Thanks. And yes, please. How did you know?"

"Are you kidding? That bag must weigh nearly a hundred pounds."

"Exactly actually, according to the neighbor's fish scale that I hung on the shower fence."

"Right. A hundred. I did find that out, which I'll tell you about later."

She massaged a gob of the blue gel into his shoulders, backing her head away from the piercing medicinal smell. He groans in relief, then turns his head to watch her skip across the hall to the sink. Barefoot and all legs, her black bikini panties and gray t-shirt knotted across her rib cage are accentuated by the light streaming through the window. Her small, tight, rounded butt bobs like tethered buoys retreating under a tide change.

"You've got a great ass, JP, anybody ever tell you that?"

A small chuckle wafts through the doorway. "All the time, Rick. How about you? I hear the girls on campus say you're a real hottie."

"Hottie. Right. This is true. But only when you're around." He leans up on one elbow.

"Oh, man, I'd love to unscrew my legs and lower back, and put them in a whirlpool for a few hours. Do you have any whirlpool-type places in mind?"

"Sure, Rick, go ahead and unscrew them. I'll throw 'em in the VW and take 'em to the laundromat." His eyes follow her wall shadows that bounce off the bathroom light.

He laughs. "Whirlpool as in hot tub, Ding-Dong, not the brand of washing machine!"

"You know, you're pretty dumb for a professor, Professor. That was supposed to be a joke. Duh!"

"Listen, I appreciate your help here, but..."

She cuts him off, "I thought you'd never ask." He takes two quick puffs from the joint stub she hands him, smothers a cough, and puts the remaining roach in his bedside ashtray. He winces as he reaches across to the night stand.

"How are your shoulders?" she asks, dimple out, head cocked to the side, one eyebrow up.

"I don't fool around with my *shoulders*," he says grinning, his eyes slits.

"But," she says, "maybe, you know, like maybe pushups wouldn't be the best thing right now...I was thinking maybe you should just stay on your back?"

"Hmmmm, that might be nice for a change."

"A change, right. You mean like since Tuesday?"

"Ha! Ha! Okay, since Tuesday. That's comedy, right? Yeah, I get it!"

"Did he get it, Billyboy?"

"I'm sure. He had no choice, y'know what I mean? Anyway, I'll know for positive in Monday's class. The story from the message he left me is that it's in the bag, so to speak, if he brings a yo-yo with him."

"What's with the freakin' yo-yo? YER a yo-yo!"

"Thanks. Same to you, Slam. The deal is that if he does a lecture with a yo-yo, then we know to proceed with pickin' up Mr. C. Puter Chip, got it?"

"Right. A yo-yo. A college lecture with a yo-yo. Now I've heard it all. Well, you better hope he does his little yo-yo tricks on Monday, Billyboy. Call me when you find out." Click.

Chapter 9

FISHUGGERS

"So, you wanna know what I found out, Rick? I mean just in case you thought I was doing nothing but waitressing and studying and teaching my aerobic dance class and getting my Dad to his check-up, and driving around in circles scouting guys at Haines' Lighthouse Pub while you were putzin' around on your swamp expedition." The dimple again.

"Well, sure," he admits, "I know you've had a few things going on, but I was definitely hoping you'd dig up some info about this turtle creature. After all, it's not like something we deal with every day, and, actually, I've been hoping we might learn something that might help us figure out what this weirdo mission is all about."

"Well sure, you say? Hey, you're just dripping with anxiety to hear the JP Report, you say? Unfortunately, I don't know that there's a whole lot we're going to learn about the blackmail deal from my research, but it is pretty interesting stuff. So, here goes. Here's All The News That Fits, I Print! (Pretty funny, huh? Never thought of me as The New York Slimes, huh?)."

She unfolds her notes and squints at them over the tops of her wire-framed granny glasses. "Okay, so I stopped at the library, and here you go: Fishuggers of America. Yuch! Some name, huh? Well, the Fishuggers have a separate independent division named Save The Turtles Action Group (STTAG, they call it. Something likes a male deer with a stutter. Ha!).

"Anyway, the deer stutter-er-er-ers represent, among other things, protection and preservation of the nesting and reproduction rights of Loggerhead turtles, which, by the way, the Fishuggers officially call Caretta caretta —kinda like Bongo-bongo." She accents her point with a little hip shimmy dance step.

His quickly raised eyebrows flash three parallel wrinkles across his forehead.

"So, Loggerheads, they say, have a reddish brown carapace— that's the topshell, and a medium yellow plastron—that's the underside. Not bad so far, huh?" She smiles, then returns to her notes: "Hatchlings are about two inches long."

She grins widely as she exaggerates the two-inch distance between her thumb and forefinger, her devious mind clearly on something else. "Imagine that," she says, twisting her lips to the left while raising her right eyebrow. Amused with herself, a small chuckle squirts out. "They're light to dark brown, aah, the turtles that is." She laughs this time. "Their flippers are dark brown with white margins, and their undersides are faded yellow/ochre."

"Yellow ochre, right," he says.

"Right! And now, get this: On the West Coast, they run — ah, swim actually." She looks up to see if he appreciates her humor. He rolls his eyes.

She continues, "They swim—you won't believe this distance— between Alaska and Chile! Long way, huh? On the East Coast, they are primarily found in Florida, as well as in Georgia and the Carolina's, in addition to the Florida Gulf Coast. But the word is they will show up almost anyplace between Newfoundland and Argentina. Like Seaport County for example?"

She looks up to see that his attention is riveted on her two pages. He nods slightly. She continues. "Thirty to forty percent of the world's total Loggerhead Turtles live in the Southeastern United States, accounting for 50,000-70,000 nests per year. Whew! That's a lotta nests, y'think?"

He smiles. She turns her notepaper sideways. He imagines her running out of paper as she takes her usual frantic notes on the nearest writing surface, which sometimes means the tabletop after the paper is filled on both sides.

"I almost forgot," she says, "You know those ugly jellyfish, the almost clear ones with the stinging testicles?"

"Ah, I do hope you mean tentacles."

"Yeah, whatever. You know what I'm talking about. They're called sea nettle jellyfish?"

"Sure. Nasty stings. Right. Could make your green eyes red!"

"C'mon, Rick, be serious. The Loggerheads, they love these jellyfish. They eat them for breakfast, lunch, and dinner."

"Er," he leaned toward her and grimaced, "and midnight snacks, when they get the munchies?"

"Well, sure. I guess. They eat 'em all the time, the book said." Not missing a beat, she continued, "Of course, that's cool for us prospective sting-ees, that the turtles feast on these yuchy things, but apparently a good number of Loggerheads choke on plastic bags that they think are jellyfish. Why can't people stop throwing plastic bags in the water? And balloons too! Balloons are just as bad, y'know?"

"Really!" he says, and sits back in his chair. "Maybe the Fishuggers should have a PB&BDD: Plastic Bag and Balloon Disposal Division. And then there're condoms, you know, they could make it PBB&CDD and..."

"Oh, yeah, very funny, but did you know that turtles can drown?

Can you believe that, that turtles can drown? Did you know that?"

He exaggerates lifting both eyebrows.

"I bet most people wouldn't know that," she continues, "anyway, many Loggerheads do drown in shrimp nets. During active periods, they need to surface every few minutes for air, you know, like to do your deep breathing thing? And getting tangled in nets doesn't let them get to the surface." She chugs the last half of a glass of water that's on the table between them, and wipes her wrist across her lips.

"And speaking of these creatures being active, Rick, you should know that female Loggerheads can deliver up to 126 eggs per clutch."

"Clutch?" he asks as he leans forward again, an expression of mock shock consumes his facial muscles. "Per clutch?" He sees that he is catching a half smile from her and continues, "As in clutch? 126 per friggen clutch? Whew! That's some pile of kids to worry about."

He lowers his head to look over his own glasses and waves a scolding finger. "Maybe that's what happens when you mess around with stinging testicles!" They exchange grins.

Yeah, you're a riot, Professor, but wait 'til you hear this, okay? This is like the grand finale. The average adult is three feet long and weighs 200-350 pounds. As they mature to juvenile stage, Loggerheads migrate from ocean depths to shallower coastal waters, and often live in marshland mud, which I guess means like the wetlands along 7 Bridges Road?"

She takes a deep breath before concluding. "Juveniles average 15-20 inches in length, and weigh, get this: 100 to 130 pounds. So you got yourself a full-fledged newbie juvenile. Cool, huh?"

"Yupsidoodle, it's cool all right. But like you said, I just don't know that it's going to help us much in figuring out this mess, or why these goons are breathing down my neck. Anyway, you get an A+."

She climbs into his lap and surrounds his head with her arms.

"Y'think I could get a better grade than that?" she purrs. "Hey, y'never know, y'know?"

Chapter 10

TURTLECHIP

It's nearly 2PM before Maddigan wakes up again. Feeling like he's just crawled out of a car accident, he talks to the ceiling. *Jesus! What a way to spend Saturday, and I have a ton of stuff to do before dark: shower, laundry, wash the Jeep, put away the bike and bike trailer, grocery shopping, get the tools and everything ready for chop-up-the-turtle-night tonight, finish grading quiz papers, and type up two student reference letters.*

He rises slowly, leaning heavily on the wobbly headboard and edge of the night table, feeling groggy, swiping at his hair and beard. He hooks his glasses on, and plods naked into the bathroom. A note from JP is taped to the faucet:

"Hi Sweetness! I'll bring dinner from the restaurant but can't get home 'til after 9 because 2 girls didn't show & El Bosso wants me to stay late. If you need to get surgery started, don't wait. But I'll help you clean up when I get back. (At least the rain stopped!) I love you. XXXXXOOOOO—Green Eyes"

Damn! Oh, well. It's the blood and guts clean-up thing I really need help with. At least I can count on a good dinner, assuming I'll still have an appetite by then.

He arrives back at the cottage after dark, and packs away the groceries, enough for JP and himself for the week. Changing into some old paint-covered clothes, he pauses to swig down the last of the leftover thermos brandy. He peeks out his windows, checks up and down the street and scopes out all the empty, blacked-out, adjoining cottages. All's quiet. He lights his pot-filled pipe and clamps it in his teeth as he heads for the backyard shower stall. The only visible sign of life is a dim window lamp in the twenty-something Mystical Mama's house a few doors up.

He drags the bag to the fish-gutting sink and 3 x 5 butcher-block tabletop next to the shower. He hefts the hulk up and onto the surface. He puffs the pipe 'til he feels a buzz, then switches on a half-black-painted overhead wall fixture that throws just enough light to see, but not enough for anyone passing by the front of the cottage to notice. He steps back and thumbs the edge of his carving knife to check the sharpness.

He pulls on a heavy rubber apron and elbow-length rubber gloves he found in the summer fisherman's unlocked garage next door. After a couple of deep breaths and some serious teeth-gritting, he steps forward, slices through the bag and tears it apart, jerking his head back from the rancid smell. Then he plunges his knife into the belly, pulling the blade mightily toward his hip to separate the body into left and right halves.

Except the blade doesn't pull. The shell doesn't slice. In fact, the knife barely penetrates the shell and hardly moves in any direction. He starts to feel spooked. *What made me think this would be like slicing pie and spooning out the filling?*

Within minutes, he's hosting his third major bout of the sweats in eighteen hours. This time, like his first outbreak in the swampland, drops are running down his neck and back, as well as his forehead. He leans down, taps his pipe into the gravel, empties the smoldering ashes, then slides the still warm bowl and stem into his shirt pocket.

The stench of the rotted corpse makes lilacs of bus fumes. The knife is going nowhere. He is soon using a saw, then his hatchet, finally a crowbar. At last, he is able to crunch and crack and separate the slime-drippings from the protective cover they cling to. The repeated squirts in his face, on his glasses, repulse him. Chop. Cut. Slice. Scrape. Spoon out. Gag. Step back. Chop. Cut. Slice. Scrape. Spoon out. Gag. Step back. His arm muscles twitch for the effort.

In two hours, he collects enough slop and glop to fill a row of plastic buckets he'd collected over three months of nighttime beach strolls. He stuffs a doubled-up black trash bag to the point where he can barely twist it shut. Broken shell pieces stretch and slash the plastic, protruding their way through a dozen openings.

His nervous system startles with muscle quivers and goosebumps at every blast of seabreeze that gushes between the narrow cottage alleyways. The occasional passing car, tires tossing road-strewn gravel from the street, causes him to snap upright from the mess he's leaning over. He covers the light bulb that can't be seen anyway, with the towel that's slung over his shoulder. He steps back into the shadows and—hands on hips—stretches his stiffening back. He raises his head to look around with every distant dog bark. *Damn this mess I've gotten myself into! Damn Slam! Where is the damn thing anyway? What if he's BS'ing me?*

She tucks the two Styrofoam-boxed $25 lobster dinners neatly into the slot behind her front seat. The chef helped her sneak them out the back door in exchange for two joints, and because he enjoys her short-skirted leg muscles marching back and forth into his work area. She imagines, after tonight's turtle mess, that Rick may never want to even look at seafood again, but The Shanty was running low on steaks.

She knows for sure that when she finally arrives home, she will need to be tough to the task, yet gentle. He will need her to be attentive and understanding.

She is already exhausted from teaching her aerobic dance class, and then turning over her six tables, twice each. She is annoyed with having had to kiss ass and smile through a parade of rude and snotty customers, including three unruly brats, five nit-picky old ladies and two idiot smalltime politicians pretending to be big spenders. But she managed to clear $120 in tips for swallowing hard while showing her teeth and dimples (and some extra leg views for the politicians), for paying attention, and for hustling the heavy trays from the kitchen. She spilled twenty crumpled ones from her pocket to give to the Green Card busboy. Muchas gracias!

Now she is confronted with having to drag her spent, tray-tortured arms, her back-and-forth-to-the-kitchen-a-zillion-times, already aerobic-spent legs, and her insult-riddled brain into the middle of the professor's ordeal...and help him through it. But he's worth it, and she knows he needs her. Besides, tomorrow, Sunday, they can sleep late.

JP rolls her VW Beetle slowly up the driveway so as not to alarm him. He glances over his shoulder and watches her pull off her apron as she gets out. She walks tentatively up to him for a kiss until she sees his strained eyes and forehead wrinkles, and the scuzz dripping off his glasses. She scrunches up her nose and caves in her smile as she backs off a step.

"Maybe I should put this back on," she says, waving her blue, grease-stained The Shanty waitress apron.

"Thank God you're here. Can you load that bagful of shell and scraps, and the buckets into the Jeep, then the whole mess in the bag to the dumpster behind the supermarket, and empty the buckets into the swamp next to the parking lot?"

"Whatever you say, Professor. Did you find it yet?"

"Yeah." He let out a deep sigh. "Just. It's wedged in here," separating a softball-sized chunk of fatty gel with his knife blade. His rubber-gloved fingers jam into what had once been the base of the Loggerhead's neck, and pluck out the hermetically sealed plastic one-eighth-inch thick by two-inch square. He holds it to the light. It's the size of a quarter.

"Jeeze! All this," she asks, "for that little thing?"

"Hey, it's 1981, you know. These little chips can actually hold a few pages worth of information."

"Can you believe it? So what's on this one?"

"Don't know, don't care! Don't want to know! Just want to get done with this."

"Okay, I don't blame you. So what's next?"

"Clean up."

"No, I mean with the chip?"

"First they were going to meet me, but then changed signals and told me to put it in a double-sealed plastic bag inside a hollowed-out textbook, then give the book to the student they planted in my class."

"Bill?"

"Yeah, Bill, if that's his real name. Bill Shill. Ha!"

"Well, Bill Shill will wait until..." The rhyme wasn't coming. "I'll load the Jeep."

"There's a lot of cleanup to do," he says wearily.

The dimple.

"Hey, Professor, that's why we're a team, right?"

He throws her a kiss with his rubber glove.

"Yuch! Save that for later, after we shower."

They trade forced smiles. She laughs as she loads the Jeep. By the time she returns, Maddigan has cleaned up the area, and himself, and is already asleep. She throws clothes in the washer, does a quick shower, and snuggles in next to him, out like a light two minutes after smooshing her pillow.

Chapter 11

CHOCOLATECHIP

"I dunno, Prof...er, Rick, like I hate to ruin your Monday here, but y'know I'm not your, uh, regular student, y'know? Like I have a kid and two jobs and the kid's old man keeps comin' around an' disrupin' our lives? So it's, uh, it's hard for me to, uh, get the time to study this stuff? Y'know what I mean? I'm like, uh, really interested in it an' all? It's jus that every time I sit down to read or write the as-signments you give us? I get this shithead, uh, oh, sorry, I mean, like this guy beats on me an' the boy, an' he's always, you know, drunk? So..."

Maddigan watches his anguished student's face pretzel up, but barely hears a word. He's still thinking about the disgusting Saturday night he'd just had, cutting up a 100-pound turtle and disposing of the parts, and the slop and stench, and the risks, and how his back and neck still throb from bending so long to the task. He's also think-ing about making sure that he gets Bill the book that JP hollowed out. He's imagining it being reported back to Slam that he'd managed to come up with the chip. *God forbid if I hadn't found it.* Carrying the chip in the book in his mailbag was making him nervous, like trying to nonchalantly chit-chat with a cop when there's pot in your pocket.

"Right, Chrissy, I can understand how hard this must be for you."

Another one of the dozen sad stories he hears every week. *I have to get out of this rut I'm in,* he thinks. *This is not the time to be feeling sorry for myself.*

"And I appreciate you trusting me, Chrissy," he finally says, "and your confidence in coming to me to discuss it, but I really can't just step into a situation like this." He had to consciously pry his brain out of the turtle innards.

"First of all, I'm not, you know, I'm not really a shrink or police-man or anything."

Though I'd love to be a cop right now, he thinks, *so I could bust this poor girl's boyfriend or husband or whatever he is, and feed Slam to the DA, and get myself out of the mess I'm in.*

No response.

"You know?"

No response.

"My job," he continues, his thumbs and forefingers preoccupied fumbling with a paperclip, "is to make sure that my students do the work that's required to get through the course."

Still no response.

He catches himself staring at the papers on his desk.

He reaches under his glasses to squeeze the bridge of his nose, then strokes his beard, and looks up. When he connects with her eyes, he sees them glisten, drops filling the corners. Her face shows fear, anger, disappointment...a hint of whimper...*all too much for such a young face*, he thinks. He knows she came to him expecting more. She drops her head and wrings her hands in her lap. The tears spill first from her sad left eye, then from her angry right one. She raises a curled up hand to wipe them away, one side then the other.

Ticks from the wall clock, steady and even, relentless, fill the void.

"So, how old is your son, Chrissy?"

She sniffles and reaches for a tissue as she holds up three fingers.

"Three, huh?" he asks. She nods. A small shivery gasp works its way out. He puts his hand gently on hers.

"You know there are people and organizations where you can get help? Have you been to the Counseling Office yet?" She shakes her head sideways.

"That's probably the best place to start. They have all kinds of information and can give you names and phone numbers, and put you in touch with someone right away who can help you and the boy." His tone is gentle. "Whadda you say?"

She nods like someone who'd just been shot might respond to the question asking if she'd just been shot.

Jesus, I'm really saying all the wrong things here, he thinks. *This isn't what she wants from me, but I've got my own damn catastrophe to deal with. I need to talk to myself: Shit, Rick, this isn't what it's about! You're supposed to be here to help these shredded-life students get their acts together. That's why you took this freakin' job. Stop with the dead turtle already. Get your damn glove and get in the game! Her life and her three year-old's life are in the frying pan!*

He reaches for his phone. "Let me call my friend Sue, over in Counseling...okay? Let's find out if she can see you right away. She's great with getting things like this straightened out, okay with you?"

She nods again with just an iota more enthusiasm this time and, looking more fragile than he's ever noticed, she continues to mop the tears. He reaches in his desk drawer and produces a chocolate chip cookie wrapped in a napkin. "Here! Munch on this while I call. It's homemade by the Seaport County College student cafeteria staff."

She breaks off and eats one little crumb at a time as he picks up the phone.

He dials. "Sue? Hi, this is Rick. Good. Listen, I have Chrissy Wescrik sitting here and she could use your help figuring out how to deal with some upsets she and her three year-old son are going through right now..."

He covers the mouthpiece and leans toward her. "What's your son's name?"

"Jason," she sputters, and eats another crumb.

He uncovers the mouthpiece. "Jason: J-a-s-o-n W-e-s-c-r-i-k." Something about the way he said the name made three-year-old Jason sound eighty-three.

"Chrissy's doing all she can, Sue, but Jason's not being treated right by his father." He listens intently to the response.

"Right. And my friend, Chrissy, here is working two jobs and trying to get through my marketing class, but she can't find study time with all the uproar, and Jason's father has been being abusive to her too...Yes..."

He glances quickly at the black and blue marks on her arms and side of her face. "Yes, just a couple here and there, but you know... right. Great! I'll send her right over."

He nods at her and raises his eyebrows as to question if the step he's taking for her is acceptable.

She whimpers, "Okay," then bites another piece of the cookie.

He covers the mouthpiece and asks if she wants him to walk her over and she manages an "uh-huh!" He winks at her as he speaks into the phone.

"Sue? In fact, I'll walk her over myself. We'll see you in a couple of minutes. Oh, and thanks. Right. Bye."

The teary-eyed student unconsciously wraps the remaining

piece of cookie in the napkin and puts it on Maddigan's desk, then brushes her fingertips together. He hangs up, stands, and reaches to clasp his student's hand to help her up.

"So, Chrissy Wescrik," he says, like he was a game show host about to summarize her winnings. She manages a half smile. "Let's take a couple of deep breaths and head on over." She does. They do.

They leave his office and walk, bumping elbows, to the back stairway. The whole way out of the building and across the mall to the Administration Building, he speaks softly to her about the need for her to regain control of her life by focusing on deep breathing and positive thoughts. Some action in a positive direction, he tells her, is always better than no action. He urges her to work harder at surrounding herself with positive people. He gives her examples. He knows he's only partly getting through to her, but he really can't just go bang heads with the loser she's choosing to live with. *What the hell makes women so weak-willed to not assert themselves in the face of violence and disrespect? I just can't make sense of it. Maybe there is no sense.*

Students who would normally stop to talk with him read his body language—head down and turned to the student he is physically close to and is obviously ushering across the mall—those who pass mostly just smile and continue on their way. He carries her books, and gently puts a hand to the small of her back as he guides her through the doorways. All the while, his mind is back inside the turtle. He fights back the urge to throw up.

Damn turtle was so repulsive, he thinks. *It should've been this simple to deal with—like walk the whole mission over to some turtle expert's office and be done with it—come back in a few hours to get the chip. Did she finish that chocolate chip? Boy, do I ever need to do for myself what I'm telling this girl to do! How come I'm so fat-headed?*

On his way back from Counselor Sue's, classes change. He checks his watch and picks up his stride. He has to work his way against the rushing current of body traffic.

He hustles up the two flights, through jabbering throngs of students, to pick up his bag, notes, props, graded quiz papers, and the peel-stick student nametags he makes every day for every class for attendance and name-learning.

Maddigan was known on campus as much for his name stickers as for his BULLSHIT stamp. He neatly hand-letters each first name in different colors with black shadowing and smaller, plain black last names underneath. He believes the nametags enhance student self-esteem because, "I call you by your name instead of 'the person with the purple hair' or 'Yo, the one without the teeth!'"

"Also," he points out to nervous freshmen, "everyone learns everyone else's name and makes more friends quicker. Your last name is your family's name and isn't unique to you, but it's there on the name badge just in case you get lost, or in case I get seven Sue's in class. But it's your first name that's all about you! Unless of course," he points out, "you have brothers and sisters who all have the same first names? Like, 'Hi, I'm Dinky and this is my brother Dinky and this is my other brother Dinky...and my sister over here...' which always gets him laughs. Preparing the name stickers for every class also forces him to spend a minute thinking about each student before getting to the room.

With Chrissy delivered to Sue, he now had to hustle back across the campus to get to his class before the bells ring in four more minutes. No time for any of the usual little chit-chat visits and talk walks with the assorted clumps of people he passes along the way. The big exchange—the chip in the book—was about to take place.

Head down and worried about surrendering the chip, but smiling for the public, and aware of his need to be on time, he starts to jog...a virtually unheard-of New Yorker-type oddity in this slow-motion area. What's the rush, anyway? people always asked him. He laughed at the thought as he picked up the pace.

In the summer, the locals would tell him, "There's no place 'round here worth running to. And winter? Everyone's either in Florida or passing their time at the local bars, pizza parlors, bait and coffee shops, or the Seaport County Mall. Running *any*where between November and March is out of the question, unless it's to keep warm.

"Oh, and if someone insists on going out for a brisk walk, even a stroll, tell 'em to wait for fall and winter. Opposite of what all the travel brochures say, those are the best times to hit the beaches. Yup. Fall an' winter's the best cuz there's no Bennies!"

"Hmmm, 'no Bennies!'" Maddigan rolled the words over in his mind. Bennies, of course, meant tourists. Something there, he thought, about cutting one's nose off to spite one's face, since tourism is clearly the economic lifeblood of the Jersey Shore. Having some less-than-straight-up nickname for out-of-towners seemed a little hypocritical. *But this: is Seaport County. Ha! After all, Bennies may account for most of the populace's paychecks, but that's no reason to have to like them.*

The "Bennies" name, he understood from some of his born 'n raised students, was apparently derived from the summer onslaught of New York City Italian guys who seemed mostly to be named Benny – each in a sleeveless t-shirt with a cigarette tucked behind one ear, gyrating along the boardwalk sloshing a paper-bagged can of beer. Some conjecture has it, though, that the Bennies name originated from a rather opposite image of uppity Princeton-ites in their quest of the "benny-ficial rays of the sun." *Either way,* thought Maddigan, *local lore was indeed a thing to behold! Jeeze! The things I think about when I jog.*

Chapter 12

STRESS 101

Maddigan is out of breath and sweating by the time he reaches to open the classroom door.

"Hey, Professor Rick!" The three words have a derisive edge. Maddigan stops in mid-step as he's greeted by the star of Seaport's football team. The hulking student is the same one whose back Maddigan had talked behind at lunch. As cocky in class as his high-stepping romps accentuate on the playing field, he must have thought he was arriving late for class, but now sports a snide grin as he realizes he has just beaten his teacher to the door by a step.

"Oh, hi Boomer!"

"Hey, Rick, you been doin' some serious workouts or what?"—a poke at the perspiration beads falling from Maddigan's brow. "Or," he said, half under his breath, eyes rolling, as they both cross the threshold into a roomful of suddenly snuffed chatter, "maybe I should ask if you're b-r-e-a-t-h-i-n-g?" They both grin insincerely.

Maddigan clicks his brain onto fast track, throws the door open and charges to the front of the room. "Hey!" He looks around. "Apologies for my delay. I'll make it up by talking faster." He smiles. Everyone smiles. Boomer slides into a back corner seat.

The day seems to drag on for a week. He has two more ninety-minute classes to do, with Bill Shill and the turtlechip book exchange scheduled for the last of these. But instead of being able to take some quiet time to assuage his edgy feelings, think through the whole chip deal, and assess his risks, he has to sit through a dumb faculty meeting. It's another debate on whether the parttime faculty has rights to the fulltime faculty's dental plan. (As far as he is concerned, all of their collective teeth could fall out!) Then, he has to race back to his office to see another dozen students who would be waiting there for personal counseling.

It's probably better I'm busy, he thinks. *At least I don't start imagining some nasty confrontation with Bill or any of his pals after class. I mean, I did get what they wanted. There's just something too—what's the word?—clandestine about this whole thing. So they've got me blackmailed, but having them force me to make like a CIA Agent is too weird.* He smirks. *Hopefully, all I do is give him the book and walk away.*

He acknowledges the clump of counselees camped in the corridor next to his office door, and ushers the first in line to his desk. He slides a chair over and motions the earnest-looking young man, Larry, to sit. He slits open an envelope addressed "Private to Professor Maddigan" that was taped to the back of his chair as he asks Larry what's up. He watches and listens to Larry describe problems he had with his boss's know-it-all assistant, all the time continuing to fumble with, extract and unfold the single page from the envelope.

Larry is waving his fist, saying how he is tempted to punch his boss's assistant in the mouth, and misses seeing his professor do a double-take on the full-page drawing of an erotic looking flower with inviting, outstretched legs. It is signed "Green Eyes" and Maddigan's face flushes fire engine red when he realizes the drawings' suggestion.

Hastily, he re-folds the paper, tucks it back into the envelope and puts the envelope into the zippered flap of his mailbag.

"You all right?" Larry asks, now noticing the heat of the moment. "I wasn't talkin' about you, ya know, I mean, my fist? It wasn't you I meant. I..."

"Oh, sure, Larry. No, I know. Yeah. Thanks. Yes, I'm fine. So how can I help you with this boss's assistant person?" He imagines JP waiting for him in bed, like the flower, with her aerobic dance legs stretched apart. It takes his breath away.

Two hours of personal calamities later, and each of the troubled students happily on their way with solutions in hand, the class bells ring in the hallways.

Maddigan "works the campus," as JP teasingly describes his friendly politicking practices, which most students like and most teachers don't. He ambles back to the Planetarium classroom, stopping often to socialize and share words of encouragement along the way.

Fifty-seven seats fill up, all pushed back to the walls to form his circular stage. The Professor slides off the top of the teacher's desk where he'd been sitting cross-legged at the front of the room, stands, rubs his achy hands together, and walks to the center of the circle. He paces and swivels as he speaks, pausing with each turn long enough to engage contact with every eye in the room.

"Today, we're going to learn to breathe," he says rather matter-of-factly, and is greeted with a hush, some amused grins, a sneer or two, some elbow jabs. "And then," he continues, "we're going to hear about a one-time, special offer you ab-so-lute-ly won't believe!" Some smiles dissolve and a few students wiggle forward in their seats.

"Let's start with the breathing. I want to make sure all of you are actually alive enough to be able to hear my special offer." He pauses, smiles, sighs, and rubs his forehead, then continues.

"All of us," he says with a slow swoosh of his arm, his eyes scanning the faces around him, "experience stress. STRESS!"

He strides to the board and prints the word with jagged saw-blade lines for each letter, then returns to stage center. "Positive stress is what allows us to sit up in a chair, so some stress, the good stress, we need.

"But negative stress, or over-stress, feelings of *dis*tress if you will, is stress that's not productive *like*, he thinks, *a damn middle-of-the-night tromp through the swamp!* It's this negative stress that makes us sick. It's this over-stress that diverts our attention enough to set ourselves up to get into car accidents."

Always the actor on stage, he pantomimes his lifted right foot jamming on a brake, and an imaginary steering wheel seems to spring up out of his hands as he turns his face defensively. "Or," he saws with a make-believe knife, "cut our fingers." His face twists up as he's reminded of trying to slice the turtle shell. *What did JP call it? Carapace and plastron? Right. Shell.* Then he shakes his hand fitfully and sucks his pretend-cut knuckle, "or we say the wrong things, get into arguments, miss making a sale, or screw up a business arrangement."

Though trite, his acting movements flow naturally with his words, and come across engagingly enough to hold attention.

"Each of us processes negative stress in different ways. Some of us," he whispers with his hands on each side of his back-and-forth tilting head, "get headaches. Some," he says, while arching backwards into his back support-positioned hands with thumbs pointing forward on each side of his waist, "get backaches." He groans. "Some," leaning forward with both hands on his stomach, "get stomachaches.

Others," he scans the room knowingly, "get diarrhea, or constipated. Some get cramps or feel tense and tight everywhere...or, maybe not everywhere, maybe in just one or two special places."

Reminding himself how sore he feels, he touches each spot as he recites: "neck, shoulders, legs, wrists, jaw. Does any of this sound familiar? How many of you can identify with any of these kinds of symptoms?" He raises his hand as a prompt. Other hands shoot up in a wave across the room, like a school of dolphins breaking the surface. He nods.

Then he waves his fists, "Some of us make fists when we're over-stressed. I have a vein that pops out on my forehead." He rubs his forehead. "What's your trigger? Think about it."

Maddigan pauses and paces. Student eyes follow.

"The more you know about how your body responds to stress, the easier it is to learn how to control and channel it."

He continues, "The thing is, you have a choice here. You can choose to control negative stress. You can choose to channel it. And, choose to make it work for you, instead of against you."

I need to make that choice myself! he zings a reminder to his brain.

"Outward Bound program instructors who prepare partici-pants for solo survival treks into the wilderness, far from civilization, discuss the stress of fear and solitude, of being suddenly left alone in the forest with nothing except a knife and your ingenuity. They advise participants, 'when you feel nervous and feel like you have but-terflies in your stomach, don't try to chase them away.'" He flutters all his fingertips as his hands move slowly outward from his stomach in opposite directions. "'Teach them to fly in formation!' is what they advise." He flutters all ten fingertips together, left to right, as if he were playing a piano fugue.

"It's your *choice*! It's *your* choice!" he points a finger and turns slowly, panning the class.

"It *is* your choice!" No one escapes the electricity that seems to connect him to each person in the room.

If you want to choose to feel, and be, happier and healthier, to get better grades, to succeed at work, you can! You can. It's your choice. Now think about how this applies to business...to sales and marketing."

He pauses and walks across the circle of chairs to write on the board as he repeats out loud in a grating enough fashion no one's likely to forget: "Repetition Sells! Repetition Sells! Repetition Sells! Your Behavior Is Your Choice! Your Behavior Is Your Choice! Your Behavior Is Your Choice! And you know what else? Repetition Sells!"

"Sounds good, Rick, but how can I choose to not be pissed at some jerk who cuts me off on the parkway?" a disgruntled voice retorts.

Good question, Tim. It's a good question because you asked *how*...tells me you're interested in the process, the steps, the how-to. The first thing you need to do when you start to feel stressed-out is to regain control of yourself, and you can do this by being more in touch with the present moment, which I'm about to show you how to do."

Chapter 13

LIKE A BLANKET

He surveys faces to be sure his captive audience is still captive. It is.

"The past, after all, is not here now. This includes getting cut off in traffic, right Tim? Which—even if we were in the car right now—would already have happened so it would already be in the past, yes? So if something is in the past, that makes it fantasy because it's over with and we can't do anything to change it! And if you dwell on the past, you are missing the present, which—by the way—you won't get back."

A mixture of faces stare back at him, some puzzled, some enlightened, some grinning and nodding, some glazed over, but all are paying attention.

"What a surprise that a big hand doesn't come out of your washing machine, like that TV commercial, and give you back the time you missed while you were busy being pissed off over something that's over with, like," he glances at Tim, "getting cut off in traffic. In fact, dwelling on past stuff can actually make you neurotic, which of course is not healthy. You probably all know some guy who's in his thirties or forties, or maybe even older, who can only talk about the big touchdown he scored in high school: somebody who's kinda stuck in the past? Certainly not a mentally healthy place to be."

Maddigan circles the circle, strokes his beard, waves his arms to accent key words. More faces look like they're joining the enlightened majority. More heads nod.

"So the past is a waste?" a voice from behind him questions.

He turns and smiles. "No, Leslie, thank you, I'm not suggesting we run out and get lobotomies or never visit the past. We can learn from the past. We can gain comfort and sometimes a sense of control from the past.

"We need to know where we've been to have a clearer vision of where we're going. So, thinking about the past is fine as long as it has some value to, or in, the present.

"For example, just the process of remembering a pleasant past experience can be a calming influence, which is a good thing. Thinking back about how we did something or failed to do something once before, can help us learn how to handle the same or similar circumstances here and now—also a good thing."

He continues pacing. He continues to process his inner dialogue. *My legs feel like that cartoon rubber guy...is it Gumby? I really beat up on my body with all that lifting!* Maddigan looks to the ceiling for inspiration.

"Ah, then there's the future, which is not yet here, and may never come anyway... this building could, heaven forbid, explode two minutes from now, and it won't have done you much good to have used those two minutes to worry about next week's test, so the future...is also fantasy!" He can see he is losing some students. *I need to slow down. It is, after all, a lot to absorb in one ninety-minute class.*

"If you bring yourself to the point of worrying about the future, which I can assure you accomplishes nothing—I know. I've tried it! You end up, again, missing the present. You can actually become as neurotic as those who hang out in the past. The bottom line is that worrying about the future is not any healthier than dwelling on the past.

"Worrying about final exams now, for example, will only serve to make you sick, or eat, drink or smoke too much, or get in an argument, or become depressed...whatever."

He observes that his last set of comments seems to be connecting.

"Worrying about the future gets in the way of the present learning that you'll need to absorb in order to deal with final exams when they actually do come."

"But we have to plan stuff, don't we?"

"Good, Joyce! We have to plan stuff! Yes, we have to plan stuff. Like you'll have to plan your calendar to be sure you don't miss the finals. So, it's not like you can simply abandon thoughts about the future, but before your planning turns into worrying, you need to return your brain to where?"

"To the present?"

"Right again, Joyce. To the present, to what's going on," he snaps his fingers, "here and now."

He pauses to let the idea sink in.

"There's an old beer commercial that says 'You Only Go Around Once In Life!' That's a hellava statement. If it's true, it makes me think I sure don't want to waste what meager time I have left on earth—or of course in any business setting—worrying about what hasn't come or fretting about what's done and over."

His mind drifts back to JP's drawing.

A muffled sneeze erupts from the corner. The professor's attention snaps back to the room. "God bless you!" he says. He searches his mind for the illustration he needs to tie the lecture together. He resumes his pacing as he once again regards the flower art.

"Business tycoon Malcolm Forbes once said, 'As you get older, don't slow down: Speed up. There is less time left.'

What do *you* think? Write it down. Go ahead, write down what you think: Right this minute I am learning about mySELF that I... Finish the sentence. Write it down. It's for your brain only. I'm not collecting these. Go ahead. I'll wait."

He walks to the center of the circle, pushes his hair back behind his ears, knuckle-bumps his wire-rims up on his nose, scans the room and smiles.

How, then...HOW, now, mind you, I'm asking...how can we focus ourselves on the reality of the present moment to regain or remain in control of ourselves and most assuredly be better, more effective business people along the way?"

He paces two steps toward the windows. "We are here to learn how to be better, more effective business people, yes?"

Nods. Murmurs.

He watches a soaring seagull swoop past the window and dip briefly into the courtyard below. "Okay, then how do we stay in control? How do we focus ourselves on reality? The answer, my friends, is breathing. Breeeeathiiing!"

A couple of puzzled looks are exchanged. He knows he left some people a few statements back still dealing with the consequences of getting cut off in traffic, but decides to charge ahead anyway. *Good teaching challenges,* he reminds himself.

"When you breathe more deeply, you: One—think more clearly, Two—perform more confidently, Three—feel more relaxed, and Four—you are more productive more often."

He recites this introduction very deliberately, making use of emphatic pauses after each of the four benefits.

"When you breathe more deeply, you become healthier, happier, and have greater control of your mind, body, emotions, and day-to-day life circumstances.

"Every deep breath you take increases blood flow to relax your muscles, and boosts oxygen supply to your brain to help you be more alert. It soothes your neurological system."

He unrolls and tacks up a window shade-size diagram of The Neurological System. It's one he conned a medical book sales rep into giving him the day he helped her start her sputtering van in the Nursing Faculty parking lot. He spotted it on her front seat.

"And because your breathing, your pulse, your heartbeat are in fact the most here-and-now things happening to you every minute—every second of your life—then paying attention to them helps your mind to return its focus from time-wasting past and future issues, to the place where you can be most productive as a businessperson and, of course, as a human being..."

A loud whisper could be heard from the hallway, directed through the open door to someone in the back corner, and a hand-covered-mouth response: "Yeah. No. Not yet. I'll call..."

"Can we kill the hallway discussions in here please, people," he asks in a rather demanding manner with a slight glare directed to the corner. "I'd rather not have to close the door."

The culprit looks up, red-faced. He folds his hands on his desktop.

"Thank you, Bill. Remember, if you can train yourself to take deep breaths in response to stressful situations," he tosses a quick return visit glimpse to the corner, "you will be responding instead of reacting. And why is this important? Because when you can prevent yourself from reacting, you flat out eliminate all risk of over-reacting, and that, my friends, is a good thing for you, and for everyone in your path!

Let's all stand now and try this. Feet flat on the floor. Hands at your sides. Close your mouth and take a slow, deep breath in through your nose. Direct the air you inhale to the bottom part of your lungs so that..."

"So what's with the Teach, Boss? Has he got the goods, or what?"

"We'll know in a few minutes, Slam. The kid'll call when he gets the word. Speaking of the word, what's the word on the shipment coming in? Did the boats connect yet?"

"The word I got is that it's top grade. Simo says no contact yet. Our boys're a hunnert an' eighteen miles out, parallel to the coast, cruisin' the Canyon. Fish're runnin' and the water's calm right now, and so am I calm too. In fact, I told Simo that's the way we wanna keep it. Calm. Okay? This boat has gotta make it through the next few weeks, 'til we get Professor Maddigan where we want 'im. So that brings Mr. Pulver to stage center. I got 'im to just keep focused on the Teach, okay? I know you don't want no screw-ups here, okay so everyone's bein' real alert."

"You got that right, Slam. 'No screw-ups' is exactly right! Okay to go with Pulver as long as he keeps his mouth shut and does what you tell him."

"Thanks, Apple. No need to worry 'bout Pulver...and me and Billy're all over the Teach...like a blanket." Click.

Chapter 14

Yo-Yo 101

"Okay, great! Now that we all know how to breathe, I'm going to tell you about my special deal without having to be concerned about any of you getting over-stressed."

Maddigan pushes the heavy, beat-up old teacher's desk into the middle of the room, then climbs up on top and stands. He takes a white Duncan Yo-Yo from his pocket, adjusts the string and loops the noose-end past the second knuckle, over his right index finger. As if he were warming up, he proceeds to pump it up and down. He lets it sleep. Then snaps it back. He lets it sleep again, then walks it along the desktop in a jitter, then snaps it back again.

"Aaah, that's called 'Walk The Dog,'" he offers as an aside commentary. All eyes follow his movements. Many mouths are agape or grinning at the eccentricity of the moment. This is college? some of them are surely thinking.

He crouches and with the flick of his wrist, throws the spinning double disk underhanded out into a circle and then swirls it over his head. Chins jerk back into chests. Seemingly choreographed bodies, like roller coaster riders, lean sideways together in their seats. Eyes follow. He clears the ceiling by an inch, then snaps the spinning Duncan back. He lets it sleep. With his right hand still in control, he grabs a length of the string with his left hand and spreads it apart the width of his fingers, then swoops the spinning yo-yo to the apex of the string triangle he created, letting it swing back and forth three times, then snaps it back again. Some oooh's and aaah's. Scattered applause. No talking. Just one trick after another, then he returns to just pumping it up and down. He looks up at the fifty-seven mesmerized grins.

"For just the students in this class, I have made such a deal."

He smiles and continues the spinning, swirls, and snaps. "You won't believe this!"

He pauses again to repeat the triangle swing trick..."This is called 'Rock The Cradle,'" he says. Even the most withdrawn, most generally disinterested students are now sitting toward the front edges of their seats. Still on the desktop, Maddigan crouches into a deep knee-bend position, the re-wound toy now securely in his palm.

"Here's the deal: I was able to work it out—for this class only—that anyone in here who wants to go to Jamaica for spring break, for—wait 'til you hear this—$35 total, I have secured a special package rate. Just imagine yourselves out in the sun and fresh air, on the beach, in the sand, with the surf rolling in. And all you'll need is a sleeping bag and money for food."

"And drinks?" someone asks.

"And drinks," he responds. He stands again, and stops talking long enough to arc the yo-yo over a few ducking heads. Another aside: "That one's called 'Around The World.'" It swirls around, then plunges suddenly into his pocket!

"The only catch is that, if you're interested in going, I need to collect a $2 deposit from each of you, right now. So, if you want to take advantage of this one-time Seaport County Community College business management trip, pass up your $2 now, or borrow it from your neighbor if you need to. Just bring the money up to my desk and take your nametag, and I'll see that you're included on the reservation list."

Uproar hits the room. Desks slide, screech and clack. Students dig through wallets, pocketbooks and pants pockets. Nervous laughter. Change clinks. Bills rumple. Instant loans are arranged. Money pours forth. He pulls the string from his finger and shoves the yo-yo further down into his pocket, then hops from the desk.

The room is silent as he counts the cash: $114. He wads it up and scoops the change, and dumps it all into the side pouch of his mailbag. He looks up, and the questions start.

"When do we leave?"

"Are you going too?"

"Can we bring friends or family?"

"Where do we sleep?"

"When do we come back?"

He holds out the palm of his hand like he is stopping traffic, and ambles over to the green blackboard. He picks out a new piece of yellow chalk and scrawls across the board: YOU'VE BEEN HAD! YOU'VE BEEN SOLD BY A. I. D. A. S.

"Here's what happened here, people. While we were learning to breathe, I ran what's called a little 'teaser' campaign. By the way, are you breathing?" He pauses.

"I mentioned a 'special deal' to you a couple of times, right? That was the 'teaser.' Then what? Then, I got up on the desk and played with a yo-yo, yes? And I managed to attract your attention. The A of AIDAS is ATTENTION.

"Next I did what? I created interest with a no-brainer price tag: who wouldn't jump at a $35 trip to Jamaica? The I of AIDAS is IN-TEREST.

"Then I painted a mental picture for you of the sand and surf and beach that stimulated your desire. The D of AIDAS is DESIRE And notice, I stimulated, not created it. You already have desire inside you!

"Finally, I got your money. Thank you very much by the way. That'll buy me a few lunches this month. When you passed your money up here, I brought about action. The second A in AIDAS is for ACTION.

"And where did I fail? I didn't get the S. The S in AIDAS stands for ensuring SATISFACTION. But I didn't do that, so that just makes you unhappy customers. You may never do business with me again, but I still have your money."

"But you lied to us, so we should get our money back!" floats an assertive female voice from over near the door.

He waltzes slowly around the circle. "Well that's a good point, Karen, I probably should give you the money back if I lied to you, but you know what? I didn't lie to you. Well, except maybe about the fresh air part!"

"Wait a minute, Rick," blurted a gruff male voice from the opposite side of the room. "You said we were going to Jamaica for Spring Break so you had to be lying because airfare alone costs a lot more than $35, and..."

"Aaaah, yes, Bob," the professor turned to face his accuser, "but you assumed I meant the Caribbean island of Jamaica. I do confess to a slight error of omission, but I was referring to the sun and surf and sandy beaches—and, uh, maybe not such fresh air—in Jamaica, Queens, in New York City. I mean you could—perhaps at risk of life and limb, or possibly an overnight jail stay—sleep on the beach. And, by the way, the bus fare is $20 per person one-way. And since I never said this was a round-trip arrangement, I figured on keeping $15 from each of you as an agent fee, and let you find your own way home." He gives the class his best cat-that-ate-the-canary grin.

We've-really-been-had looks crossed every face. Moans and groans.

"AIDAS, Ladies and Gentlemen, is a guide. (Remember, in business: *There Are No Rules!*) AIDAS is a guide for creating and for sizing up almost any successful marketing, advertising, and public relations campaign. It is also a guide for how to approach direct one-on-one and mass audience sales presentations. Tomorrow, we will have an open discussion about the morality issues attached to AIDAS. You will prepare a one-page report citing three examples of AIDAS that you discover between now and tomorrow's class. I strongly recommend that you tackle this tonight, and not try to wing it at the last minute, unless you really want to see my 'bullshit' stamp."

He dumps the cash back out onto his desk and turns his back to the class to erase the board, talking over his shoulder: "You can pick up your $2 on the way out. Any money left over will be donated to the Fishuggers of America research fund for their Save the Turtles program. Have a good night, all. Oh, and Bill, will you please see me before you leave."

Fifty-six people were certain Bill was going to get reamed out for talking to someone in the hallway during class. Instead, Bill got a textbook that no one would ever realize had been hollowed out. The Professor picked up twenty-seven one-dollar bills, tucked them into a "Save The Turtles" envelope, and left whistling.

Chapter 15

SIMO SAYS

"PULL YOUR PORT TO OUR STARBOARD!"

Moroccan-American Captain Simo yells across his bow to the captain of the other boat as he barks out orders to his own crew and holds the trawler steady between waves. He understands boats and respects the sea, but he knows this dress rehearsal run, and especially the next, the real thing, would test his mettle.

Swarthy. Surly. Intimidating. Six-foot four. Simo's 240 pounds of tattooed muscle creep up out of his collar to frame a crooked nosed, scar-ravaged face that sports a stiff upper lip, and a week of stubble under steely deep set eyes. His unruly graying hair is half hidden under a black knit watchcap. The captain commands attention as readily at the helm as he does on his corner barstool at Gilligan's, across from the bulkhead where his trawler ties up between trips. No one bucks his orders at sea. No one crosses him up at the bar.

Gusts from the Northeast had stirred up Hudson Canyon waters after a relatively calm forty-eight hours and the resulting whitecaps plunk some nasty slaps and knocks against the two gingerly approaching hulls as they slowly come alongside each other—ninety-five miles out at sea, hours away from the Barnegat Light Inlet Coast Guard Station.

"PUT THEM BUMPERS OUT! CLEAT THE FOOKIN' LINES! MOVE IT! MOVE IT! MOVE IT! WE CAN'T WAIT FOR THE WEATHER TO GET WORSE. HURRY IT UP! CAREFUL WITH THOSE BOXES...ONE GOES OVER-BOARD AND YOU GO WITH IT...FORTY-DEGREE WATER DON'T MUCH GIVE A SHIT IF YOU GOT IN IT BY MIS-TAKE OR NOT! YOU'D BE UNCONSCIOUS IN THIRTY MINUTES AN' WE AIN'T WASTIN' NO TIME TO HAUL YOUR SORRY ASS OUT! HURRY IT UP! WE AIN'T GOT ALL FOOKIN' DAY HERE! MOVE IT! MOVE IT! MOVE IT!"

The deckhands hustle as they exchange and stack the boxes. The passing and carrying is awkward and clumsy. Nets and fishing gear stowed, the crew is out of its element. They trip and bump into one another, once nearly losing grip on a box, but a panic-stricken last minute grab retrieved it before it could hit the ship's rail and fly over. The actual exchange of parcels takes about twenty minutes. Prevent-ing collision while separating the two boats so they could get under way, takes twenty more.

"OKAY, CAPTAIN!" shouts Captain Simo to the departing boat while taking one hand off the steerage to wave the thumbs up sign. He turns back to his controls and yells back over his shoulder, "GET THOSE FOOKIN' BOXES DOWN IN THE HOLD THEN GET READY TO ROLL...WE GOT TO OPEN HER UP WIDE TO GET THROUGH THIS BAD-ASS BLOW!"

The men scurry to pass the packages below, and lash them to the uprights and standing blocks. They close the hatches and move themselves into the cabin below deck where they hang onto rails and fixtures. Smoke billows at once from their pipes and cigarettes. They pass a bottle of rum that came on board with the boxes, as they settle in for the long pounding ride back to shore.

No one except the two captains knows that each box contains half a dozen worthless newspaper-wrapped building bricks salvaged from a demolition site.

"So what's the story, Billyboy? You got it, or what?" Slam has a habit of holding the dial phone receiver eight inches in front of his face when he speaks, and stares at it like he is expecting a piece of live film footage to roll across the little holes in the earpiece.

"Yeah, I got it. The professor did all right, Slam. Heather and I tried following his Myrtle the Turtle trail and he left none...like zero. He did what you told him and got rid of everything clean. Him and that girlfriend of his make a good team."

"Whadda youse, his PR agent or sometin'? Just get the freakin' thing over here quick. You got fifteen minutes before I put out an APB to slice up yer ugly face!"

"See you in a few." Click.

The two men sip and stir their cappuccinos while late afternoon light floods Apple Solamente's library through mahogany French doors. The library is Apple's favorite of twenty-three rooms in the hand-laid stone castle-style mansion, across a gated private bridge from the mainland to the Solamente Family's Gwyneth Bay island compound.

"Things are lookin' good, Apple. Yer niece and..."

"You mean Heather McGrath?"

"Yeah, Hedder M'Gratt. And Billyboy. They got the goods from the professor. And on top of that, the ships..." He sipped from the steaming cup, "...the ships did a dry run and they met at sea and

Captain Simo says it went like clockwork."

"Good job, Slam. Clockwork is good. And practicing with boxes of bricks is also good, but now we have to concentrate on getting the chip info processed so we have the exact details we need to set up for exchanging the real stuff."

"Well, tell Billy and Heather they're doing a good job, and before long they'll have enough money to raise their baby the right way."

Apple gives his cup another stir. As he raises the cup to sip, he squints over the tops of his reading glasses under a thick tangle of eyebrows that give a certain wildness to his metallic gray eyes.

Slam nods obligingly.

Apple puts the cup down and stares absently out the bay window at nearby gulls gliding over the entrance bridge to his property.

"You know, Slam, we don't have the date yet, but we can bet the drop's going to be in the next four to five weeks at the latest, and we're going to need another boat to be the 'safe boat.' We need something to run alongside the mother ship and be there just in case there's some kind of screw-up: about thirty-five, forty foot should do the job. Got any ideas?"

"I jus' maybe do, Apple. I jus' maybe do. I'll let you know something in the next day or two." He smiles when he realizes he'd just rhymed his response.

"Good." Apple rises from his leather reading chair to take a phone call in private. His twenty-year-old son, Benjamin, had beckoned him with a thumb-to-ear-pinkie-to-mouth fist from the other side of the French doors.

Apple leaves the steaming cappuccino on the side table where his nautical maps hang over the edge like paper drapes, and an open copy of Chapman's *PILOTING—Seamanship and Small Boat Handling* covers most of a yellow legal pad which covers dozens of scattered index cards full of notes.

After a while, Apple was still not returning. Slam leans out the French doors to check up and down the hall, then drinks the rest of what's in his mug, and finishes his boss's too. He slides the two empties across the conference table, wipes his chin with his sleeve, and leaves quietly through the side entrance.

Chapter 16

THE BOARDS

"So, Professor, did you, uh, give Bill Shill a thrill when you, uh, handed him the pill?"

"You mean chip? I gave him a chip, not a pill."

"Chip doesn't rhyme."

JP stands in front of Maddigan at the kitchen table while he grades papers. She's munching on a variety of treasures from behind an open refrigerator door while peeling off her aerobics outfit, and changing into her waitress uniform. When he looks up, pleased to discover the view, she has a baby carrot in her mouth and is reaching for the cream cheese with one hand while pulling up her stockings with the other. *She's always in a time crunch,* he reminds himself, *doing two or three or four things at once.*

"He said whoever hollowed it out had a real knack for espionage. I told him my source would have to remain a professional secret."

"Well good. I certainly don't want to do that again." She closes the refrigerator door with her foot and finishes the carrot. "Y'know what it's like cutting squares in the middle of all those pages? Did he say anything else? Was he taking it straight to Scam, or whatever his name is?"

Now she's chomping on a celery stalk plastered with a lump of cream cheese, while she steps and slithers into her sexy, little blue and white, short-skirted uniform dress. He is enjoying the sideshow.

"Slam. Yeah. He said Slam would be pleased, and that I'd hear from the bastard sometime this weekend. Hopefully, this will end the whole blackmail thing, though I'm not sure what I'll do if it doesn't. These are pretty rough people. I've really got to watch my step. I sure as hell don't want anymore dead turtle jobs. What are you thinking?"

"I'm thinking we need to buy more cream cheese." She scrapes the foil wrapper remnants onto her last bite of celery. "No, serious. I'm thinking they should be passing out smiley faces for you doing their dirty work, but I still don't trust that they're going to leave you, us, alone, if you know what I mean. Like they got what they wanted, but as long as you keep scoring pot from the channel you've been swimming in, they can keep you on a short fishing line." She stands staring at him as she buttons up the blue and white front.

"Great. So I should give up my only vice to kiss a bunch of mobsters' asses?"

"Your ONLY vice, Rick? Please! Remember we live together, and I'm twenty-one and you're thirty-three, and we have sex ten times a week, and we drink beer on weekends until we can hardly walk, and when our cokehead friends from New York show up for their monthly boat visit, we do lines. On top of..."

"Okay, okay, okay. You're right as usual." He is mesmerized watching her tuck her breasts into her waitressing bra. "I'm sorry. You're right. I'm sorry. It's just that I'm really not ready to give up pot. It keeps me relaxed and feeds my creativity."

"That's terrific. You're relaxed and creating, while I've become your accomplice in a mob-related caper involving a dead hundred pound turtle and God knows what else, and now we're both at risk because you have to keep scoring your illegal smoke from a connected source."

He puts down his pen and pushes his papers to the side. She fusses with her hair.

"What source isn't connected?"

"I can get it from Vanessa at work. No one will even know you're involved. It's just between her and me."

"Yeah, but I don't want your neck out too. What if somebody sees you?"

She reaches for her little red The Shanty apron with the big pockets.

"My neck is already out, Professor. And besides, nobody's going to notice us in her car in the dark at the back of the lot, after the restaurant's closed. So why don't you just let me handle this for you, okay? I'll see her Friday night. She's always got some with her. I'll pay whatever it is and you can pay me back. As long as you let me have some with you whenever we fool around. It, you know, makes me... creative!"

The return of the dimple.

He picks up his pen and twirls it between his fingers. She, elbows out, is tying an apron string bow behind her back.

"Hey," he says, "speaking of which—the creative thing, I mean—what if you and I start up a weekly group counseling session?"

The question stops her in her tracks. She takes off her small, wiry glass frames to rub the lenses on a kitchen towel that hangs from the refrigerator door. He sees that his wild shot question actually hits the target.

"We can't legitimately call it *counseling* 'cause, technically speaking, neither of us has the right professional credentials, but, informally speaking, we can be *consultants!* I thought maybe something like:

New Age Group Consultants for Personal and Professional Growth and Development. Whadda you think?"

She touches a drop of saliva to her finger and onto one of her lenses, towels it again then rehooks the delicate frame over her ears and smiles pensively.

"Where'd your inspiration come from for this one? We've only seen two movies this year: *On Golden Pond* and *Chariots of Fire*. No, wait, I know. Your spirit was moved by our favorite Christopher Cross song—*Sailing*, right?"

"Ahhhh, c'mon Green Eyes, how about it? I mean you're getting qualified in elementary education. I've got degrees in management and philosophy, and almost in human development. We've been to a zillion practical psychology and psychotherapy conference sessions together, and we've both worked with a slew of top trainers and authors."

JP swipes her hair behind one ear. She squints her right eye closed a couple of times, but stays fixed on his movements as he rises and begins to pace a few steps in one direction, then a few steps back in another. He's speaking faster now.

"We're always helping friends and students with problems, right? What if we just put a flyer together, pass it around discreetly, and see what we get? I'm sure we can make a difference for a lot of people. Besides, we can probably make some extra spending money at it. Does this work for you? For us?" He grabs the chairback and leans forward.

She'd been staring at him the whole time while nibbling a last bite of pretzel and crawling, slow motion—caught in thought—into her down ski jacket. She glances up to the cottage rafters momentarily, then straddles a kitchen chair, leaning her arms and chin over the back, facing him.

"Hmmmmmmm." She straightens herself, skirt, jacket, hair, and tries to act unfettered, but her white shoes jiggling under the chair rung give away her enthusiasm.

"And how long has this groupie deal been on your fuzzy little brain, Mr. Rick?"

He smiles. He likes the way she straddles chairs and acts boyish.

"Actually, I had this idea last summer. I thought about calling the sessions 'Anchor Outs,' where we would take ten or twelve people on the boat and throw the anchor out and sit around on the deck and do role-playing and psychodrama and Gestalt techniques to help them solve their problems. We would charge a fee to cover costs. Nothing much. Just enough to put a little change in our pockets, and prompt our sign-ups to feel committed. We could throw in beverages and snacks, or a box lunch. In the winters we do the sessions in our living room. He pauses to catch his breath. So?"

Her steadily growing grin is now a bright toothy white display.

"Oh, Rick, it's a G R E A T idea! Working together? I love it. Besides, it'll be fun to rattle those tenure-driven colleagues of yours who are always on your case, and they'll be dead-ended since it has no involvement with the college, and we wouldn't be claiming to be shrinks." She reaches for another carrot from the foil wrapper on the table, puts it in her mouth and holds it there without chomping, like a cigar.

"Of course we'll need a bigger living room in the winters. When do we start?"

"Why don't you draft the flyer? I'll start telling some folks I know who I think might be interested in participating. We'll need to hurry to get the boat ready so maybe it can go in the water the week before St. Patrick's Day, like Tuesday the tenth. That would give us enough planning time so we could start the first weekend in April, uh, with a couple of space heaters thrown in!"

"Heated Anchor Outs. Neat. It'll be good experience. And between my college loans and your endless boat expenses, some extra bucks wouldn't hurt any. I'll start on it right away." She snaps off a piece of carrot, and crunches the rest between her teeth.

"Super. Lets' do it!"

She tosses him the leftover hunk, which he pops into his mouth and chews noisily.

"By the way, Professor, 'Let's Do It' is a new aerobic dance I just learned that I'm going to be teaching to my class next week. Do you think you might be interested in seeing me 'do it' for you tonight? And I don't mean to disappoint you ahead of time, but before you answer you should know that—even if nothing else—I really do have to wear sneakers so I don't twist my ankles."

"Well, if that's the case, please schedule me in. And I don't mean to disappoint you ahead of time, but before you book the event you should know that if you're not wearing anything but sneakers, I don't think it'll be your ankles I'll be watching."

She bats her eyes back at him.

"And, besides, you won't need to do your usual warm-up exercises because I'm already warmed up having just watched this changing of the outfits ceremony."

The dimple.

"I might keep my gold neck chain on."

She turns, pecks him on the cheek, and leaves.

Chapter 17

34° AT 7:30PM

"Apple? Slam here. Listen, the boat thing...how much can we spend to get a good backup escort boat for this haul?"

"Figure 'bout one-fifty, Slam. Nothing more though."

"Good, Boss. I think I got just the right thing."

"Let me guess, Slam—our professor friend?"

"Yeah, the Teach. He's got a thirty-eight footer, fourteen foot beam, sleeps six, twin Daytona four hundreds on Chrysler blocks. Like new. Fast Eddie does the engines. He's on the boat every week or two doing tune-ups that ain't really needed. He says the Professor is a head case about the engines, and the girlfriend is a looker if you know what I mean."

"Is that a problem, Slam? Eddie?"

"Nah. Eddie's old enough to be her grandfather. He just gets the hots for any skirt that's nice to him. Says she smiles at him. He's harmless."

"I'll take your word for it, Slam. So the boat's okay?"

"The boat's in good shape, Apple. I hear it runs like a top. Eddie says it flies. He says the Prof paid eighty-two a year ago, and put about seven or eight into it, plus winter fees. He should be happy to take thirty down and a promise of ten a month for a year of payments, which of course we'll short him on. I'll talk with him."

"Maybe a good idea to invite his girlfriend into the discussion, Slam, y'know? She'd probably jump at the money before he would, and that would seal the deal."

"Yeah, Boss. Good idea! I'll talk with the brawd too if that's what it takes."

"We'll speak tomorrow, Slam. Let me know."

"You got it, Apple. Later." Click.

"Billyboy? Hey, Apple says to tell you 'good work!' and now we need to speak with the Teach again. Can you get him the message to call me at this number tonight at nine so I can tell him how pleased we are with his job that he did us, and that I have a very special piece of good news he'll want to know?"

"Right, Slam, get him to call you tonight, nine, got it."

"Thanks, Billyboy. Later." Click.

An hour later. "Hey Bill! It's me again. I just heard from Apple, and he says he needs you to set up something with Captain Simo, so skip the message thing that I told you about for the Teach for now."

"It's no big deal, Slam. I can still take care of it."

"I know it's no big deal, but just do as you're told, Billyboy. Stop off at the castle and get the scoop direct from the Boss. I'll make sure the message stuff is taken care of. Pulver and yer old lady Hedder..."

"Heather, Slam. It's Heather!"

"Yeah, well, Hedder and Pulver can find Maddigan for me. It's better you should do what Apple needs. Call me after you get back from Simo. And don't let him drag you into no card games or drink-

ing contests. There ain't no way you can win either one against him!"
Click.

Maddigan pulls on his thermals and bright blue nylon work-out pants with zippered ankles and a gold stripe down each leg. He scootches his matching hooded jacket over his head, and laces up his running shoes.

The hood-framed beard and glasses, he thinks, as he glances at the dark entrance hall mirror on his way out, makes him look like a monk or a serial killer. He's not fond of either image. He pushes the hood away, and flips on his blue and orange New York Mets cap. He tucks a house key into his zippered jacket pocket and stuffs a pair of insulated gloves halfway into his back pants pocket, fingers flopping with each step. Locking the door behind him, he skips down the front steps, and heads toward the beach. He shakes out his hands and wrists to get the blood flowing, and animatedly stretching his neck, arms and shoulders along the way.

Eyes half closed, he notices two window lamps and the driveway spotlight immersing the twenty-something's cottage in a pale yellow glow as he breezes past, following his ears to the ocean.

It's thirty-four degrees at 7:30PM—time, he decides, to get himself back into pre-turtle excursion condition, and an invigorating evening jog along the boardwalk will get him recharged while he waits for JP to get home.

The roar of the shore increases steadily as he approaches the beach. A distant foghorn bellows its muffled warnings every five seconds. A mile and a half of sand would lead him to the Southern end of the boardwalk, or "the boards" as locals call it...snowfenced-in and accessible only from street parking and periodic entrance ramps.

Two or three round-trip laps on the 1.1 mile stretch will get his heart rate up and work out some of his muscle stiffness.

As pleased as he is with JP's take on his idea to team up on running an informal counseling group and doing sessions on the boat, he feels panicky thinking about Slam's other shoe, and when it might drop. The bastards have their microchip, but now what will keep them from blackmailing him further?

He picks up his pace as he leaves the sand and starts up the ramp. At the top, he breaks into an easy jog.

With his career on the edge the way it is, he keeps imagining the worst. He'd be a basket case if he didn't have the classroom and counseling interfaces he thrives on. His advertising years produced record client sales of hot dogs, cigarettes, useless appliances, habit-forming drugs and stupid vanity products, and rewarded him with a plastic, capitalistic lifestyle that he hated, that his ex-wife cherished.

Now, thank God—good riddance—he is done with both. Now it is only his teaching that's important—his teaching, making a difference, JP, the boat.

Yet he stands to lose it all because the wrong people discovered his weakness, a problem he hasn't been able to solve for himself. He's tried everything he knows, but can't shake the cravings. Maybe, he thinks, he can at least shake his tormentors. Maybe he should take JP and move somewhere new and start all over. Maybe they should just sell their cars, load up the boat and like the song, go *Sailing*... disappear into the sunset.

He sometimes feels so untrue to himself for not following his heart and taking off like that.

He jogs. Even with the near-freezing temperature, he begins to break into a sweat.

A boat escape had great emotional appeal, but it would leave her family to deal with. He'd have no problem bon voyaging her parents. They just pretend to like him anyway. He knows they can't cut through the age difference thing. Trying to explain that their middle daughter lives on a boat with one of her professors paralyzes their vocal cords at family and community gatherings. He sees them smile through gritted teeth.

On the flip side, three of her four sisters—the oldest and two younger—accept him at face value. He wouldn't want to leave them behind anymore than JP would. But the other, JP's second-oldest sister, Birdie, is an insufferable egocentric working on her third husband. She barges her way into the family spotlight at the expense of anyone else who manages to get near the stage.

He hops deftly around a mound of windswept sand that covers a major section of planking in front of him. A pecking seagull there skirmishes out of the way.

The thing is, he knows that even if he and JP could get past leaving her family ties on the dock, the creeps who crunched him into this corner would probably find him again anyway.

Every hundred feet, lamppost quartz bulbs cast down fuzzy mist-filled puffs of light across the boards—enough to outline every nearby structure along the mile plus of "Air Conditioned" honky-tonkness.

Well-worn, concrete-braced wooden benches line the stretch of railings adjacent to the beach and ocean. Large black trash barrels stand sentry, chained to railing uprights.

"CLOSED FOR THE WINTER" arcades, bathhouses, miniature golf courses, and lucky number wheel-spin booths loom out of the darkness awaiting their thirtieth or fortieth layers of April paint.

Boarded-up baseball, basketball, dart throw, and ring toss amusements are jammed in between cavernous alleyways filled with canvas-covered kiddy rides, a dismantled Ferris wheel, and racks of dented bumper cars.

Dingy, faded signs fight haphazardly for attention: "Daffy's Taffy," "Harry's Hot Dogs & Hamburgers," "Ben N. Sherry's Ice Cream," "Limey Lois's Lemonade," "Charlotte's Cotton Candy," "Candi Butts' Candy Apples," "Angelo's Pizza & Fudge," "Pete The Greek's Pancake House."

He laughs out loud at the visual hodge podge, even though he sees it every day.

He passes the four tables and seven counter stools at "Ken and Carol's THE COTTAGE Breakfast and Clam Chowder" next to "Danielle's Souvenirs/Sun Products and Pet Hermit Crabs."

The more he pays attention to what he's passing, the more he seems to be heating up and perspiring. He raises his elbows out to draw more air up into his lungs.

He remembers begging to go to all of these places as a little kid, pulling on his mother's skirt, his father's sleeve, whining for a custard, or ten pennies to split with his kid brother for a full half hour of arcade entertainment—now limited to fifty-cent games that last two and a half minutes. It's nuts, he thinks—less time for more money?

Accentuated by the distant foghorn blasts, his jogging sets him into a trance, producing exactly the mind-freeing state he sought. The wind and sand-battered buildings he trots past, with cartoon castle turret and animal figurine silhouetted rooftops, are backed by a sea of tourist bungalows—row upon row of empty, 20 x 30-foot cookie-cutter shingled boxes with tiny, screened porches and a car's width of space.

He thought of his daily childhood trips to the beach and rowboat crabbing expeditions. He recalled the rarely affordable sea-breezed evening boardwalk rides, probably on the same winter-after-winter stowed bumper cars he just jogged past. He and his little brother, Jordan, would play endlessly in the shady sand between cottages.

Daddy always proclaimed his delight that the boys were enjoying the fresh ocean air while he slugged back his "vacation drinks." Mommy passed her time at the kitchen table, reading paperback novels, stripped, as they were, of the "smutty" covers she was afraid the boys would see, or that she was afraid her husband would find out that the boys had seen.

Like the commercial facades along the boards, most of the bungalows near the beach had withstood another winter of nor'easter winds sand-blasting their exposed walls, doors, and window frames. All but the most freshly painted surfaces were reduced to smudges of bare wood, as if they had been dragged through a tunnel of giant steel wool pads.

He notices some form of excitement, blurred lights and muffled sounds shooting out across the boards a couple of hundred yards in front of him. He picks up his pace.

Chapter 18

~~~

THE FOGHORN

Two bundled-up elderly couples stroll across Maddigan's jogging path to lean on the railing and gaze at the rolling waves beyond the blanket of sand. They are laughing, pointing, tossing scarves over their shoulders, and pulling caps down tighter. They don't notice him.

Another jogger, headed his way, nods a flash of eye contact as he passes close enough to deliver sounds of labored breathing between puffs of condensation. Maddigan almost asked about the clamor ahead when he saw it was just the arcade. He'd forgotten how overbearing its pandemonious presence could be on dismal, empty winter nights.

The boardwalk railings, thickened by years of seasonal coats of paint, are interrupted every eighth of a mile by entrance steps to the beach. At the top of each entranceway—New Jersey, having perhaps the only oceanfront beaches in the world requiring payment to enter—stand claustrophobically small beach-badge purchase and badge-checker gazebos like so many phone booth sentries guarding the granules of sand.

Next to each of these structures, heavy upside-down lifeboats are rust-encrusted-padlock-chained to heavy beach lifeguard chairs lying on their sides, which are rust-encrusted-padlock-chained to the wooden boardwalk deck railings.

But he has stopped noticing what's around him. He is beginning to concentrate instead on his breathing, his pulse, his sweat, the swishing noise his nylon sleeves and pants legs make. He pushes his sliding, fogged-over eyeglass frames up to the bridge of his nose.

Now, a third of the way along, his senses seem to re-ignite as he passes the source of all the activity he'd found worrisome only minutes earlier: the only sign of winter nightlife for miles around—Lucky's Year-Round Arcade.

A conglomeration of amplified clinks, clunks, bells, whistles, sirens, and recorded witchy-sounding laughter, layered under blinking colored lights, simulated gunfire, hot air blasting from two overhead heater fans, and the smell of popcorn, all explode out of the dark across the boards, interrupting the stupefying trance his jogging is prompting, overwhelming the distant foghorn.

Lucky's was never crowded during the off-season. He heard that 'the take' of summer months filled the owner's Cadillac trunk three or four times a day, and nightly, with buckets full of quarters— a bounty that must surely cover winter staff and electricity expenses.

He thinks he sees a familiar face flash a look at him as he passes. Then, before he can glance back, it is gone. He keeps jogging. Perhaps he would step inside on his return trip to survey the handful of people he imagines are huddled around the games. Maybe the face belonged one of his students. Or maybe it's just his levitated state of mind, or his drizzled lenses. He'll stop to clean them at the North End turn-around.

He feels his legs warming up and lengthens his stride.

Arcade sound and light fragments dissipate as he starts to approach the fringe of a "runner's high." Even the collection of shifting peripheral visions is giving way to the running experience. Moving now at a good clip, he is starting to perspire. His eyes tear at the corners, and he pulls his jacketzipper half-way down to get more air. His leg muscles limber, he starts kicking into a slight bounce off the wood surface. His thoughts turn to feelings and he is starting to feel physically renewed.

As he reaches the more isolated North End, the air feels colder and denser, but he is now sweating freely. He's glad to see the familiar sea-salted gray condos spring up into sight on the left as he hears the racing waves rushing along the inlet rock walls ahead and knows he will soon make the welcome turn that would put the onshore winds at his back. Warning cries from the distant foghorns seem to sweep closer.

A hundred or so feet after his turn, at a particularly dark spot that manages to escape the spires of misty light thrown to the boards on either end, he slows to a rapid walk, removes his glasses and rubs the lenses with a tissue from his jacket pocket.

As he returns the wireframes to his ears and takes two steps back into a jog pace, someone steps abruptly out of the shadows in front of him and stands just ten feet away, directly in his path. He slows again and is about to say good evening, and toggle to the side, when two vice-like arms grab him suddenly and silently from behind. He stumbles and loses his balance but the set of workout arms hold him in place like he was a giant tent peg being readied for sledge-hammering.

"Hey! What's..."

"Shuddup, Teach! Move over here behind this building with us. We just wanna talk, okay?"

"Yeah, but I..."

"I said shuddup! It's cold out here an' I don't want to waste no time so I'll ask the questions. You give the answers, okay?"

The vice closed tighter on his arms. He thought about being sledge-hammered into the boardwalk. He nodded.

"That's better, Teach. Now, first I'm gonna tell you that you did the turtle thing good, you and yer girlfriend."

"You leave her out of this! I..."

"Teach, yer not listening good, here. Now shuddup! Or if you don't listen, my friend Mr. Pulver, here—as in Pulverizer, get it?—he makes pixie dust outta yer shoulder sockets, got it?"

Maddigan nods. Of course he knows the voice, but the restaurant building shadows and his re-steamed-up glasses keep both mobster faces a mystery. He feels his wrists being tied. He thinks about yelling and trying to make a break for the open arcade until an image of pulverized shoulder sockets, not unlike a handful of pebbles in a cup of cornstarch, flashes past. He shudders.

"Now, here's the scoop. Billyboy was supposed to call you, but he got sidetracked to another assignment, so Mr. Pulver here and me decided we'd see you in person, okay? Soooooooo, let's take a nice quiet stroll down by the water while Pulver helps me explain what you and me gotta settle."

The three of them walk down the North End ramp to the beach and out toward the water's edge, Slam remains six to ten feet off to the side and Pulver, an arm's distance behind him, tugs every couple of steps on the wrist bindings. The waves are whisking out the last of a low tide. Shells and stones clatter maniacally under the rumbling of the surf. Boardwalk lights are almost lost to the growing fog. The fog warnings, still five seconds apart, are now more muffled...more like groans than horn blasts. The men stop inches from where the last wave sprawls across the sand. Slam moves to face Maddigan and looks up into his captive's face with a big, greasy smile. Pulver, who is still holding on as if in a steer-roping contest, takes up Slam's post on the side facing Portugal.

"I'm gonna make you an offer, Teach, and for the sake of yer little JP girlfriend there, and her VW, and her job at The Shanty, and her dance class, and her old man's health problems, I'm sure you'll find the offer I give you is going to be totally irresistible."

Maddigan's face. In instant rage. Eyes shooting daggers. But the slight tug on the rope he feels in response to his clenched jaw and squinted stare, is damn near pulling his arms out of his armpits. He somehow manages to grit his teeth hard enough to keep from screaming in Slam's face.

"Besides, that job you got at the college still depends heavily on us keeping our mouths shut about you buying pot from the Pine Beach boys. The way you handled the turtle deal helped yer cause, but we got o-n-e m-o-r-e thing we still need yer help with."

Maddigan is shaken to the core. His anger quickly gives way to fear. He's doing everything he can to keep his knees from knocking.

"Okay, what's the story, Slam?" he mutters between tight teeth.

"Good boy, Teach! I knew you'd see things our way." He pauses to light a cigar. The windblown glow outlines a hard face filled with tough and sinister lines. "We want to rent yer boat."

"Now, wait a minute, I..." He pauses to take a deep breath and collect his thoughts, put more calm into his response. But he is too rattled. It comes out as desperate begging.

Chapter 19

THE DEAL

"Listen, Slam, I need my boat. I mean I really need it. It's not for rent. I don't have anyplace else to live in two weeks. I..."

"Yer starting to get under my nerves, Teach! Yer not listening so good!" On cue, Pulver tightens his grip. "I didn't say we was taking yer boat, but yer making that a tempting idear. I says we're wanting to rent yer boat. We'll pay you more than what it's worth, and in one year—after it's all paid off—we'll give it back to you for free. So just consider it a twelve-month rental. We rent it for ten thousand a month for twelve months, and we'll even throw in ten thousand bucks deposit up front to help you an the ladyfriend find a place to live. Okay? How 'boutcha, Teach?"

"Are you crazy? The boat's not for rent OR for sale. And it's worth more than $130,000 anyway!" Maddigan starts to struggle with the rope, but then sees Pulver's huge shadow outlined against the distant glow of Lucky's arcade, and eases up.

"You're pretty good at doing arithmetic there, Teach. But we know you paid eighty-two and got—at the most—another ten into it, so one-thirty is a good deal."

"I'll consider one-fifty with twenty-five more up front."

"HA! I don't think you're in much position to bargain here,

Teach. This ain't no flea market, but I like yer spunk. I'll get you twenty up front with ten a month for twelve months, and that's it. A hundred and forty total and you get the vessel back in one year. Take it or Pulver here breaks yer arm...good deal, right?"

Maddigan grunts. Slam looks away into the darkness, spits into the waves, and takes a series of short puffs on his cigar.

Still facing the ocean, Slam continues, half-shouting over his shoulder, "So it's a good idear you should take the deal. In case you decide to leave it, by the way, you might want to know that Pulver here snaps your arm in half right now, and nobody's gonna hear you screaming all the way down here by the water, so think about trying to get back home with yer arm dangling in pieces."

Slam puffs again. "Oh, and Teach, you should know that yer visit to the Point Pleasant Hospital Emergency Room to get yer bones put back together, followed by three or four months in a sling with pain pills for breakfast, lunch and dinner, and arm aches the rest of yer life every time it rains, is just for openers!"

Slam puffs. "We will also have to send a couple of 'marijuana revelation' letters to the Jersey Shore Times-Observer and Seaport County Press, plus pay some damaging-type visits to Dr. Stafford's office at the college, and to your little girl's car, and job, and dance class. Oh, yeah, and to her sick daddy too, you got it?"

Maddigan feels his lips quiver. "Yes, dammit! I got it," he says.

He looks out over the only three waves he can actually see rolling in from the blackness, then turns back to Slam.

"What do you want my boat for, and when do I get it back, and what happens if it's damaged, and how can I be sure you won't bother my friend or her family, or me or my job, and—since I obviously have no choice—when do I get the twenty and when do the monthly payments start and how will you make those payments and when and where? And can you please untie me. I'm not a criminal here."

"Jesus, Teach. You ask a lotta freakin' questions." He takes two quick puffs.

"Pulver, take the rope off!"

He flicks a long ash off the end of his stogie and looks up to the distant boardwalk, which is gracefully slipping away into the night fog.

"What we do with yer boat is none of yer business. Let's just say we're planning a little—" he gestures with the sweeping glow in his fingertips, "—fishing trip. You get it back in twelve months. We ain't gonna damage it, and if we do, we'll pay to have it fixed by anybody you want. We catch the right kind of fish and you don't need to worry about the boat, or your little girlfriend, or her family or yer arm, or yer job because me and the Pine Beach boys is outta here—gone from yer life forever—headed to another country and another professor with another young honey somewhere."

Slam kicks at the sand and gazes absently over the restless sea. He flips his cigar stub into the water.

"You'll get the twenty smackers next week, in the same book, back from Billy. We take the boat next week so yer first ten is next week also. That makes thirty big ones in the book. You'll get ten more on the first of every month mailed to you at yer college box from different book company return addresses so it looks legit. I'll call you when to meet Bill. He gets the keys and you gets the book with the do-re-me. Now go back to the boardwalk before yer muscles decide to—aw-trophy— is that the word? Or before Pulver here decides to take up joggin' and follow you home.

'Night, Teach!"

With Pulver's grip and shadow fresh in his mind, Maddigan runs two-thirds of the way back on the hardened packed sand along the water's edge, looking back over his shoulder every hundred feet. He cuts across the beach to re-enter the boards back in front of Lucky's. He finds himself thinking about the face he glimpsed there earlier, now long gone. But it wouldn't matter. His aching arms and wrists, this sudden turn of events, now had his undivided attention.

He's back at the cottage, shedding his sweat-soaked layers after venting his frustrations in four more laps on the boards, and returning to the driveway just minutes after she pulls in.

"I'm telling you, JP, this "Slam" character and his muscle friend are more dangerous than a starving speed freak with a hatchet and grill in a room full of chickens. And they've got me up against the wall." She might normally have smiled or one-upped his analogy to something like a handcuffed, shackled pothead in a chocolate factory, but not this time. The tide has turned serious. He reenacts the confrontation.

Her mouth agape and eyebrows raised, she leans heavily toward him over the kitchen table, standing defiantly over her coat and apron on the floor where she had thrown them in anger when he explained about Pulver tying his wrists.

"Shit, Rick, what do we do now? What else did they say to you? And give me a look at those wrists of yours." She steps toward him and reaches for his hands. "Let's put some aloe on them. So what did they say? What did they say?"

She helps him to a chair and lays the backs of his hands gently on the table exposing the red-scraped rope burn lines. She scoops a wad of waitressing tips from her dress pockets and plunks it on the kitchen table, coins spinning deliriously. She quickly opens the two top buttons on her uniform, kicks off her white shoes, and produces a bottle of aloe from some cabinet as he continues to explain what happened and what was said.

"I don't know what to do here except go along with them, and of course I don't trust them, but I'm concerned about your getting caught in the middle. I actually thought about you and me taking off in the boat but I know the family thing, well, you know, but, dammit, I feel like I'm somewhere between having to choose death by thumb tacks or potato-peeler."

She gestures to move his wrists closer.

"Okay, okay, here's the...OW! That stuff stings!"

She withdraws the bottle of green gel, closes the cap and stands it on the table, then very gently rubs the aloe into the rope burns. He winces and looks to the ceiling.

"The money thing isn't bad, Rick, if they live up to what they say, but what do they want the boat for anyway? It's not like it's an ocean racer or something."

He shakes his head slowly side to side.

"Taking off in the boat with you is tempting, R E A L tempting, but maybe we'd be smarter to just do what they say."

She strokes his temples and forehead gently as she speaks, "Just take the money, find us a nice place on the water, or even another boat, lay low, mind our own business, run our groups, keep our lives and our habits more private, stay out of the headlines, and hang out for a year 'til we get the boat back?"

She kisses his cheek and hugs his head to her chest. They stay that way for two or three very long minutes. He feels calmed.

"You know, JP, I love you so much. You are so good to me, and for me. I'm sure you're right about things. You always are about stuff like this, like life decision stuff. You seem to have a sixth sense about which road to take. It's just the way these dirtbag guys operate, and their threats, and how they keep controlling me, us. It all makes me feel jumpy. Ah, sorry, I know, it's all something I choose to feel nervous about, but I do get afraid when I think about anything coming between us."

She swarms on him with kisses. He responds. Embraced and eyes closed, they stumble and bump their way to the bedroom. Pushed back into the pillows, she arches her back as he slides her panties over her thighs to her ankles. His head jerks back in response to sporadic twinges of pain as his wrists come in contact with the blanket edge. He kisses his way up her legs, slowly, deliberately. He wants her on the same edge he feels every time their skin touches. The burdens on his shoulders dissolve as she pulls his head up to hers, then spreading her legs into one of her dance-step splits, reaches for him. Consumed. Filled. One. Fear and anger go away. The world goes away. In the dark there is light. Bursting first with hunger, then joy. Then calm.

Chapter 20

ON-DECK CIRCLE

Gloosh, crackle, gurgle, gurgle, HAAACHT! THUMP! Gurgle. The swift slash comes with so sudden a thrust of the precision-sharpened machete it almost decapitates the first mate, who has seen his last sunset—the horizon giving way to moonless skies over the turbulent inky black Atlantic. The near silent steel blade sounds of unexpected death somehow penetrate through all the decibels of roaring engines in an angry wind and splashing sea.

Glop, glop, glop, glop, glop. Throbbing spurts of blood run wildly in every direction, connecting the rubber booted feet that stand in a wobbling circle across the deck as the fifty-six-foot *Maltese* rises and falls rhythmically on the eight-foot waves that spray walls of saltwater up the hull along the port side, that give the white foam of their wake a serpent-like appearance.

"Remember this spot where we are, right here, right now! Remember it! Remember Jocko's blood here on the deck that's working its way to your boots! REMEMBER THAT I FOOKIN' TOLD HIM TO KEEP HIS FOOKIN' MOUTH SHUT ABOUT THIS TRIP!" Spittle flies from Simo's brown-toothed mouth. "And he went and told his old lady we was running drugs here!

"THE RAT TOLD HER WE WAS RUNNIN'' DRUGS!

This here's a fishing trawler, for fishing! Anybody else here got an old lady they want to make a widow out of? If not, then you better remember you're fishing on a fishing boat. Got it? GOT IT?"

Heads nod agreement, slowly, deliberately. Knees knock, wobble. In the cold, sweat pours freely.

Simo swings his dripping bloody blade in one fell swoop and swipes it across a towel that hangs from a deckhand's waist. The man jerks his head back and shivers convulsively as the glistening machete twice passes breezily by his crotch, coming stainless clean along each razor edge.

"Well," continues the frenzied captain, "Jocko's old lady bought it too. My friend Slam took care of her. What couldn't be fed to Mrs. Rat's own garbage disposal unit went to the bottom of a dumpster headed for oblivion two states away. So unless you're lookin' for the same treatment for you and your woman, don't rat on what's goin' on with this boat! You'll SHUT UP WHEN I TELL YOU TO!"

Simo turned and slung his now drooling cheekful of chewing tobacco at Jocko's gurgling body. "Now get this piece of shit overboard and clean up the goddamn deck! I don't want to see no trace of blood here, and none a you seen Jocko here since we put into port at The Highlands! He never got back on the boat. YOU GOT IT?"

Heartbeats are pounding wildly against the gathered chest walls, each crewman hoping the next is unable to hear his thumps, or see the fear behind each twitching eye.

Two of the men with more seaworthy stomachs than the rest drag the gushing red smeared body and barely attached head to the rail, tie the feet to cinderblocks and shove it over. A couple of thumps and a triple kerplash are the only sounds to mark the occasion. The boat never slows.

Still shouting, Simo continues as if nothing more had happened than that someone had skimmed a piece of burned toast to the gulls, "He got off the boat the other night and never came back by the time we left this morning, got it? GOT IT?" He continues to poke the machete toward them to accent each shout, and glares into each grimaced nodding face.

"All right, get your asses moving! We're going to be at sea for two weeks here so you better get with the game plan or the sharks are going to think you and Jocko is like a double dessert."

Simo goes below deck while the unnerved crew scurries about with buckets of soapy water, scrub brushes and mops...daring scattered whispers of weak reassurance to one another.

A worried, apologetic voice follows a timid knock at the v-berth cabin door. "Ah, Capt'n, if I follow the course you charted for tonight, the radio reports say we may run straight into a major storm. I just wanted to check with you..."

"Don't gimme them asshole radio reports, Charlton! Just toe the line. Don't ask questions and don't fookin' think! You got it? You ain't paid to think. Follow the course and blow through the fookin' storm, and don't bother me again until sunrise, got it?"

"Yessir!"

Simo sleeps.

"Yessir, Apple, I think we got ourselves one hellava good safe boat here from the professor. It'll sure make Simo happy that he's got an emergency backup ready to go. It's like having prune juice in the cupboard if you know what I mean." Slam lights a cigar, grinning and bearing his yellowed teeth over the match flame.

"Well, I'm glad to hear that, Slam." Apple paces across the library, dividing his attention between Slam's billowing cigar smoke and a five-by-eight index card he carries that's filled with inked-in columns.

"Anything that helps insure that this job goes through with no hitches is worthwhile, and it is indeed always a fine idea to keep Simo in good spirits."

Slam nods agreement. Any kind of reassuring comment from Apple is a verbal pat on the back, a point scored. Life, to Slam, is a game of points.

"When do you and Pulver pick up the professor's Chris Craft? Is it in the water yet? Is Billy squared away about paying the guy? Even though we've got the professor in a squeeze, we don't want him shooting off his mouth about the boat. Once the job's done, that's another matter. Then the professor's little cabin cruiser might as well have *Titanic* painted on the transom." Apple laughs smugly at his own analogy.

Slam smiles appreciation for Apple's humor. Keeping the climate lighthearted with Apple is an ongoing goal because it serves to set the table for more points. Slam knows better than to do or say anything that raises Apple's eyebrows.

"Here's the bottom line, Boss. The professor's little 'love boat' goes in the water tomorrow. We got Fast Eddie overseeing the event. He will also get the engines up and running and have the Chris ready to be picked up the day after tomorrow. Pulver knows what to do and where to take it."

"Good, and Billy?"

"Billy gives the professor the book with the cash tomorrow night after class."

"Yes, right. After class. This is good, Slam. Let me know when Billy's done the book thing, will you?"

"Sure, the b-o-o-k t-h-i-n-g. You got it, Boss!"

Slam, Apple thinks, is not the brightest light on the Christmas tree, and not someone he particularly cares to have in his presence when he is trying to make a good impression, but Slam always does ask how deep when he's told to dig, and that obedience makes up for his dim wit and crassness.

"And have we heard from Simo?"

"Yeah, he's on the way. Says he lost Jocko at sea. And I had Pulver take care a Mrs. Jocko. Simo says he's ready anytime the mother ship gets to the Canyon. What does the microchip say about when and where, Apple?"

"I'm working on that now, Slam. Check back with me in the morning. Call around eight. I'll let you know the next step." Slam responds with a silent half bow and half salute that his boss doesn't see.

Apple takes a dismissive step sideways to the table to lean over the ocean charts, but Slam misses the hint. Apple mumbles under his breath as he picks up the magnifying glass, "Too bad about Jocko," he says quietly like he's talking to himself, "but I bet it had something to do with him not being able to keep that big Mick Jagger mouth of his from flapping when it should have been zipped. I'll just bet that's what it was."

Slam picks out only a few of the mumbled words, but gets the gist of Apple's comments and understands the probable accuracy of his conclusions. Apple stares hard at the index card, then looks up, suddenly aware of Slam's continuing presence.

"Oh well," Apple mutters. "Listen, Slam, I need some time now to concentrate on the codes if you don't mind. Oh, and tell Pulver good job taking care of the Missus."

Slam waves his cigar dismissively and turns for the door. "Roger that on the Missus, Boss. Talk to you at eight," he says as he leaves.

Apple returns his concentration to figuring out the guts of the microchip message he had copied onto the card, along with longi-tudes, latitudes, tide changes, storm fronts, currents, projected vis-ibility, knots per hour, moonlight coverage, number of crewmen, groceries required, coast guard routes, shipping routes, air traffic, channel markers, radio signals and codes, static interference, military traffic, engine conditions, fuel, emergency supplies, inflatable rafts, life-jackets, flares, guns, ammunition, bilge pumps, decoy fishing rigs, and spotlights.

He considers the complexity created by that assortment of items and concerns, and weighs it against everything he knows about the two delivery and receiving ship captains. He's convinced that both men are so strong, bullheaded and skilled that they probably don't need any of the information or supplies that he has made himself so crazy with thinking about in order to get the job done. Probably, but not certainly. The only thing that's certain, he thinks, is uncertainty... plenty of that to go around! He intercoms for a cappuccino.

Chapter 21

WISHBOOK

"Hey, Professor?" The quiet voice turns the corner and joins Maddigan as he crosses the building entrance and hallway leading to the room.

"Hey, Bill, what's the word?" Maddigan asks through a nervous half-smile as other students rush past them on both sides, jabbering away, laughing, brushing Bill's and Maddigan's elbows, bumping the professor's bulging mailbag.

"I got a management book to show you after class," he says with not a lot of exuberance. "There's some stuff in it I don't get, but I thought—somebody told me," he fumbles for the right words as more students cluster about, "er, I guess I thought you'd know what it was all about? So, after class? That okay?"

"Fine, Bill. I'll see you then."

Maddigan smiles his best fake smile and steps onto the platform at the front of the room, walks to the board, and draws a large upside-down triangle. He almost draws a hollowed-out book.

"This," he says with a sneer and twist of the lip, "is an upside-down triangle. If you go to Harvard Business School and pay fourteen zillion dollars a semester, they'll put this on the board and tell you it's the upside-down triangle approach to management. Well, here you go. I'm giving it to you for—what are you paying, twelve-bucks a credit or something? Bargain City!

"The idea is that you need to go from broad—" he turns a small piece of fat blue chalk sideways to thicken the top line, "—from broad to specific in your decision making process."

He squiggles a fat line across the top of the giant upside-down triangle, then zig-zags the chalk sideways, plummeting down to the V point at the bottom, where he adds an arrowhead. Then, with yellow chalk, he slashes two equi-distant horizontal lines through the upside-down triangle.

Across the top of the diagram, he writes:

"Define The Problem."

The problem is I'm getting screwed on this boat deal. I can just feel it. In the top section, he writes the word: Objectives. *I've got to get JP and me out of this mess.*

In the middle section, he writes the word: Strategies. *I can play along with them for now, but this one-year plan isn't about to happen, and I've got to make a move soon.*

And in the bottom section, now a small upside-down triangle itself, he writes the word: Tactics. *A trick is the only way. I don't have any other options. It's the police or Dr. Stafford or an awfully good scheme—otherwise I'll be finished on the spot, and I'd lose JP too!*

He rubs his forehead unconsciously. As he speaks, he realizes that his eyes are darting back and forth to the book on Bill's desk. He begins to think his attentions might be noticed, and he repositions himself to eliminate the book from his line of vision.

"This, ladies and gentlemen, this Objectives/Strategies/Tactics or 'OST' approach to problem solving will work for your personal lives as well. It is actually derived from the military, and can be effective in even the most stressful situations."

He thinks of his wrists being tied behind his back and tugged on by Pulver.

"Let's see, an example: If the Marines had a wartime objective to take the hill in forty-eight hours, their strategy might have been to approach it from the North and do it at night under the cover of darkness. And their tactics could have been to use teams of six, crawling under the shrubs, and targeting the machine gun nests with hand grenades at a precisely coordinated time."

A precisely coordinated time is exactly what I can make work because Slam and Pulver and the rest of those creeps will never expect it. I have the element of surprise on my side.

"The hardest part, believe it or not, is to define the problem. The second hardest part is to do that in a short single statement."

He paces. "You may think that sounds easy, but I can assure you that when you sit down to write out a short, clear definition of what the problem is that you seek to solve, you will find it difficult to express it accuratelyly in writing. And, by the way, if you're genuinely committed to solving the problem, you really do need to be able to put it in writing.

"Now, imagine if you will, how much more difficult this task becomes in a real management setting when a group or team of people is involved, and you need to achieve consensus—where every person must, at least somewhat, buy into the single statement description.

"That's like getting everyone here to agree on what makes the best sandwich."

He pauses for them to grasp this exponential outgrowth of his original diagram. He thinks about how complicated it has become to state his own problem in clear simple terms, now compounded by the involvement of so many other people and events. He walks back to the diagram and taps his chalk on the board.

"The Objective then is kind of the flipped-over version of your problem statement. To be a true Objective though, or goal—instead of a wish—it must meet four separate criteria. Objectives must be: One, specific. Two, flexible. Three, realistic. And four, have a due date."

He writes the four criteria on the board next to the triangle, and brackets them, running a swirly blue chalk arrow from the bracket to the word Objectives.

"So, if your problem statement is that your actual sales are on target for this quarter of the year, but twenty percent lower than you had projected for the last quarter, you flip it over and your Objective becomes: 'To increase actual sales by twenty percent for the coming quarter to compensate for last quarter's shortfall.' Specific, flexible, and due-dated. But of course you have to know that it's a realistic possibility that you can in fact actually achieve a twenty percent increase."

He underlines the word 'Realistic.' Next, he underlines 'Flexible.'

"You have to be flexible enough to move the date, or move the percentage, or change the Objective, or goal, if—over a reasonable time period—achieving your target starts to not look realistic."

Applying that comment to his own predicament prompts him to rub his forehead vigorously for two or three seconds. *Flexible. Flexible. How do I be flexible? Somehow, I've got to think differently about this tangle I've gotten JP and myself into.*

"The reason, by the way that so many people fail to make and achieve goals is that they think that—to be a goal—something has to be etched in concrete, and if it's not achieved then we're looking at failure with a capital 'F,' which is simply not the case. What a meaningful goal has to be for me, uh, I mean has to be then, is flexible."

His thoughts keep returning to the book on Bill's desk. $30,000. *It certainly would be great if the rest of the deal happens the way they said, but JP is always right, and my window of opportunity is going to be a short one. I can't just take the money and run, because I will have lost too much—but I can't wait twelve months either because they'll never honor that arrangement. They're thinking they've got me for thirty, they'll keep the boat and that I'll just quietly disappear until the next time they need something. I can't allow a 'next time.'*

"The goal in our example also meets the other criteria. It has a due date, right? We've used the term, "this quarter," so we're talking about, these next three months. And our statement here is specific, right? So, realistic, flexible, specific and it has a due date. Without all of these criteria, you have only a wish!"

Instead of the way he would normally understate something, maybe even whisper it, his voice sounds a bit forced. He seems to be punching out the words he wants to emphasize.

"A wish. And wishing gets us where? To Disneyland. Why? Because a wish is not here and now, and that makes it fantasy, right? A wish gets us nowhere!"

He picks up different color chalks, and draws a looping blue arrow from the center Strategies section to the top Objectives section, and then another looping blue arrow from the bottom Tactics section to the center Strategies section.

"The Strategies are the thinking avenues that take us to the Objectives. The Tactics are the implementation of those thinking avenues." As he says the words Strategies and Tactics, he smashes two pieces of red chalk to smithereens, flakes flying frantically to the floor, making an overkill asterisk in the middle Strategies section.

"The Strategies have to be right. The Strategies have to work. We have to think through the Strategies and then RE-think them before trying to execute the Tactics."

His eyes return to Bill's desk, the book.

Chapter 22

GATOR AID

"So you got my prize piece of paper-cutting craftwork back?" she says, running her arm through the hollowed-out textbook pages. The covers flop inside out and backwards. The entire volume hangs from JP's elbow, as she sits cross-legged on the kitchen counter, between the dish rack and the coffee pot.

"Yeah, Bill left it for me after class."

"And the, ah, thirty, uh, big ones?" The shaky words tumble out between nervous giggles. She grins coyly at the thought. She's never seen that much cash at one time. She drops her legs to dangle in front of the pots-and-pans cabinet.

"Yeah. Here." He tosses the three rubber-banded packs of hundred dollar bills on her lap. Her face flushes and she lights up like a row of Lucky's pinball machines as she flips and slaps the packs of bills, not sure how to handle them. She pulls the band off one stack and passes it to the side of her nose. Peeking seductively over the edges, she strikes an erotic pose then waves and fans the hundreds as she starts singing, *You Got The Money Honey...I Got The Time...*

"Serious, JP," he says, trying hard not to smile, "I have a lot to think about here and I can use your brain."

"That's all I'm good for, Professor, my brain?" she quips. Still clutching the three wads of cash, she slides off the counter and into his arms. "How about we do the other parts of my body first, and then the brain junk later, okay?" Clutching two packs of bills against her chest, she smacks the other against his, and covers his mouth with hers.

"Mmmmmpf," he responds.

Another night. Another run on the boards. The face is back at Lucky's. That same face. A flash again, then gone again. He knows the face but can't lock it in long enough to recognize it. This time he breaks stride and steps straight into the arcade. But the person he saw is gone so fast he thinks maybe he is hallucinating.

He stands, hands on hips, panting and scanning through the hovering clouds of cigarette smoke, his ears sorting through the clatter and rumble of near deafening sounds. He squints to focus his eyes beyond the bombardment of blinking lights that necklace small clusters of ragamuffin teenagers absorbed in video and pinball games.

No face. He nearly blurts out to the nearest clump of kids huddled around a change machine, "Hey, did any of you happen to notice a face?" The stupidity of the question surfaces before the words and stops his tongue in its tracks.

So many unresolved issues. *This damn face puzzle is making me crazy. The boat is gone. Pulver and Fast Eddie drove my Chris away. God, I hope they take care of it. At least I managed to get the $30,000 into the bank before it closed. At least I still have JP—and my Jeep— and my job, and my students and, thank God, no more dead turtles to deal with.* He smiles and turns back to his run.

"Wipe that smirk off your face, asshole," Simo waves a menacing finger, "or you'll end up keeping Jocko company down where the horseshoe crabs dig in, or, by now, he's probably being digested in some shark's belly!"

In the wake of their dump-the-concrete-anchored-body-off-the-deck-and-scrub-away-the-blood burial at sea, an eerie silence has grasped the crew. In the aftermath, no one is speaking above or below deck, except to state their bearings, pass along instructions, or bum a cigarette. Simo is pleased. He'd counted on creating silence. He knew he had shocked the men, even the most rugged and fearless. He wanted to use the first mate slicing—and stunned silence that followed—as a control device. It is working.

Gator appears at the bridge, obviously seeking to restore some semblance of balance by approaching the captain with a friendly but forced grin. Simo takes it as a wise-guy signal, and flashes Gator a warning sneer as he stoops to pick up a tire iron used to prop up the engine room hatch. Gator backs away slowly.

"What's that smart-ass smirk all about?"

"Sorry Captain, I don't smile so good since I had that fight with Tongs. I kicked his butt, but Tongs, he got a good shot into my jaw with that kick-box shit of his, and it makes my mouth a little crooked. Looks like I'm smiling when I'm not. Anyway, you can be sure the Jocko thing won't happen again. The guys we got now are quiet as ants feedin' on a chum bucket. Nobody says nothin' to nobody an' when we go ashore, they'll only talk that the fish was runnin' or that they wasn't. That's it. The guys need the work, Captain. Like Charlton—you know he's got a sick kid. I, uh, listen, I can tell you there ain't nobody sayin' shit to no one, including their old ladies. The guys ain't even talkin' to each other."

Simo squints and lays the tire iron on the console above the controls. He rubs the inside corners of his eyes with his gnarled thumb and scarred forefinger. He'd heard Gator vouch for the crew before.

"Listen, Gator, I'm trustin' you on this one, but we can't afford no loose cannons runnin' round, so you better sure as hell be right or I'll cut off yer balls an' skin 'em and use 'em fer fishline bobbins! You know what I mean, right?"

Gator's hand drops like a rock to cover his crotch as he nods agreement. Gator is a tough guy. He doesn't take well to most threats, but he knows if he wants his job—and his life—that when the captain speaks, you jump, and you never question him, and you lick his boots if he tells you to. Gator had very little doubt that homemade testicular fish floats was not a new notion, or practice, to Simo.

"I swear to you Simo," he taps his thumb-covered fist to his chest dramatically. "It's under control."

As if the two had just reached agreement on a major real estate deal, both men take a swig of whiskey from separate pint bottles they suddenly produce from their pockets and that each is now holding aloft. It's like they are mentally toasting each other but wouldn't think of reaching out to tip bottle tops, or clink glass, or in any way formally acknowledge or commemorate the occasion, even though lives are on the line.

Gator swipes the back of his wrist across his mouth. "Listen, Captain," he says, "the guys want to know how long we'll be at sea, and I'm concerned about when the safeboat arrives 'cuz I gotta start to chart some times and directions to make sure we don't lead no marine police or Coasties into our paths."

Simo scratches a wooden match across the mottled surface of the hanging brass lamp and lights a cigar stub he fishes out of his shirt pocket, then flips the smoking match to the cabin floor.

"Tell the slimeballs four weeks max. Then, if we get done early, they'll be happy, and since it won't be more than four, they won't be bitchin' every time the wind turns. And keep this to yourself, but this weekend we'll be putting into port for a final ready before heading out for the big drop. The crew will have time for a couple of shots, but that's it. The backup boat? Don't worry about it. Pulver and Eddie are gettin' it as we speak so we should see them with it at the marina by the weekend. You'll have time to brief them. Now get outta here!"

As his new first mate turns to leave, Simo stiff-arms the closed cabin door and puts his face inches from Gator's. "Oh, and Gator? Once we're back at the marina and leave shore with the safeboat for the big run, you'd better be s-u-r-e a-s s-h-i-t there won't be no badges around—Coasties, cops, or otherwise—if you ever want yer balls to see land again! Got it?"

"Roger that, Boss." Gator sounds obliging but looks shaken. He gives the visor of his greasy baseball cap a two-finger salute, which Simo half notices and half nods at.

"Later," he mumbles, as he turns and heads back above deck to join the others. The remaining five on-deck crewmembers stand quietly, smoking, looking numbed, beyond earshot, at the bow rail. Two others, the cook and Charlton are below in the galley and engine room. Simo warms up the CB radio, and looks for an empty channel in between the chatter. He would talk in codes to Apple, but now it is time to do that directly and bypass Slam.

Chapter 23

KBE8321

"You did WHAT? What are you, crazy? They could have killed you! And what happens if they find you with it?"

His arms are extended with both hands open as if poised to catch a medicine ball, but the rest of him doesn't look so receptive. He leans his head forward, and her attention is drawn more to his fiery eyes and wrinkled brow. His face looks like he is ready to lead a SWAT team charge. He is glaring at her over the tops of his glasses. She reaches to take his hands and he pulls away. She flinches and backs up a step.

"Hey, Rick." Her tone is soft and slightly pleading. "Please don't be so upset that we can't even hold hands, huh? How about one of those deep breaths you advise everyone else to take?" Her voice quavers a bit. Her face is flushed. She's feeling like the now cavernous lines running across his brow are contagious, and the bridge of her nose just caught a bad case of his worry wrinkles.

"Yeah, right, like a deep breath is going to undo the risk you took? His voice has a touch of panic. He hits the word "risk" with emphasis. He shuffles around in circles. Then, he comes to an abrupt stop. Someone looking through a window might think he is praying as he lowers his head, brings his palms together and presses the tips of his joined forefingers to his upper lip. His neck is slightly askew and his angry eyes carry a hint of sadness as he focuses his attention down and to the left, on nothing in particular.

He strokes his beard and continues, "And don't you think those thugs are going to notice that the CB unit is missing? Where do you propose we hide it when they come knocking at the door? I should put it in the oven? Up my sleeve? Inside my pants? I can't believe you took it! I can't believe you actually went to the boat? Jesus!"

Though the temptation is great to pursue his comment about hiding it inside his pants, JP resists. She picks up instead where she left off. She resolutely refuses to acknowledge what she categorizes to herself as his 'stage performance,' the same kind of provocative routine she's seen him replicate many times over in the classroom. His theatrics never fail to get a rise out of his students. He certainly knows how to use his acting skills to get people thinking.

"Y'know, Rick, a deep breath will help you process the fact that the deed is done!"

She considers her words carefully, then continues, "And, if you don't choose to be insulted at my giving you a reminder, a couple of deep breaths will get you focused—as you always say—on the *productive present*. I think I've heard you say that dwelling on the fantasy of past events is a waste of energy because the past is over and can't be changed—and which is where the risk you're scolding me about should now be filed." She smiles angelically, "Right Professor?"

"I am not scolding. I..." She has him nailed. He stops pacing to fight back a grin, then loses the fight as he blurts into laughter.

"Damn you, girl, you keep all this psychotherapeutic crap coming and you're going to end up co-director for some personal and professional growth group!"

He takes the deep breath. She smiles her best dimple smile.

"Like on a boat?"

He grins.

"Thank you," she says, taking the pause as a signal to continue her presentation.

"Now let's look at this a little more rationally, can we?" He nods approval.

"If these sleaze bags are even half as dumb as you make them sound, they're not going to notice the CB missing. They'll just think you never had one, or that it's being winterized or repaired or something. And by us having it, we increase the odds of finding out what they're up to, which increases our odds of being able to do something about it. I mean, we DO want the boat back, yes?"

"Howcum all your questions can only be answered by agreeing with you?"

He pulls on the corners of his moustache and straightens his glasses.

"So, okay, Green Eyes, even if you're right about this, remember that Fast Eddie's going to be giving them an engine orientation and he knows our boat inside and out. If they ask him about the CB, you and I are going to have lower survival odds than one of your Loggerhead turtles crossing the Garden State Parkway on a Friday night in tourist season."

She lifts her chin and batters her eyelashes.

"Surely, Professor, you wouldn't want to disagree with me would you? Besides, Garden State Parkway crossings at any time, in any direction are unhealthy—even for gold medal sprinters, never mind turtles!"

She does a little toe dance swirl around his chair while sliding her hand around his neck, past the unbuttoned top of his shirt, and into a slow swirling motion over his chest.

She leans over to peck a kiss on his ear.

"First off, as truth will have it," she continues, "though I know you don't like hearing this, 'Mr. Fast Ed' is far more interested in looking up my skirts and down my shirts than he is taking inventories of our boat equipment. Probably, by the way, that's where he got his *Fast* name considering it certainly didn't come from his work ethic, what with his ability to drag two hours of engine work into a full day by the time he hands over his bill."

She's clipping her words at a rapid pace to get past raising any jealousy issues and get to the point of her rebuttal. Maddigan bites his tongue to keep from reacting to her Fast Eddie comment, which he hates to admit but knows instinctively to be true. With his own mechanical skills in the minus zone, he's come to depend on Eddie's engine services. She's right that he doesn't like hearing that the guy looks through (and into) her clothes.

"Second," says JP, "the radio is old anyway. Tell them it belonged to your grandfather and has a sentimental value. Or tell them that you don't want to be out of touch with your boat friends. Or tell them you sold it to get pot money. Or just tell them the truth, for Christsake, that the CB is yours and was not part of the sale terms. Tell the bastards they should just screw off and buy their own damn unit!"

She stomps her foot in punctuation, and turns briskly away from him, then spins abruptly on her heels and waves a pointed finger at him.

"And, by the way, Professor, they're not MY Loggerhead turtles. I seem to recall it was you with the apron and hatchet?"

"Okay, okay, okay. I give. It's just so weird to me that you, that, that you're the student and that you have better answers than I do."

"Man, that's a lotta that's!"

He tosses her a look of mock sadness, straightens his posture, takes another deep breath, then pulls his glasses off and gives them a tacit wipe-off with his shirttail. He bows his head to hook the glasses back on, and looks more forlorn than she's seen him in a long time. Her attack clearly rattled his cage. Conscious of his seeking to regain composure, she shifts into lower gear.

"Listen, Babe, you are the world's most brilliant professor and counselor, and you've helped thousands of students and other people, and I love you. Now it's time to sit still, shut up, and let someone you trust—me—do the thinking. I grew up here, remember? My father was a boat builder; remember? I was literally a Gwyneth Bay Brat. You just inherited the area and the water and boating when you took the position at Seaport. Me? It's in my blood."

His eyes are locked on hers. He nods agreement.

"You're right," he says.

"Now," she continues to build her case, "as for the CB, I never actually used one, or got FCC-licensed, but I do know how to do boat wiring, and I can connect CB radios. I can tune in channels, and listen to the gibberish with the best of truckers. Plus you need to be reminded that I also know from how to deal with the Fast Eddies of the world, as well as bottom-feeding gangsters like the Longshore-man's Union representatives that tried arm-bending my father into membership.

"It cost him money, equipment, and some bruises, by the way, but he never did join. Well, it's the same dedication to your work and sense of fairness you share with him that appeals to me—not as much as the appeal of your body of course, but pretty much!"

"I know you're right, JP, and I love you too, and I appreciate you. And I appreciate your assertiveness—yeah, and even your CB wiring skills—more than you'll ever know! My body, eh?"

"Of course, your body. So you know how to use this thing or what?"

He covers his nose and mouth with a cupped hand, producing a nasal resonance to which he adds a convincing Southern drawl: "Hey y'all, breaker, break, break...this is The Perfesser heah: K-B-E-8-3-2-1 lookin' for a sound check. Y'all c'mon back now, y'heah?"

She holds back her dimple to stay on the subject, "Okay, so we gotta hook it up to a battery, right?"

"No problem," he says. "I have a spare in the shed."

"Good. Let's get it cranked up when I get home from work tonight, okay?"

"Absolute!"

"And before I leave for work, suppose I get you cranked up, okay?"

"Absolute."

"You're always doin' vodka commercials!"

"Absolute."

Laughter. Hugs. In one sweeping motion, she lifts the sundress over her head, letting it fall to the floor, and stands smiling, in her necklace and bikini panties, arms outstretched.

"Abbbb-so-lute!"

Chapter 24

CB or Not CB?

"Billy, I'm telling you he absolutely recognized me, or he's close to it anyway. He actually stepped into the arcade and scoped it out. I ducked behind the pinball machines, but I have this feeling like he knows he saw me. I think he just can't piece it together yet."

She stops pacing and squeezes her eyes shut. Her cheeks are beet red. A hint of perspiration glistens at her temples. She stammers. "C-Can't you p-please move me and Brianna off that street? It's just a matter of t-time, you know."

"Stop worrying, Heather, will ya? Even if he figures out you've been watchin' him, he's harmless. Besides, he'll think it's just flirting. He's pretty hot lookin', right? Anyway, he'll never make the connection. Apple says you gotta cozy up to his old lady and find out if they're up to something. He doesn't trust them to just roll over, and he doesn't want anything going wrong when this next run goes down."

Fists now press against her hips. She's turned her back to his remarks.

Billy tries to resurrect the discussion by addressing what he thinks is her issue, "Brianna? She likes this street. She's doing fine here. The ocean's good for her. Look at how she plays in the sand."

"I know, but she's just..."

"You just need to calm down, Heather. Apple says maybe after this deal, we can all go to the Islands for a long vacation. Whaddaya-say? I'll tell him you're movin' in on the JP broad to find out the scoop, okay?"

"Oh, Billy!" She slaps her forehead. "Why don't you hear what I'm saying? Why do we have to be mixed up in this?"

He pretends not to hear her questions, and charges forward instead for an answer to his: "Okay?" he asks again.

She heaves a deep breath. "Okay," she lets her exasperation register with the way she says the word.

He tips his fisherman's hat to a group of students huddled into a cloud of cigarette smoke in the classroom building stairwell, then— with a smile—grasps his neck and makes an exaggerated choking sound as he passes. He bounds up the flight of stairs two at a time, his leather mailbag slapping at his hip with each lunge.

"He's a buster, isn't he? I guess he's right though. We probably should quit smoking sometime. Hey, speaking of smoke, I heard he's burning incense in his classes today. What's that about?"

"What?" a second smoker asked incredulously as she snuffed out her glowing filter.

"Yeah, I heard that too," said a third, "Something about marketing that smells or something."

"Okay, people, so you walked in here today and I'm doing what? I'm sitting in a dark room with some blinking lights, burning incense, and listening to Rick Wakeman's *Journey To The Center Of*

The Earth album. Ah, and there's candy on your desks and balloons on your chairs. So what's the story?"

"It's a drug party?"

"It's a trick!"

"You've been smoking funny stuff in your pipe?"

"You're starting a new cult!"

"You're trying to get fired so you can collect unemployment?"

"Well, those are some good tries, folks, but what else is going on?"

He begins the rapid-fire-challenge-people's-brains barrage of questions he is known for: "Do you smell the incense? Taste the candy? Feel the balloons? Hear the music? See the blinking lights? Are you reminded of the boardwalk? Or MacDonald's? Or the casinos in AC? Did you know savvy realtors urge home sellers to bake bread, play soft music and have fresh flower arrangements scattered around when prospective buyers come to the door?"

He is reciting the right phrases for the right class, but all he can think of is the dizzying effect on his own five senses that JP created when she lifted that sundress over her head. *Unbelievable!*

Continuing his volcanic spew of questions, "Did you know used car dealers spray cans of new car smell into vehicles on the lot? Have you noticed grocery stores cutting a couple of token fruits and vegetables in half and mixing them in with the other watermelons and apples and oranges? Did you know some places actually spray orange scent on the oranges, and lemon scent in the cleaning aisle?"

And, he thought, *someone I know sprays strawberry scent on the insides of her thighs.*

"Some retailers will break open a bag of chocolates in the candy aisle, or they'll cook up and distribute food samples in the store. Did you ever wonder why you always buy more than you intended in a deli after getting a sample piece of cheese or lunchmeat or salad?

"Do retailers market to your five senses? Do magazine ads include perfume 'Scratch 'n Sniff' samples? Do billboards show Cokes sitting in ice, with drops dripping down the bottles, or cans or bottles of beer being poured into overflowing glasses with foam running over the top? Radio and TV commercials use the power of suggestion and all kinds of special audio and visual effects to try to stimulate your five senses..."

She turned the scanner channel control knob.

Click...static...

"Hey, y'all got the fuzz made at the Bricktown weigh station? They're pullin' over all the eighteen-wheelers..."

Click...static...

"This here's Futa L-F-A-2-7-3-2, come on? I'm lookin' for a sound check, come on back, Sunshine..."

Click ...static...

"Well, will you pick up some eggs when you stop for milk? We got..."

Click...static...

"Y'allllllll ainnnn go-ennnn ta thad thar parrrrrty Sattttaday, isss ya? Aaaaaaah shure isssss..."

Click...static followed by static...

Click...static followed by more static...

Click...static...

"I'm glad you can hear me, Elppa. Young Nimajneb wasn't sure about puttin' me through to you direct, passin' by Mals on this call, but you said you don't want nobody taking in the details at this point, and being as I smelled one rat, which ain't such good swimmers as you know, so the rat caught a shark ride home, an' I hear Mrs. Rat went interstate, so all's well while we're waitin' on Revlup and Eidde. When they get here, Seuqcaj goes with Eidde at controls and Revlup heads back to you. I'll catch you again empty number midnight Sat. Ciao."

Static...

"Roger the rats, Omis, and the controls switch. No problem either with the bypass on Mals. You're right that it's probably best to keep these calls between us right now. I'll talk to Nimajneb so he knows. Ciao."

"Rick, Hi! Glad you're home. Look at this conversation I just wrote down."

"Hey. How'd you get the battery out and hooked up so quick?"

"Hey. Muscles and brains! Look at this will you!"

"What the hell?"

"I wrote it word for word. There was some static, but when I plugged it into the battery and flipped the dial around, that's what I got. It sounded too strange to be real—like who ever heard of names like those? The names are so weird, they don't even sound like they come from the same language. And what's up with Mr. and Mrs. Rat?

"Anyway, the discussion sure didn't sound like anything else I've ever heard, CB or not CB." She grins at her little literary quip. "You know what I mean? So I scribbled it out. What do you think?"

He leans over her shoulder, adjusts his glasses, and breathes heavily as he reads her notes.

"You know, JP, you just might have stumbled onto something here. There's no doubt about this discussion being off the wall. I mean even my most far-gone druggie students don't talk like this. And you're certainly right about the weird names...and reference to the rodent couple! But, without a little more information...it's hard to know what to think." He scratches his head. "I do know I'm getting hungry. How about we talk this through over a burger and beer at The Ark? What do you say?"

"Medium rare with pickles and a Rolling Rock!"

Chapter 25

APPLE FRITTERS

Apple has no neck. He is thick, something like a slightly hunched-over fire hydrant. But soft. For all the power he wields and all the tough guys he surrounds himself with, running up a flight of steps would probably collapse his lungs. His nails are manicured. His curly gray hair looks like a stylized steel wool pad, and a matching moustache twists every cartoony which way when he speaks.

The left side of his face predominates. It's a few millimeters higher than the right side. But the gun-gray eyes that never seem to blink, that peer over the tops of his reading glasses, are on such an even plane, and so riveting that most people never see beyond them to notice his mushy physique.

"Okay," he says, "I'm glad you're all here."

He paces the library, gingerly sidestepping the maps, charts, and tide tables spread across the floor. He stays within the temporary, connect-the-feet shaped, oblong border. Fourteen filled shoes adjust intermittently to track Apple's movements and keep themselves pointed toward him. Two of the shoe occupants are filled by his son Benjamin, who stands in the corner, arms folded. Slam, Billy, Pulver, Fast Eddie, Heather, and Apple's bodyguard Lava round out the balance of show inhabitants. Most are leaning—against bookshelves, desk corners, the conference table, and the two polished mahogany pedestals. One holds an ornate, museum-worthy globe. The other is home to Apple's life-size swooping bronze eagle with outstretched talons.

Apple's Walkman-Radio-wired maid, Mayetta, lurks outside the French doors. She is visible in spurts as she Windex's the glass squares, carpet-sweeps the floor, and busily dusts in no particular order, apparently in rhythm to some flamenco guitar station. She seems oblivious to the gathering inside.

Apple gestures to the seats around him, "Will you p-u-l-*lease* all sit down for Crysake? You give me the heebie-jeebies standing around like that." He sips some syrupy clear liquid as the gathering moves toward the middle of the room.

Three of them sink into the big leather sofa and the rest settle into the polished mahogany captain's chairs at the polished mahogany conference table. No one speaks. They are there to listen to Apple's thought process. They know it and he knows it. It is his idea of a meeting.

"Here's where we are, people: the Colombians couldn't travel past Mexico without what?" He answers himself: "Without arousing suspicion and risking crew arrests! Colombian fishing rights go just so far, you know."

Needing only a handheld mike to complete his act, he plays to them as a nightclub audience, striding about his stage, periodically pausing for effect, knowingly silhouetted in the glare of his dozen angled track-lights, he poses strings of rhetorical questions while feigning interest in having their input and approval.

"So, our South American friends stitched a microchip, with all the details of this run that we're going to be making, into some Mexican turtle's neck. They didn't want to risk a phone call tap or a personal messenger being followed, so they attached a sonic tracker to the shell and sent the thing out to sea from Isla de Mujeres. That's The Island of Women, in case you didn't know. That's a place I know that 'Pulvy', Billy, Eddie and Benjamin here would like to be, right boys?"

A grunt. A couple of nods. A half-hearted smile.

Apple's nose flares as he tilts his head condescendingly when he mentions the name of his embarrassingly effeminate son. Benjamin misses his father's body language. He's preoccupied with checking out Billy's ass while Billy is shooting glances at the inviting contrast of Heather's pale white legs against the dark brown leather couch. Her hoisted skirt and the track-light shadows accent her thigh muscles. Pulver's lips twitch in a slight smile when he hears his nickname. He is watching Mayetta through the French door glass squares searching for her occasionally visible cleavage as she stoops to her tasks.

"Anyway, this women's island is somewhere between Mexico and Cuba. So, the Colombians did this neck surgery thing at the beginning of turtle migration season, knowing that the creature would start swimming for the Florida Keys, and then head north along the coast, which it did. With Lava's help, while he was on vacation there, we were able to monitor the tracking device from the time it passed The Keys to head this way. Lava drove north and followed the turtle to Fort Lauderdale."

Apple tugs gently on the bottom edge of his favorite gray sweater vest, thinking he is hiding his over-the-belt belly. He likes the vest because it matches his hair and eyes and moustache. He is enjoying having a captive audience of devotées to his storytelling, unaware it is only his money and threats that hold their attention.

"So then, what happens next? Well, wouldn't you know: along comes our associate Captain Simo. Simo is a fearless, top-notch, trained and experienced sea captain. Anyway, he and his crew took over monitoring the tracking signals by boat, and followed the thing all the way up to North Carolina from Lauderdale. Then they found the animal tangled up in a fishing net, off the Outer Banks, where it died from drowning."

Heather gasps and, to Billy's delight, uncrosses and crosses her legs in the other direction as she shifts deeper into the leather corner.

"Yes, Heather, turtles can drown. Anyway, this particular turtle had been giving off tracking signals for a couple of days from one spot, so they realized something was wrong, and zeroed in and found it, then pulled the deceased creature aboard their trawler, and removed the tracking device."

Apple does a quick take around the room to make sure he still has everyone's attention. He does, so he continues.

"Trouble was that Simo doesn't have the best of reputations as a stellar citizen, if you know what I mean, and his trawler was being watched by some nearby Coast Guard guys. So Simo's boys didn't want to make a big scene out of cutting the thing up on deck—especially since it was one of those endangered species deals—and the damn thing was too big to drag in the water and it was starting to stink up the place."

Apple grins as he sees some noses wrinkle up. He takes another sip from his glass.

"So, anyway, Simo says there was no place to dissect it near the Outer Banks without calling too much of the wrong kind of attention to what we were doing. You know what I mean?" Heads nod.

Apple pauses to pour himself some more of what turns out to be sambuca, which he does not offered to anyone else. He takes a hefty swig and crunches his teeth on one of the "three for good luck" floating coffee beans.

"Then Simo's boys," Apple says, "chugged themselves up the

coast to Jersey, with the Coasties following along a few hundred yards behind with lots of binocular reflections coming at them. Figuring it was best to get rid of the thing before the Coast Guard got too curious, they tied cement blocks to the bag to act as anchors, and then used their lifeboat one night at high tide to drop it out near 7 Bridges Road. That's on the edge of Gwyneth Bay, across from Atlantic City." He turns his back to his audience and takes another sip.

"Then," Slam chimes in, not wanting anyone to think he wasn't intimately involved and informed of every step, "along comes our friend, the teach, and his p-u-b-e-s-c-e-n-t young main squeeze old lady."

"Yes, Slam," said Apple, "that's right! Then along comes the professor and his girlfriend. And with Pulvy's help, Slam was able to convince the professor to go get the turtle, bring it ashore, cut it up, locate the microchip, dispose of the animal's parts and get the chip back to us here."

Pulver leans back and folds his arms, pleased with Apple's recognition of his part in the successful intimidation.

"Next, Benjamin and I examined the chip and figured out how to activate it on our computer system. I know you don't all believe in computers because they're so new, but I can assure you, that someday, even people you know might have one. Anyway, Benji and I were able to identify the locations we needed by deciphering the chip's codes which spell out exact shipment dates and times, plus longitudes and latitudes, for the boats to meet."

Benjamin snaps to attention when he hears his name. He'd been staring at Billy's neck and fantasizing.

"Right," added the younger Solamente. "We have people working for Billyboy here who checked the codes to make sure we had the details right."

"Yes, Benjamin," Apple is quick to regain stage center. He reads from an index card, "and we got the code: 3153A412156N-722322W722322W from them for the first run. That code, Benji and I figured out, means March 15th at 3 A.M. at longitude 41-21-56 North and latitude 72-23-22 West. We were also able to I.D. the mother ship. It's a hundred-eighty-five-foot freighter, twin-masted motor sailer, named *Hombre,* commanded by Captain Ruiz Reyes from Bogotá. The repeat of the last six numbers also adds up to 18—the weight (that's the last 'W') of the delivery: 18,000 pounds!"

"Uh, how do the Colombians know we got the message?" asks Billy.

Apple turns to face Billy, grins with the left side of his face, and tugs on his moustache before answering. He loves being The Answer Man in his own meetings.

"The message we got includes a coded response arrangement to let the Colombians know that we got the info, and that we'll make the connection as they have specified."

Apple stops pacing to explain the sequence of events, then renews his room circling routine. He looks out the windows at the moonlit night sky and tree-bordered wall of blackness that surrounds the estate, then continues to amble around the room. He smoothes the sweater vest over his belly again, and checks his Rolex. Slam and Pulver exchange looks as if they know what's coming next.

"So," Apple says as he heads toward wrapping up his monologue, "now we know what's going to happen, we know when it's going to happen, and we know where it's going to happen. And," he eyes Billy, "we are in the process of letting our Colombian friends know that we are making the necessary arrangements."

He takes another sip of sambuca, then wipes his moustache with his sleeve before continuing.

"As far as you are all concerned though, the bottom line is that when this exchange is a done deal, A N D everyone in this room has kept their mouths shut about everything you know, about everything I've told you, A N D you have all done everything I've asked for, then all of you are going to be my guests for the summer, maybe longer, at the new oceanfront estate I just bought next to a gorgeous tropical rainforest in Belize."

His listeners exchange looks, wary grins and raised eyebrows— all except Lava—whose menacing deep-set eyes and expressionless mouth never change.

Responding to the cluster of puzzled expressions, Apple embarks on his travelogue narration, "Belize. That's south of Mexico, on the Caribbean. Average temperature is around eighty degrees all year with tropical breezes every day. You'll have your own servants, your own boats, your own Jeeps, and great beer (it's called Belikin, and it comes in dark brown bottles that are so thick and heavy you could use them for clubs... ha, ha, ha, ha!).

"You'll also have plenty of good rum, and the absolute best vegetables, homemade bread, and seafood you've ever tasted! They got snorkeling, sport fishing, kayaking, rainforest trips, exotic birds, and it's also the best place outside of Africa to buy homemade drums.

"When we visit a bar in the jungle called The Drumming, and you see the native kids play the drums like nothing you've ever heard, you'll want to get one to bring home...a drum, that is, not a kid! Ha, ha, ha, ha!

"Each of you," he continues, "can even bring along anyone you want...husbands, wives, girlfriends, boyfriends, whatever uh, lifts your skirt, if you know what I mean. Oh, and of course that includes bringing Brianna," he says with a lecherous smile at Niece Heather's legs. All expenses including airfare, meals and booze will be covered, and you'll each get $5,000 pocket cash to spend on gifts, t-shirts, jewelry, whatever you want...that's equal to like $50,000 in New Jersey!"

The grins widen. Some merge with dreamy stares into space.

Anyone entering the room at the moment would undoubtedly think the daydreamers were part of a mass hypnosis session or a Stephen King story. Most who knew Apple would agree he wasn't particularly skilled at much of anything, but he certainly could command a presence and paint verbal pictures.

He pauses to let the details sink in.

"Now, here's what each of you needs to do in the next few days..."

Chapter 26

THE APPLECART

Word-by-word analysis is taking place back and forth across the dimly-lit, high-backed booth table filled with laminated hand-carved names, initials, and philosophical utterances that seemed to run right off and over the edges. The bartender thinks the two of them are working a crossword puzzle and keeps sending the waitress over with napkins full of his scribbled three-letter odd-ball words for them to consider—pun, ort, ark, nil, gnu, tor, eke, axe, lob.

Bob Seger and the Silver Bullet Band pumps *Against The Wind* out of the jukebox. Four loud laughing men in the booth behind them share–between pitchers of beer–jokes about fish, and blondes, and blonde fish. They've reached the point of pouring sloppy and the waitress mops with a towel swipe or two each time she passes them.

"Here, Rick, look at this reference to an 'empty number' tied in with Saturday night.

"Whaddaya suppose that's about?"

"CB channels with no one transmitting on them are referred to as 'empty.' So maybe Saturday night we need to be monitoring the whole range of channels to try to catch some follow-up discussion.

See what we can paste together. I don't get all the words they're using, JP, but from the sounds of what you heard and wrote down, it's possible that something major could be on the cusp, y'think?"

"Major Cusp. Wasn't he the guy that had Cusper's Last…"

"Yeah, a 'Last Stand,' but it was G-e-n-e-r-a-l and the last name was C-u-s-t-e-r, woman, not Cusp!" He takes a swig of beer. "Listen, how are you going to be able to be home from work before midnight Saturday?"

"I'm thinking I'm not going to be feeling well along about nine o'clock, my stomach, you know? It'll be on the cusp of throwing up. Hahahaha! Besides, I'll have made most of my tips by then."

"Don't risk the job for this, Green Eyes."

"Not to worry. Vanessa will cover for me. I'll be back home by 9:30."

"Let's get out of this smoke. How about a walk on the beach before bedtime? I've got some ideas we can talk about just in case this CB dialogue is related to our boat. Oh, yeah, and if you're really gonna miss the smoke in here, I just happen to have a nice little rolled bit of Jamaican under my hat brim"

"I've always liked that about you, Professor, that—y'know, not like other guys—you've always got something under your hat, and you're usually filled to the brim too!" She laughs.

"Beep! Hiiiiiiiii Rick! This is Joyce. Sherri and I were wondering if we could stop by Saturday night for a little private tutoring? (Giggling in the background.) And…and a chance to talk kinda off the record about some problems we're having at SCCC. (More giggling.) We'll, um, catch you after class Thursday, okay? That's like, uh, both of us would like to get, um, tutored at the same time, if y'know what I mean? Mmmm. Niiiight, Rick!"

"What the hell's that about, Professor? We're doing threesomes now while I'm at work?"

"Oh, please, JP, you know what this bimbette stuff's about. You also know that I love you and that I live and breathe for you. I…"

"I know. I just get jealous, and worry you'll, you know. Besides, I like when you tell me that you live and breathe for me. It makes me live and breathe better!" The dimple reappears. She tosses her hair.

"Okay," she says as she reaches for the machine button, "what's the next message? God, we go to The Ark for a beer and burger and you'd think the roof fell in. What's with all these calls?"

"Beep! Hey, Teach! Fast Eddie says you used to have a CB on the boat, but Mr. Pulver says it ain't there. Yer not trying to pull a fast one I hope. I'll call you back."

"Oh, shit! What did I tell you, JP. Now I'm going to have to…"

"Going to have to tell him that you pulled it out to get it fixed, and that they should probably just get a new one? What's he going to do? Kill us over a $300 missing radio? Lighten up, Rick!"

"Beep! Hi JP, this is Heather? I'm in your Elementary Ed class? I was wondering if you could call me when you get in to tell me what we're supposed to read for Thursday's quiz? My number's 899-1731? I'm up 'til 12:30, one o'clock? Thanks?"

"Who's Heather? And howcum everything she says is a question?"

"I guess she's not sure about whether it's Major Cusp's last stand or not." She smirks. "No, serious, she's nice. Lives around here someplace. We've talked a couple of times. She's helped me with class notes. I guess she likes to sound like a Valley Girl, you know? Anyway, she has a kid, and a boyfriend who's also a lot older."

"Whaddaya mean *also* a lot older?"

"Well, you know, like you've been married with kids, and you're twelve years older than me, which I think is great because I love you so much, and I feel so important to be with you, and I learn so much from you, and I want to be with you forever, and..."

"Okay, okay, enough. You can have my body if you want."

"Oh, yeah, well what makes you think I want?"

"Do you?"

"Yeah!"

"Case closed. Call your Heather friend, then I'll meet you in under the comforter."

"How, um, comforting!"

"Listen, Billyboy, I'm telling you, she's holier than thou. I've talked with her a few times, even helped her with some class notes. She doesn't have a clue. JP is a dumb little bimbo who's getting off on having a fantasy fling with her professor, which probably won't last another semester. It's like the world's biggest ego trip for a student to be fooling around with her teacher, especially to be living together. And that's where it stops. Maddigan is just like any other guy. He's got his brain between his legs and thinks he's hot stuff because all the young honeys in his classes want a piece of him, mostly because they think it will buy them a good grade!"

"I hope you're right, Heather, because Slam says everyone is depending on you to make sure those two don't upset the, um, Applecart, so to speak."

"Very funny, Billyboy! I'm telling you, Maddigan would jump my bones in a heartbeat if JP walks or gets tired of having an old man who's twelve years older. I should know, Billy. I'm a woman. Women know things like this. Besides, look at us. I know our nine years difference isn't the same as their twelve years difference, but it's pretty damn close! Apple doesn't need to worry about those two. They're too busy having sex ten times a week to be thinking about anything else."

Intermittent slithers of streetlight reflections dance through the windblown needles of the front door sentry pine tree. Maddigan leans forward from his pillow and lightly lifts her leg, letting it drop with a soft frumpf into the snarl of blankets. She never blinks. Her breathing is steady, as drone as the rotating murmurs of air escaping from the space heater across the room.

He sits back to admire her slight but tight muscular body, her hair splayed across a disarrayed sheet. Absorbed by the vision of JP washed in the shadows, he watches her breathe. The streetlight glimmers dart sporadically between the wooden windowslats and ripple across her shimmering back and buttocks. He pulls the kicked-away sheet and blankets to her shoulders. She stirs for a moment, yawns, stretches one arm, gathers a corner of comforter and returns to her dreams.

He rises in the dark, steps into his sneakers, pulls on his sweatpants, sweater and windbreaker. He wishes he could crash as hard as she always does but—this night—sleep is nowhere on his mind's horizon. He kisses her forehead, and tosses the spare blanket from the foot of the bed over his shoulder. When he reaches the kitchen counter, he pockets his front door key, then picks up a marker and paper towel and scribbles:

"Gone to beach. Back with the sun...and a shell for you! Sleep tight. Kisses—me"

He tiptoes back into the room to leave the message next to her on his pillow. He locks the door behind him and steps out into the brisk night air. He shuffles, deep in thought, up the sand-strewn street to the roaring surf where he pulls up the windbreaker hood, wraps the blanket around himself, and curls up to sit in the sand, knees to chest. He picks up a shell that was shoveled into a nearby mound of sand and pockets it. Hugging his knees, the professor stares blankly into the murky black sea, rocking gently to the uneven rhythm of the waves. He sees a shooting star out of the corner of his eye. He is feeling melancholy.

He thinks about the past three years since moving to Seaport County. Long gone is the short-fused emotional tangle he'd left behind—haunting rubble beneath the idyllic surface of his suburban commuter existence.

He cringes as he recalls the daily battles with a disillusioned wife led astray by the advances of a close friend...someone he at first naively encouraged to intimacy with her, then later regretted. In the endless sleepless nights that followed, he admonished himself to the point of self-abuse. He grits his teeth remembering her next two affairs, one with a greasy, pipe-smoking town politician who pretended a happy marriage while bed-hopping with a dozen other town politician wives who pretended happy marriage.

The other, astonishingly overt by any measure, was with a sleazy aging hack playwrite.

Maddigan's fists tighten as his mind drifts deeper into past despair, and the events he fought so hard to keep contained. Predictably, the devastating memories come to him whenever he is alone. The two-edged sword of divorce and custody hearings that wrought havoc on his digestive system, that pounded the inside of his forehead to a pulp even though the judge ruled maternal abandonment and mental cruelty and awarded him full custody of all three children...all three in diapers.

Unprecedented in the State of New York for children so young, the judge said. *So what,* he thought. He wanted his family back, his wife, his life, his self-esteem. But it was too late and too far gone, all of it. He had his children, his house, and barely his job. But the legal tribulations had taken his life from him.

Chapter 27

SPIT HAPPENS

Here he sits behind a small dune, sheltered from the wind by a sand-embedded blanket, continuing to rock himself into a little crevice. Here he sits, listening to the omnipotent night sea he can't see, managing somehow to yet cling to his earthly existence.

His mind goes to the survival strains of a testy marriage that parented a profoundly retarded daughter, and the near-suicidal stress he came to know of raising her alone. Too much stress for a twenty-five-year-old father. *Dear sweet Maddy. She cried all night every night.* He walked the floors with her, humming, stroking, kissing…trying to sort out what this baby's tiny world was all about.

Single parenthood loneliness sucked. How, he wonders, did he ever get past the thinness of his spread-out, fragile emotions? But spreading himself thin was all there was then. It wasn't of course just the helplessness of Maddy that tangled up his nights.

Wrapped around his stressful workday hours, there was his oldest and most beautiful child, Holly, an insecure loving puppy dog of a four and a half-year-old daughter. And there was Maddy's two and a half-year-old cherubic but rambunctious twin brother, Marty.

Ah, yes, he also recalls, there were actually three to four almost solid hours of sleep every night. Handcuffed as he was by twenty,

twenty-one hours of fear each day that his children would be taken from him by the State (he'd heard so many stories) brought him to within a hair of demolishing his career, to within a blink of tossing himself off a cliff.

Light-years seemed to pass before his estranged wife's shrink was able to rewire her brain. Somewhere between her running up $10,000 on his charge cards and absconding with the family car, which she and her druggie boyfriend managed to total, Maddigan became accustomed to bad news surprises—sometimes jarred to inaction. *Catatonic,* he would describe it later to a judge.

As he withdrew mentally and emotionally from the havoc, he became increasingly preoccupied with raising his children. Then the ultimate humiliation: he lost his job because—Maddigan was told by his boss's shoeshine boy—he was "too preoccupied with raising his children."

It didn't take long for finances to crash, leaving him to seek grocery loans from friends, and enlist homemaker/baby-sitting services from a parade of public assistance agencies. These options—and ultimately having no choice except to collect food stamps and unemployment checks—became his lifeline. He wanted to hide in the attic.

Somewhere along the way, Maddigan exchanged threats with his wife's boyfriend who, in one of his stupors, threw toddler Marty down the stairs. Maddigan struggled frantically with his rage when he arrived home from a long day of desperate job searching to find his son swollen and bloody, being bandaged by the day nurse. *Dear Jesus, he's only three years old. Was this what life was supposed to be?*

And then, the icing on his wife's cake: his misguided irate in-laws arrived at the house, driving seven hours nonstop from Pittsburgh to threaten him in the living room, throw belongings of his out the door, and yell at him in front of the children. Then the grand finale: his wife shrieked curses, punched him in the jaw and pushed him to the floor. He rose to his feet angry and shaken and—with clenched fists buried deep in his pockets and all the restraint he could muster—he spit in her face.

Then the lawyers. Charges and counter-charges. Nearly two years. And all of that time, he juggled four fragile lives day-to-day. He somehow managed also to mentally pull his bitter wife back in to work with him, to confront and implement the inevitable—that Maddy had to be institutionalized.

Finally court. She never showed up. He won. But he lost. He kept so much inside.

After the court ruled in his favor, he let this woman, who two years earlier had virtually left him for dead, return and manipulate him into believing she was recovered and fit enough of a mother to raise the other two children.

They would live in Brooklyn. Okay, he could drive there. Then once she had them with her physically, overriding his concerns, she took them to Syracuse—a long tough drive in ice and snow. He kept so much inside. Finally, over his raging objections, she violated court orders and took them to Miami, knowing he couldn't afford more lawyers. A totally too far trip to make, and she knew that too. The bitch. He kept so much inside.

Then he faced years of intercepted letters and cassette tapes, interrupted phone calls followed by dial tones, packages marked "Refused" returned to his doorstep. How could he be their Father if he couldn't communicate with them? Even if he could afford more legal fees, he believed her fragile mindset might prompt flight to another country. She did, after all, speak fluent French and had spent a summer in Switzerland. He'd never even been to Europe. He would never see them again.

She added fuel to the fire at every turn. "Disrupting the children while they were trying to establish new lives was not," their Mother insisted, "in their best psychological interests." Presumably, her string of transient boyfriends was. He should have known better. He should have acted when he could.

A crashing wave advanced up the shoreline and snapped him back to the beach.

"B-I-I-I-I-I-I-I-ITCH!" he screamed now at the roaring ocean.

"*Bitch!*" he whispered under cascading tears, rocking harder, huddled to his knees.

The waves sprawl before him in the moonlit stretch of his peripheral vision. Edged like the shoreline in gradations of gray and black, memories of his life's deepest, darkest upsets are delivered with each clatter of small stones and broken shells.

Was it Maddy's plight that drove his wife to disown the child, and drive such distance between him and their other two children?

With each uprooting, he yielded "for the good of the children." *For the good of the children* became her battle cry thrown in his face whenever she saw that it served to immobilize him. Her determination—and that which she covertly delegated to insolent boyfriends—to control and keep the children away from him, and away from the phone and mailbox, thwarted his every effort to reach out.

Holly's and Marty's mother-smothered hearts left no room to know their Father's rage. And sadly, children's eyes don't see great distances. He wipes a tear from his cheek. And another. Ocean spray hits his face. He takes a deep breath.

But now, he begins to think, is a different time, a different life. All is no longer so bleak.

From the day he first met her on one of his between-class jaunts across campus—JP sitting cross-legged with friends on the lawn in front of the library, throwing her head back in laughter as he approached, then inviting him into the discussion saying she'd heard he was new and asking what classes he'd be teaching—from that first moment when he saw the glint in her eyes, her small bright white teeth, her dimple, her fresh-scrubbed look—from that first moment of accepting her uninhibited un-intimidated invitation that paused him long enough to squat down to eye contact level, to shake hands and exchange introductions, from that moment forward, she nurtured him with sunshine.

It was JP who lifted his spirits from darkness. She prodded him to excel. She convinced him to learn psychotherapy by getting psychotherapy, and he sat in hundreds of group sessions, absorbing, adapting, sculpting his own techniques. It was JP who seemed to give him purpose, who helped him reconnect to his growing children.

He wipes his cheeks again, but this time, he smiles.

His new teaching career unearths enormous feelings of joy, self-satisfaction, and accomplishment for all the positive new perspectives of life he knows that he's been serving up to his students.

He sniffs at the thick salt air. A wave spills itself across the sand.

And living on a boat has been a dream fulfilled.

But now his addiction to pot threatens to undo it all. Just the thought of quitting his de-seeding pan, rolling papers, pipe and tobacco pouch, and those long deep inhalations that relax his body and take his brain into creative, uninhibited outer space is like facing divorce and custody hearings all over again. Yet something is about to happen. He knows that some thing has to change.

His empty stare catches a sand crab. It pops up in front of his feet and scurries to the water's edge. It dances, nimbly jittering along the foam, accompanied by the vacant applause of rattling shells pulsing through each rush of surf.

This is the kind of dance and disappearing act I need to do, he thinks. *I need a plan that lets me scurry off into the distance, me and JP. I need to get rid of these shitty memories. I'm here, now. And I'm about to be swallowed up by this rising tide—these evil, mindless gangsters who've no regard for our lives or values. If JP and I can just find out what they plan to do with the boat, we'll be in a better position to catch them off balance. If we can catch them off balance, maybe we can improve our odds to be left alone.*

Another large wave, this one harder than the last few, roars to the beach.

We've got to figure out this damn message JP uncovered. It has to be a code of some kind. I have to believe the boat, my boat, is involved up to her brass rails.

The thing is, like JP says, neither this guy Slam nor his goon sidekick is smart enough to be working for someone who's smart. Figuring them out shouldn't take a Mensa I.Q. Maybe we're just over-thinking this thing. Maybe the strange message names are just alphabet equivalents of numbers, maybe they combine to say something secret, maybe they're...

A large wave spills up the beach and reaches his running shoes before he can pull his feet away. He stands quickly, stumbling as he tries to collect the blanket, and retreats ten feet up toward the dunes, where he sits again, this time on the blanket. He takes off his wet shoes and socks, shoes he had hurried into to when he left and only now noticed were on backwards.

Backwards. What an idiot I am. Backwards. He shakes his head in disbelief that he'd switched shoes for the first time since he was five or six. *Backwards.* He starts to laugh, but something clicks...he swallows hard instead.

What if...what if those CB voices were saying things backwards? That would mean that "Mals" could be..."Slam." That's it! Mals. Slam. That's it! I've got to wake JP.

He rockets to his feet, pulls the blanket up over his hood, grabs his wet shoes and socks and double-time jogs it barefoot back to the cottage.

Lights, loud music, wet washcloths and twenty minutes later, JP is groggy but awake, sitting next to him on the couch, wrapped in the comforter she dragged from the bed, and brushing sand from the shell he presented.

"Mals? Mals is...Slam, JP! They're saying names backwards. We need to go over your notes again. We need to see how many other names there are. Are you up for it?"

"Up. Yup, I'm up. How could I not be up? You could probably raise the dead, for Chrissake."

She stretches and yawns. "I was having such a good dream. We were on a beautiful, big new boat, cruising the Caribbean...okay, okay, let's look at what we've got."

She hands him back the shell he gave her as she swings her legs over the coffee table and pulls on one of his t-shirts that was draped over the back of the sofa.

"My notes are in the child psych book on the end table next to you." He reaches and passes it to her.

"Backwards, huh? You know you might just have something here, Professor."

Chapter 28

BLACK LEATHER JACKETS

Three hours 'til midnight Saturday.

JP should be leaving her waitress job any minute now with that stomachache she said Vanessa would be covering for with the boss. Half-hour drive, she should be here by 9:30.

That run I took on the boardwalk hasn't done much for my nerves. And the blackberry brandy shots might as well have been V-8 Juice. My legs feel like they're still running–jittering when I stand, jiggling when I sit. Maybe I should just grade test papers or something? Nah! With the headspace I'm in right now, trying to concentrate on grading tests would be like trying to read Armenian rocket ship assembly instructions by Bic Lighter.

If we're right, and JP's got this dialogue nailed, and we've got the names figured with this backwards stuff, something big-time must be happening here, but what? "Simo" CB'd "Apple." And "young Benjamin" and "Slam" and "Pulver" and "Eddie" are all part of the hornet's nest! Plus we got Bill Shill hanging out, and what's with the "Mr. and Mrs. Rat" (or "Tar" if you do that backwards), but the rest of this has got to be right so far. And who else is involved that wasn't mentioned? Hmmm, I'm thinking: Aifam eht? Jesus!

It's all too weird. Where does my boat fit in? Moonlight dinner cruises? I don't think so. Then that whole freakin' turtle thing. What was that all about?

Where are you, JP? I can't run this half-assed wired-up radio without you.

Maddigan steps to the kitchen table; he's about to light a joint but—flame-tipped match in his hand—he freezes as he hears a car roll up on the pebbles outside. He checks his watch. *Too early for Green Eyes.* Two doors slam shut. *Maybe she left early and brought someone with her? No. She wouldn't do that tonight. Besides, the car doors sound heavy.*

He blows out the match and tucks the joint into his sock. He sweeps a quick spray of NO-Zone across the room and tosses the can under the sink on his way to the window. He looks between the blind slats just in time to see two guys throwing their arms and legs to the side as they lumber awkwardly along like workout freaks to his front door.

Shit! Now what? They must be more of Slam's thugs here for the damn CB. With lightning speed, Maddigan lifts a two by eight floorboard under the corner of his throw rug, yanks the CB wires off the battery, shoves the transmitter under the board, re-covers it with the rug and slides the battery under an end table.

Five assertive knocks rattle the wood through his plastic insulated, hooked screen door. He turns tentatively toward the raps while his eyes flick around the room looking for potential problems to prevent.

He remembers the joint in his sock as he sees the roach clip he'd been headed for, sitting in plain view with a pack of EZ-Roller rolling papers on the kitchen counter. He steps back from the door to empty his sock and sweep it with the clip and papers into his silverware drawer. He flicks on an overhead track light fixture and the outdoor spotlight.

Three more knocks.

"I'll be right there!" he calls, as he does a final inventory. His baseball bat stands in a dark corner next to the bedroom hallway. His Buck knife is on top of the hutch by the front door. He spots the screwdriver, pliers, and small spool of wire JP had left entangled on the table after she had connected the CB. He shoves them into the same drawer he'd just visited.

He plants his left foot behind the door and opens it a few inches. "Hi!" he offers at the two hulking shadow-faced men in boots and black knit caps, who appear to be struggling with keeping their muscles from bursting through their black leather jackets. "What can I do for you?" he asks in a shakier than normal voice as he pushes more weight onto his left foot and considers how quickly he could grab his knife or dive for the bat.

"Are you Professor Maddigan?"

With the spotlight he'd flicked on shining behind them, he has to squint to see their faces. Their penetrating hawk eyes, a scar, beard stubble, a chipped tooth all come into focus.

"Yeah, that's me. I'm Professor Maddigan. What is it you want?"

Both men, near eye level with Maddigan even though they stand a step lower than the threshold, reach inside their coats at the same time, sending an instant shudder up his spine and accelerating his flash thought about diving for the bat.

"We're DEA Agents from Newark, that's Drug Enforcement Administration. I'm Special Agent Jake Hartley, this is Special Agent Rusty Leeds," says the smaller of the two, who stands about six-four. They produce gold badges and hold them out. Maddigan feels totally confused. He leans forward and stares hard at the badges wondering if the I.D.'s are legit.

He eases up pushing on his left leg, but thinks again about the bat, until he sees a packed shoulder holster on the big guy as he opens his jacket to re-pocket his badge.

These guys are an hour and a half from Newark and it's nearly 9:30 at night...D-E-A? What the hell's this all about? Christ, did someone see me smoking dope? Please, dear God, don't let this be to arrest me.

His voice still a bit quavery, "Wha...what's this all about, Gentlemen?"

"Do you own a boat?"

"Well, ah, I guess so...I..."

The two glance quickly at each other.

"Mind if we come in Professor?" the smaller one asks as if he had just bumped an old lady in a grocery store with his shopping cart. "We have some questions we'd like to ask you about an investigation we're conducting."

"Well, ah, sure..." *An investigation they're conducting.* "That's fine. You can come in."

Maddigan steps to the side. As they pass him in the doorway accompanied by a rush of cold air, the smaller guy pockets his hat and sweeps his long blond hair back with his hand. Both do quick scans around the room. The big guy with the chipped tooth steps a stride into the hallway. He snarls under his breath and leans cautiously left, and then right, into the bedroom and bathroom doorways, flipping wall light switches on and off and probing each corner like he was expecting to see fifty-pound bags of cocaine piled up against the walls.

"Are you alone right now?" the smaller one asks.

"Well, yes. My girlfriend's on her way home from work, and..."

"Your girlfriend lives with you?" the big one questions over his shoulder as he bends forward to look through the window that abuts the kitchen sink.

"Yes. Listen, you want to sit down?" Maddigan asks, attempting to keep things cordial. "Can I get you anything? Water? Soda?"

The two agents sit on opposite sides of the combination kitchen/living room, leaving him the couch in the middle.

"Thanks we just had some coffee," the smaller one responds. "And your girlfriend's name is...?"

Maddigan feels another shudder. This one tingles his neck. "Ahhh, JP. Her n-name is JP. Listen, I don't understand why you're asking about her, or why you're here. Lots of people own boats, you know?"

"Thanks Professor Maddigan. Yes, we're aware of that."

The smaller guy is a schmoozer, disarmingly gentle, Maddigan surmises.

"It is 'Professor,' right?"

"Yes, I teach at Seaport County Community College."

"What subjects?"

Again an engaging tone. He's catching me off-balance.

"Ah, business and psychology. You know, management and marketing stuff?"

"Underpaid, no doubt?" the bigger one tosses off the probe as he turns to look at the closet door behind him, a small blue and green-painted wood placard hangs there with the message in bold white:

NOW is the only time.
The past is over.
The future not yet here.

Chapter 29

APPLECRISP

"Underpaid? Hey, who isn't?" Maddigan chirps back, annoyed with the big guy's preoccupation with the room. The agent turns back to face the professor.

"But I'm not in it for money." *I'm sounding too defensive.* "The boat, my Jeep—I paid cash for those with money it took me ten years to make in New York City. Advertising agency work. Before moving here..."

"...To teach because you get intrinsic rewards from teaching," the big black jacket interjects with a hint of sarcasm, while focusing on Maddigan's nervous hands.

Maddigan holds his breath. *I'm a damn wreck here,* he thinks. *What's going on?*

"Right," he responds, pulling at his beard, "and with what I had managed to save, and after forcing myself to scale back..."

"By," the big black jacket squeaks as it twists, "living here?" the agent asks with one eyebrow raised.

"Well, yeah, but this is only a three-month rental. JP and I live on the boat the rest of the year."

"What kind of boat, Professor?" the smaller black jacket asks politely.

"It's a refinished classic 1959 Chris Craft Constellation—all wood, bull-nose hull, teak decks, twin Daytona 400 engines on Chrysler blocks. But I don't have the boat."

The jackets sit up straight. Mouths open in a hint of surprise as both heads shift slightly back. Eyes squint. Brows raise as if to say, "You gotta be kiddin'."

"Serious. I rented it to some guy. The deal is I hold the papers, and he pays me monthly, and then returns the boat to me in a year."

"Can we see the ownership papers?" the big one cuts to the bottom line.

Maddigan rises and ambles to the bedroom. He's followed by the XXL-sized agent who stands watching from the doorway. The Professor proceeds to rummage through his important papers box that he retrieves from the bottom drawer of his dresser, while the L-sized guy meanders around the living room and kitchen, bending, stretching, and looking. He pokes at Maddigan's jacket hanging in the corner, the loaf of bread on the kitchen counter, the sofa padding.

"Here they are!" Maddigan proclaims like he'd just turned up some tyrannosaurus shinbones at an archaeological dig site. "The deal just happened a couple of weeks ago," he offers. He slides carefully around XXL to cross the room and hand the folder marked "BOAT" to the smaller, friendlier agent. "And I'm supposed to get some paperwork on it in the next few days. The guy seemed legit though. I visited him at his business. He owns a big seafood restaurant up in the Highlands. Grand Slam's Clams it's called."

Second thoughts about what he had just said cross Maddigan's mind. He doesn't want them to think he was so stupid as to not have a signed agreement, and he certainly doesn't want them to know the threatening circumstances of the deal, but he feels nervous all the same for telling them something that isn't true. He also knows he shouldn't be volunteering so much information. A twinge of worry ramrods through his brain for having given them the restaurant name.

While the two agents lean over from their seats on the couch where they had repositioned themselves to examine the papers, a second car hits the driveway pebbles. Both men jump to their feet, reach inside their leather and are suddenly standing at the window looking through the slats.

Jeez, they move faster than the crab I watched scrambling along the water's edge last night. "Hey, you guys, take it easy, will you? It's just my old lady. It's JP!"

"Benji, get Slam on the line. Find out what he hears from Pulver and Fast Eddie."

Benjamin dials some numbers as Apple circles the library, absently shifting papers, books, maps, charts and index cards that cover the conference table, from one place to another. Within sight through the French doors, Lava stands in the hallway talking to Mayetta. Benjamin is laboriously untangling and stretching the long black coiled phone line across the room to where his father stands fidgeting. Apple, who had been running his fingers nervously through his hair, finally strides toward Benjamin and snatches the phone from where it was tucked between his son's elbow and ribcage. "Gimme that damn thing, Boy!" and clamps the receiver to his ear.

"Slam! What's happening with the two safeboat sailors?"

"Oh, hi Apple! They was delayed puttin' the boat in the water. Something about frozen water jugs holding down the tarp cover. Anyway, they're moving now, lickity-split, to the destination, and should be there by ten when the restaurant's almost empty."

"Good. Next time they call in, let them know to gas up, then dock next to the north end of your restaurant. No lights. No engine. No noise. Tell them to go find Mother Simo at Gilligan's, and remind him I'll be looking for him on a quiet. He knows when. I'll fill you in later." Click.

"¿Qué passa, Billyboy? How's that tight-ass bitch of yours?" growls the grinning sea captain from his cigar-smoke-clouded corner barstool.

"Hey, Capt'n Simo. Busy times we got here—says Apple. Heather and the baby are doing fine. Thanks for askin'."

"What's up with the Macintosh, Billyboy? I'm supposed to talk to him in awhile. Howcum he sent you here?"

"Apple doesn't want anyone else to know that whatever time he tells you on midnight CB is the delivery time, you should subtract ten hours just in case someone picks up the chatter, you know?"

"That guy thinks of every fookin' thing. How do I know that you're telling the truth, Billyboy? You wouldn't be tryin' to set me up, would you? You know I could make dog meat out of you faster than you could chug this beer, don't you?" Simo slides a sweaty brown bottle along the bar to him. Billy picks it up and tilts the neck to toast the captain.

"Apple said you would say that, so he told me to tell you to say to him that I stopped in to see you, and that he'll ask you, 'around ten?' and you'll say 'yeah.' Okay?"

"Whatever Apple says is crisp, my boy! Got it? Ha, ha, ha, ha!"

Billy chugs the beer, smiles at Simo's humor, slaps the bottle bottom on the bar, gets off the stool he'd been sitting on, and considers patting Simo on the shoulder, then thinks better of it.

"Gotta get goin' Capt'n. Apple's got me on the run, but thanks for the beer and thanks for not makin' dogmeat outta me. That woulda made it hard for me to collect Workers' Comp." Simo returns the smile and Billy leaves.

She swings through the front door, one arm out of her coat, apron slung over her shoulder, "Hey Rick! Whose car..." She stops in her tracks. "Who are you guys? Don't tell me you're Rick's students."

"No, Ma'am," offered XXL-size as he pulls out his shield again, "We're Federal Drug Enforcement agents. I'm Special Agent Leeds. This is my partner, Special Agent Hartley. We're here to ask the professor a few questions. You're welcome to sit in if you like."

"Well, thanks, big guy, but this is my house too, so I don't think I need an invitation to hear you ask my old man some drug questions! Do you have a warrant?"

"No, Ma'am, we..."

"Easy JP, they're here to find out about the boat, about our deal with the boat," Maddigan turns to the friendly agent, "Isn't that right, Agent...er, what's your name again?"

"Hartley. Jake Hartley. And this is Agent Rusty Leeds." Hartley's eyes are fixed on JP.

"Right. Hartley and Leeds. Listen guys, JP and I are more than willing to help you with anything we can, but we need to understand what's involved, and what's with the boat?"

"I'm sorry, Professor, we're not at liberty to disclose that information. We..."

"Well you damn well better change that rule, Agent Jake Hartley, because—unless you can tell us what's going on—there's really nothing more that the professor or I have to say. May I remind you gentlemen that you do not have a warrant, that this is Saturday night and we have both worked our butts off all week, and we have plans to relax and recharge that do not include sitting here telling you about a boat that we do not have, and…"

"JP, wait! It won't kill us to spend a few minutes…"

"Bullshit, Rick! These two muscle-beach boys have no right to barge in here and…"

"Listen up!" Agent Leeds barks like a Marine drill instructor, "The two of you can calm down here and answer our questions, or keep up the hostile attitude, and we'll have to cuff you both and bring you in to our Newark office to question you there."

He turned an intimidating stare to JP, "If you're looking for a warrant, Missy, we can get one within the hour, and we're not going to be turning this place upside down looking for a boat. We'll start with the twelve-volt battery shoved under the table, the loose floorboard under the rug, the marijuana flakes on the kitchen counter, what your NO-Zone spray is used to mask, and the plastic bag of herbs sticking out of your apron pocket!

"Now, I suggest, you unruffle your feathers, begin to settle down, and start cooperating, and—if you help us out here—we might forget waiting around until one of our other partners brings that warrant over that will allow us to turn this place, and you, inside out. Now let's stick to why Agent Hartley and I are here. If we can get your help, we might decide to overlook the other issues I mentioned. Understand?"

Maddigan and JP both nod sheepishly.

"Good. Now, tell us about the boat deal. What it was? When it took place? Where it took place? Who was there? Why did you agree? And how is the deal being done? We want to hear names, dates, times. And don't skip any details!"

Chapter 30

HOW'S THIS?

By 11:30, Maddigan had outlined a scenario that had Mr. Slam and Mr. Pulver of Grand Slam Clam's Wharfside Restaurant in Highlands, NJ, plunking the first $30,000 cash boat lease payment down on the table. They were in the restaurant's private dining booth. The table was hosting Maddigan's compliments-of-the-house lobster and champagne dinner around 9PM on the first of March.

Somewhere between dipping the claws in butter and sipping a second free glass of Moët, Maddigan says he was promised eleven more $10,000 payments to come by mail on a monthly basis. The boat was promised to be returned undamaged at the end of a year.

Maddigan assured the agents that the $30,000 cash was immediately deposited. He explains to them the money will be used "less, of course, the appropriate taxes" to start a new group consulting business he plans to launch with JP. Both pair of black jacket inhabitants' eyes turn to her. She nods confirmation.

The Professor itemizes projected expenses to include office supplies, books, sound and video recording equipment, promotional flyers, professional association and journal subscription fees, insurance, legal fees, accounting fees, signage, postage, telephone, etc. He re-emphasizes that a signed boat lease agreement is forthcoming.

As if thinking that by stalling them, the issues would somehow go away, Maddigan embellishes his story with sidetrack explanations of his teaching and counseling approaches. He itemizes the experience and credentials he and JP have to offer. He even suggests that Hartley and Leeds enroll in a session.

The two men look impatient, but before they can prod Maddigan back to addressing the boat issues, the professor's comments quickly circle back around to the deal he made and that—he shrugs emphatically—he simply was made an offer he thought he should take advantage of because, he reasons, it allows him to keep his boat and make money on it at the same time.

He makes a point of underscoring that he has no idea of what is planned for the boat or why it generated so much money in this agreement, but that he just felt it was best to not ask questions. He assumed it was going to be used in conjunction with the restaurant running moonlight customer cruises or something.

"Yup! A clam restaurant running romantic midnight cruises. Or maybe it's so they can just lean customers over the railing—your boat has a railing?--and save floor cleaning expenses when people have to throw up bad clams?" offers Agent Leeds.

Maddigan hints at a smile and tells the agents that he did ask once about their plans, but never got an answer.

"Okay, Mr. Professor and Ms. JP, we appreciate your help," the big guy stands. "I think we've got what we want here for now. At least we know everything we need to know about the boat, where to find it, and where we can get a good profitable lobster and champagne dinner at the same time." Leeds sneers as he trails off the rest of the sentence and moves toward the door.

"Well, you will keep our names out of this, won't you?" JP asks with a creased forehead and far-away glimmer of hope in her eyes. "I mean there's really no need to say who gave you the information, is there?"

"Probably not," Hartley moves to join his partner at the front door. "We really can't guarantee anything, but we'll certainly do our best to keep your identities under wraps."

"As for tonight," Agent Leeds says, looking down at the tops of their heads, "we'll let you get on with your 'relaxing and re-charging' activities." A small half-cough served as his accent mark.

Agent Hartley shifts gears, "We'll probably be back in touch with you sometime in the next few days, so we strongly advise you to stay in the area. Here's my card." Maddigan thumb-and-forefingers it, unsure if he should pocket it or just keep holding it. He keeps holding it.

"Call us if you think of anything else. Agent Leeds is at that same number. If I'm not available, ask for him. Oh, and we'd like to see a copy of your written agreement when it arrives. You can fax it to this number." He points to the bottom right corner.

"In the meantime," Hartley's voice lowers to a pat-on-the-back whisper, "I suggest you might want to clean out whatever you've got stashed away, Professor, including what's in your drawers and under your floorboards." He pauses for effect. "We may not be looking the other way on our next visit."

His voice level returns to normal as he reaches for the doorknob, "I assume the battery is for your car?" Nods. Uh-huh's.

"Right. Well..." He pauses again while both men put their hats back on. "Have a good weekend, but we expect you to let us know immediately—and I do mean immediately—if you should have any contact whatsoever with this Mr. Slam or any of his associates. Is that clear?"

"Crystal," Maddigan responds.

"One more thing," says Hartley. "Let us know right away if and when you get your next boat payment, okay?"

"Absolutely!" Maddigan's relief that they are finally leaving makes his response sound almost too exuberant. JP chimes in quickly to cover the miscued enthusiasm with an obliging "Right" to close the conversation. The two men leave.

"Whew!" A major exhale gushes from the professor as he and JP peek through the window-blind slats to watch the black Lincoln Towncar back out of the driveway, barely missing her side mirrors, churning up pebbles.

Maddigan turns to flip the business card on the kitchen table. JP is still staring out the window, trying unsuccessfully to gain composure.

"Goddamit, Rick! What written agreement?" she blurts out as she wheels around to face him.

"Please, Green Eyes, give me a minute to recover from this." He swipes at his forehead, his ears, his beard. "My knees are still shaking from seeing them pull their guns out when your car hit the driveway, not to mention that they knew I had pot in the house."

"Bullshit, Rick! You acted like a wuss with them. You're always so forceful and preaching to people to be assertive and here you are sounding as convincing as a dishcloth, for Chrissake! What came over you?...And what's with the Moët?...Why are you holding back information from me? Haven't you figured out that I am your only..."

"Easy, JP, easy. Their visit could be just what we needed. Here's what I was thinking..."

"We've got maybe twenty minutes, Rick. Where's the CB?" She's oozing exasperation. "Where's the damn CB?"

"Under the floorboard. Chill. I had to yank the wires off when the TV Starsky and Hutch wannabes showed up. I thought they were Slam's slime when I saw them in the driveway. Will you be able to re-connect everything in time?"

"Are you kidding?" Still impatient, JP beams momentarily. "Put it all on the kitchen table, plus the pliers, screwdriver and spool of wire that I'd left out, but can't find. Do you have that tape recorder you use for class?"

He pockets the joint and clip from the drawer as he reaches for the wire and tools. "The recorder, yeah. It's in the closet. I'll get it."

"Here, Professor. Hold this wire while I connect it to the unit and the battery cables, and stop looking worried. Even though I probably should, I won't zap you."

"Should?"

"Yes, since you ask. Listen, Rick, I understand now what you had in mind by acting so timid with them, but what the hell did you have to lie to them for? They're federal agents. They could hang our butts in a minute. I got the wire. Here, move this antenna around 'til we get a clear signal."

Hisses and crackling static bounced off the cottage walls. "What's on this tape that's in the recorder? Do you have a new cas-sette?"

"Jesus, woman! You getting a little carried away with this femi-nist assertiveness stuff or what?"

He shifts gears quickly before getting a response he knows he doesn't want to hear about his assertiveness training sessions she went to when they first met.

"To answer your first question, I had to steer those guys away from finding out we'd be doing this midnight gig. They're not after us anyway. They want Slam and his crew. And just like us, they want to find out what's up with the boat."

He stops circling the antenna around the room when the static fades and the speaker hits a point of clear reception. "How's this?"

Chapter 31

Hiss. Static. Click.

Some local cowboy is spouting off to a passing trucker on the Garden State Parkway about how to avoid center lane construction on the approach to Atlantic City exits. Their nasal drawls are clear. *Click. Click.* JP switches channels.

Static. Hiss. Static. Hiss. A husband and wife are dickering about his night out with the boys. He's defending his right to get drunk. JP clicks again.

Static. Hiss. Another channel. A three-way discussion of how much authentic cranberry milk glassware is worth. Another click.

Static. Hiss. Another channel. Southern twang truckers discussing the pros and cons of the showers at Pilot Truckstops.

"That's good, Rick. Prop it up right there. Get your tape machine ready." Unwilling to drop her anger, JP prods, "Still, you didn't have to lie to them, Rick. They're bound to find out at some point, and where are you getting this 'written agreement' you told them about? Honestly, Rick, I..."

"Okay, okay. I screwed up. Let's not screw *this* up. What do you think our chances are of catching this exchange and getting it down on tape? We have only three more minutes. Are you ready? Is our microphone off so they don't accidentally hear us? Is the..."

"Shhhh! Rick, please! Yeah, the mike's off. Let's concentrate on listening. Turn on that cassette recorder. Here goes."

She flicks around a dozen channels. *Static* and *hiss*es follow each *click*. All twelve channels are occupied. She *clicks* some more. A blanket of *static* and *hiss*es. Four empty channels in a row. Here's where we'll concentrate, she says. As the clock hands mate at twelve, she clicks to channel thirteen.

Static. Hiss. Static. Hiss.

"Breaker, break, break. Omis here." JP's head jerks. "Anyone on this channel?" *Static. Hiss. Static.*

"Rick, did you hear that? Omis! He's the guy, right?"

"You're a genius, Green Eyes. Stay on it."

Static. Hiss. Static. Hiss.

"Gotcha Omis. Elppa here. Do you copy? Come on." *Static.*

As they listen in from the cottage kitchen table, JP and the professor exchange knowing looks.

"We got 'em, Rick! It's the rotten apple guy and that Captain Nemo dude."

"Yeah, Simo. He's the one, they is them!"

Static. Hiss. Static. Hiss.

"I copy, Elppa. Looks like we got an empty channel. What's the word?" *Static.*

"Did Revlup and Eidde get there?" *Static.*

"Roger that. Yllib was here too." *Static.*

"Good. Around ten?" *Static.*

"Yeah. Ready to rock 'n roll. What's the lucky number?" *Static.*

"OK, Omis, get some ink and meet me one up. Copy?" *Static.*

"Roger the ink and one up." *Static. Hiss. Static. Static. Static.*

JP looks panicky. "Rick, what the hell are they talking about?"

"Chill, Green Eyes! Apple told Simo to get a pen and switch to channel fourteen...quick, go to fourteen. They're switching channels in case someone's listening in."

"Yeah. Like us."

"Right, like us. Tape recorders don't always work. Gimme that pen and pad behind you. If they're switching channels just to write something down, I want to be sure we've got it too!"

Staring at the receiver, right hand glued to the channel knob, she reaches to her left for the pad and pen and hands it to Maddigan.

Click. Static. Hiss. Static.

"Omis here. Go Elppa!" *Static.*

"Ides. One. P. Copy?" *Static.*

"Loud 'n clear Elppa, you an' Shakespeare both. And the two lottery Pick-6 numbers you want me to play?" *Static.*

Maddigan is writing frantically, checking with JP to make sure he's hearing the message right.

"Go!" *Static.*

"412156 now and 722322 Wednesday. Come back." *Static.*

"Roger the 412156 now and the 722322 Wednesday...sounds good as any. Hey, Elppa, I almost forgot: How's your Mother?" *Static.*

JP's face scrunches up, "HUH?...how's your Mother???"

Maddigan lifts a finger to his nose, "Shhhhhh...later. We'll figure it out later." He keeps writing.

"Thanks for asking, Omis. She's like a hunnert an' eighty-five, but still motoring around on two legs." *Static.*

"Hey, good for her. I forgot—what's her name again?" *Static.*

"Erbmoh. Strange I know, but she was named by a strange uncle named Seyer Ziur before she immigrated here." *Static.*

JP's chin jerked sideways. "Erbmoh? Apple's mother's name is Erbmoh, and she's *185* years old?"

Maddigan gave her a palms-down response, "Shhhhh. JP, please!"

"Roger Uncle Seyer. What made him so strange, besides the name stuff?" *Static.*

"Meet me three up." *Static. Hiss. Static. Static. Static.*

Maddigan had been leaning over JP's shoulder. She was seated. He slapped the Formica tabletop. "Quick, JP...go to channel seventeen!" *Click. Click. Click. Static. Static.*

"Hey, you there?" *Static. Hiss. Crackle.*

"Gotcha. Just wanted to make sure no ears get locked in on us. Yeah, Uncle wasn't exactly 'strange' like you might think, Omis! He just drank a lot, according to my mother." *Static.*

"Roger the beverage damage, Elppa. Some capacity, huh?" *Hiss. Static. Crackle.*

"You got that right. I heard he could drink anybody under the table. The word in the family is he put away eighteen doubles one night!" *Static.*

JP and Maddigan exchange puzzled looks.

"Whew! That's alotta booze!" *Static.*

"Yeah, well, he drowned in it when he tried to go to nineteen. End of Uncle Seyer!" *Static.* (Pause) *Static.* "Anyway, catch you three one four, Omis. Over and out." *Static.*

"You got it. Over and out." *Static. Click. Static. Hiss. Static.*

"We got it. We got it, Babe!" Maddigan squeezes JP's shoulder, and brushes his hair back off his forehead.

"Good work, Green Eyes! How about you disconnect all that shit and we stow it away? If we work with just the tape recorder, it'll be easier to hide quickly in case someone shows up." Maddigan is excited but clearly still shaken by the earlier black leather visitors.

"Hi, Apple. When's the communication with Simo? I been putting everything on hold until I hear from you."

"Sorry, Slam, I already spoke with him. There wasn't time to plug you in. He was on the run. You know how it is with trying to schedule around the weather and tides and all?"

"That's okay. I understand. I just wished I knew. Anyway, I assume everything went okay?"

"Absolutely, Slam. Thanks for your diligence on this. I'll try to keep you in the loop next time. Why don't you stop over here tomorrow night so we can review details. Around 7:15." *Click*.

Chapter 32

HEAVY FEATHER
AND THE IDES OF MARCH

By 1:30AM, after repeated peeks through the blinds to check if the driveway was still free of agent-types, after playing the tape forward and backward twenty times, after smoking the joint he'd retrieved from under the kitchen drawer full of knives and forks and spoons and tools and wire, and after mixing in a couple of slugs each of blackberry brandy, Maddigan and JP managed to decipher all the names.

They now know that "Simo" is the one who had called "Apple." And that "Pulver" and (Fast) "Eddie" and "Billy (Bill Shill)" are all part of the Grand Slam's Clams gang that is at least partly accountable for New Jersey being referred to by some as the "Greaseball State."

They agree that—based on voice alone—Simo sounds like a tough guy, and that Apple sounds like a fruit, but a fruit that is unquestionably the boss. They added "Young Benjamin" from the earlier exchange JP had captured. As for Apple's mother, they could only conclude that she just *acted* one-hundred-eighty-five years old, was a twin, and that her name was *Hombre,* which made no sense. They figured that Apple has a weird uncle with a big-time drinking problem named Reyes Ruiz, which also made no sense. They are completely stymied by the numerical references.

"This 'Ides' thing and them mentioning Shakespeare is like some kind of warning, I think," JP murmurs.

Maddigan turns suddenly. "What? What'd you just say about Shakespeare?"

"Well," JP says, "it's like I seem to remember the Owl mentioning that in Shakespeare's play, Julius Caesar in 1599..."

"Jesus, JP! Fifteen ninety freakin' nine?" He scratches his head, "And WHO is 'the Owl'?"

"Ha, ha! WHO is the owl. I get it. Hey, you know the answer. 'Hooty Judy' you call her, the one looks like a bird? On the English faculty?"

"Ah, right. 'Hooty Judy the Owl.' The one who's been politicking her way into deanhood for years now." Rick swipes his hair back off his forehead. "Probably SINCE 1599," he mutters to himself.

"Okay, JP. Julius Caesar in 1599. Right. Anyway, what's with the three-hundred-freakin'-eighty-two-year-old Julius Caesar warning? You saying a warning could be THAT old?"

"No, that's pretty fast math though for an UN-math professor, but Julius Caesar the play was in 1599. See, there was this astrologer named Spurinna who's identified in the play only as a soothsayer, you know, a person who predicts the future? Anyway, Spurinna warned the Roman ruler to 'Beware the Ides of March.'

"Then, on March fifteenth in 44BCE—that, uh, stands for forty-four years Before the Common Era, or we could just as reasonably say 44BC, for forty-four years Before Christ. That was a really long time ago, huh? Even before you were a teacher!" She smirked playfully as she poked at his chest. "Anyway, it doesn't much matter," she continued, "but, as fate would have it, that was the year that Caesar was, like, assassinated. So, first of all, 'Ides' is generally believed to mean March fifteenth. There's some doubt about whether Caesar might have maybe thought that 'Ides' actually meant the thirteenth of March because at that time..."

"WHOA! Hold on! So, if what you're telling me is that something's going down on March fifteenth, we don't have a shitload of time to get ourselves sorted out and moving in the right direction. It's like being five runs behind in the eighth inning with one out already in the books."

"Well, yeah, Rick, that's what it's like. But you know what? WE are just about to get up to bat with the bases loaded, and all we have to do to tie the game is for one of us to hit a grand slam and the other one of us to just hit a solo home run, right?"

He laughs at how plausible she makes the nearly impossible sound. He strokes his beard and squints at her. The left side of his mouth is skeptically upturned, his left eye half closed.

"Listen, JP, let's put baseball aside. The bottom line is: how fast can you hop?"

"Me? What about you? I can cut classes and call in sick to work, but what do *you* do?"

"Well, if need be, I'll just have to get sick too! Maybe we can catch some germ that requires us to stay in bed together for a week?"

A twinkle and half grin brings the right side of his face into symmetrical alignment with the left. His thoughts though are solemnly fixed on March fifteenth.

"Seems a lot safer than screwing around with these bastards," she continues, sounding more chipper than she appears. "Serious, Rick, we're looking at devoting a major chunk of time here if we're going to save your job, get the boat back and slide away under the radar."

"You're right, Babe, but like my old friend Roger always used to say: 'you gotta do what you gotta do!' If you can swing it, I need you. And I want your help. If you can't, I'll understand, and I'll go it alone."

"My hero! You must be whacked out, Ricky-Dicky if you think for one minute I would leave you to try this alone. Whaddaya think, you're like that video Pacman game or somethin'? Like you can just eat Energy Spots then gobble up the bad guys?"

She stretches and yawns.

"Let's get some sleep and make our plans over morning coffee."

She grabs a blanket from the back of the old stuffed lounge chair, plunks herself into the pile of pillows that nest in the corner of the couch, rolls up into a ball, and is fast asleep before Maddigan can even reach to turn out the lamp.

"Coffee. Right. Good idea," he mutters. "Ricky-Dicky? HA!"

He takes the other blanket to the lounge chair, pushes it back to sleeper position, and sinks in.

"Sleep tight, Green Eyes."

"Y'know, Rusty, something about the professor's story doesn't jive. It's like he's not giving us the whole picture. Did you get that?"

"Yeah, that was my take too. That's some feisty little honey he's shacked up with, huh?"

"Feisty, yeah. That's a good word. Feisty, but definitely a looker. How do you figure a guy like that does it? I mean she's at least ten years younger than he is."

"Not to worry, buddy, we'll only ever end up with broads that are older than dirt. Our work is too serious to attract young muscle, if you know what I mean. How about that written agreement shit? Don't you think a deal that big would be put on paper before you'd ever hand over the keys to a boat that you live on?"

"Yeah, it doesn't fit that there's nothin' real on the deal."

"It's coming, he says. But you know what, pard-ner? No matter how I think it through, the thing doesn't sound right. I mean this guy's a professor, so he's not stupid. Do you get that he's hiding something?"

"Yeah, but what's he hiding?"

"Maybe he's cut in on the next drop. Let's sniff around Grand Slam's Clams in the morning. See what we find. I'll pick you up at five. Coffee at WAWA. We can be there by six. People who run restaurants don't get up 'til nine or ten. That gives us three or four hours to do some discoveries, yes?"

"Discoveries. Sounds like the discovery expedition in that new hit movie *Raiders of The Lost Ark*. Anyway, I'm in. See you at five."

"I don't care, Billy!" Heather shouts as she storms across the cotton braided oval rug to close the door to Brianna's room, afraid of waking her.

"Belize schlamize! So what?" she stammers. "I don't want to-to-to to be here anymore. I don't want us to be part of this, this, this gang of mobsters anymore. I don't care about Apple Snapple or Lava Soap or Pulverized Brains or any of those other jerks. I care about you, about us. I want to go someplace in life with *you*." She reaches with both hands to pull her curls away from both sides of her head. "*Any*place!"

She paces in circles, waving her hands, pausing here and there to point a finger at him. "Anyplace away from here. I want us to have a life together with Brianna, for her to have a chance to grow up happy and healthy, and be proud of her parents. I don't want her being a Mob Brat. I'm supposed to make friends with this JP, and she's in a different league from me. Apple doesn't understand that. I've called her and she never called back. That should tell you something."

Billy stands quietly, shifting his feet. He thinks about saying something, but decides it would only aggravate her further.

"Here we are," Heather continues, "like just a few houses away from the people that Slam is looking to knock off, and where do you think that leaves us? I'm telling you, Billy, we're too close to the middle of this mess. We're going to end up in jail just because we're too close."

She scoots around the room like a helium balloon would skitter across the ceiling.

"Maddigan saw me twice watching him from the arcade, Billy. Both times were just for an instant." She takes a deep jittery breath.

"I don't think he recognized me. I bolted quick enough to have him miss me in case he came back, but he must have caught on that someone was keeping an eye on him. It doesn't matter that I am just monitoring his comings and goings. But if he nails me doing it, I won't be able to lie to him about it, especially since I feel sorry for the guy. He maybe thinks too much of himself, but he doesn't deserve all the crap Apple and Slam are sending his way."

She wheels at him. Her face is flushed in anguish, "You can't really think no one will connect us to this game? I don't want us to end up in jail, Billy. Please Billy. Please!"

She takes his hand tightly in hers. Tears stream down her face. She brushes her hair back with her other hand and looks forlornly to the ceiling for help. Her staggered breathing turns to small gasping whimpers, then sobs.

"I, I, listen Heather, I, I love you too, you know that. You know that. And you know I love Brianna, and I want the best for her too, but you gotta understand that we're too far into this to just up and waltz away, here. I know how hard this is on you and how much you want to get out, but we've got to see this deal through or risk ending up in Gwyneth Bay with cement shoes."

She lets go of his hand and steps back, looking like a sucker-punched boxer.

He steps toward her, "These are not nice guys, Baby," he says, "and they got us by the shorthairs so—for now—we don't really have any choice. I promise I'll do everything I can to get us out of this as soon as this drop is made."

He reaches to pull her toward him, but she turns away.

"A n d w h a t h a p p e n s, dear Billy," she cries, "w h a t h a p p e n s if this drop goes belly up? Then what? Don't you see the risk we're taking by seeing this through?"

"The risk," he says through clenched teeth, "is in *not* seeing it through. You'll just have to trust me, Heather. I love you. I'll do the best I can as soon as I can to get us out of town, out of state, out of country... whatever it takes. Okay?"

She lunges to hug him, tears filling her eyes, her breathing in knots.

Chapter 33

A KING-SIZE BUST

"I'm telling you, Agent Hartley, it can't wait! I need to see you tonight...before I head for work. I'm on the late shift. Oh, and...alone. I have information you need immediately, but I only want to deal with you. I'll explain everything when you get here."

(Pause) "Right. 6PM is fine. Thanks. I'll see you then." Click.

"So, Green Eyes, what's the story? He's coming without the chip-toothed gorilla?"

"Yeah, alone. He assured me of that."

"Good. Now we need to get our ducks in a row before he gets here. Let's start by writing down everything we know so far, and exactly what it is that you need to bargain for, yes?"

JP nods and they set to work filling a legal pad with dated transcriptions of the CB messages they intercepted. They itemize some of the coding points they had figured out and list other tidbits that they suspect but could not decipher. They create a "cast of characters" listing.

Maddigan writes out a complete description of the "boat lease deal" that he was forced to work out with Slam and Pulver—plus the blackmail threats that hang over his career. They fold those blackmail description pages into the back of the pad, to be revealed only if JP feels it is absolutely necessary.

As if the experience of rehashing all the boat deal details was clogging up his brain like the mud from that midnight turtle-trek swamp, Maddigan stands and says he has to take a break.

He paces a couple of circles around the room and then stops at the kitchen counter and dumps scrapings from his pipe, together with the contents of a plastic bag of pot seeds, and an entire twenty-five-dollar ounce of Colombian into a pie tin. He stares at the tin for a few seconds before marching resolutely with it out the door. Then—like he was feeding chickens—he stuns JP, who had moved to watch him through the window, by tossing handfuls of the contraband over the fence and into the wind, spraying across the sandy lot next door.

"A party for the gulls and squirrels," he says, prefacing an awkward silence as he reenters the cottage. The quiet is loud.

JP finally speaks up, tucking away his abrupt actions for future discussion, "So, you're pretty certain that this scuttle we've dreamed up will work?"

She stares at his face for an answer and some clue about the surprise disposal of his stash. Though she long worried that it was slowly gaining control of his life, she never dared to question his pot habit.

I would be so happy if...but, no, I won't say anything. He will if he wants to, she thinks, and when he is ready.

"I mean the information we got makes sense to me and all," she offers when he doesn't respond, "but we have to rely on this Narc to pull it off."

He poker-faces her in return.

Then, seemingly out of nowhere, as if he'd just caught up with JP's narration, he starts to summarize. "Absolutely, it is one of our better genius ideas, Green Eyes." He smiles. "As for our DEA guy, he may be the only one who can pull it off. He has the contacts and authority we don't have. It'll work if he gets behind it. I'm more worried about getting him to buy your story and keep us involved because if we're not part of the action, we're not likely to ever get the boat back. And what's to keep him from leaking the blackmail details, even unintentionally, into a campus-bound channel?"

She keeps fighting back the urge to hug and kiss him for his toss-it-to-the-wind action, but thinks it best to not raise any triumphant flags of valor just yet. Maybe a few days.

"Right," she acknowledges, "but don't worry, Rick. I'll get him to buy it. You can count on that!"

"Benji, get Simo on the line. I want to check his brain, make sure he's tuned in."

"Should we use the CB, Dad? In case...aah, the phone. You know? The wiretap thing, you know?"

"Yeah, yeah, okay, but make it quick and make sure nobody's nosing around the channel you use! Oh, and call Lava in here will you?"

Apple adds a slug of sambuca to his coffee, takes a gulp, then flips through his rubber-banded game plan—a carefully sorted, color-tabbed, and numbered deck of caffeine-stained, worn-edged, index cards—cards that foretold when his ship would come in, and when and what he should pack for Belize.

Lava appears at the glass-paneled library door. His hulk blocks the streams of daylight that spill a serious-looking trapezoid of shimmer into the wood floor and carpet edges. Now, as he fills the doorway, the room becomes a fallen shadow. Another inch or two, and he'd have to duck to get under the doorframe. He ducks anyway.

"Lava, stay here while I talk with Simo. I may want you to get up there and check him out. If he's on the way to getting drunk, or mean, we're going to have a big problem."

Lava nods repeatedly. He's rocking gently on his heels like an Orthodox Jew at sunset, while he watches Johnny flip through the staticky channels and crank up the volume. Simo's voice breaks his trance.

"Hey Nimajneb, whadda ya doin' callin' me on my portable CB in the middle of my boilermakers? Where's yer old man?"

"Ah, er, Elppa is here. Stand by."

"Omis. What's the word?"

"Thunderbird's the word, boss. Whasupwitchew? I jus' told da kid I'm busy bending elbow. Is this a quick call or what?"

"It is now, yeah. I'm looking to send Aval over to keep you company and to make sure that that Erbmoh brings the piño for the coladas, if you know what I mean."

"Roger that Elppa, good idea—Aval, but I don't need no muscle, and Aval don't know nothin' about boats, so let's skip it an' I'll talk to ya later."

"I know, Omis. I understand how you feel about Aval, but he's still my main man and I'm sending him all the same, so I expect you'll keep him at your shoulder, got it?"

"Haaaaaght!" Simo clears his throat and unleashes a huge glob of flem, swipes his chin with his sleeve, then answers, "Shoulder, yeah. Catch ya later." *Static.*

"Okay, Lava, you heard him. He's already three sheets to the wind. I need you to get there, get him sober, and get him to do the job we're paying him to do. I know there's no love lost between you, but this is a big-time drop and we can't afford for Simo or anybody else to screw it up!"

Lava nodded. "You got it boss. Consider it done. But after this run, I don't want that asshole in my life anymore."

"We get this job done, Lava, and you can pick and choose any-one you want in your life. Uh, including Mayetta. I notice you've been noticing her? So you just give me the word. Maybe we take her to Belize too, okay? Now, go get this captain and make sure he's sea-worthy."

The two of them are hunched over the kitchen table. An hour's worth of briefings and Q&A exchanges. Notepaper and diagrams are everywhere. From the moment of return of the black leather to the cottage, the two of them appear to hit it off. Not having Agent Leeds along serves to loosen up the conversation.

It also helps to have Maddigan off teaching his evening class. JP doesn't hesitate to flash her short-skirted legs and braless look, freely accented as it is by a mostly unbuttoned shirt. She describes Mad-digan's turtle trek and gutting episode. She talks about his various in-person and telephone encounters with assorted members of the mob squad.

She makes a strong case to Agent Hartley—Jake, as he asks to be called—for the two Narcs to support her and Maddigan's involve-ment with DEA pursuits.

He expresses serious concerns about the risks involved for the two of them, as well as the risks he and Leeds would be taking with Agency regulations. She acknowledges that she knows it is against procedure, and responds with her best waitress flirtation skills.

"Uh, how do you like your coffee, Jake? I'm gonna put a fresh pot on." She stands.

"That's okay. No need to bother."

"No bother. I'm gonna have some anyway. Milk and sugar?"

"Sure. Thanks."

Smiles, dimples, a few little leaning forward excesses over the table, as she brings two mugs from the cabinet, two spoons from the drawer and milk and sugar to the table. She pushes some papers aside to make room.

"Excuse me a minute. Now, where did I put those filters?"

He starts to tell her to forget it, but some long-legged bending from the waist, that allows him a good long look at her buttocks and crotch as she conducts a prolonged search of the bottom shelf in the cabinet under the sink, catches his tongue. She had, of course, purposely squirreled away the coffee filters there before he arrived to let him know that she knows that his eyes are following.

He understands, without her directly saying so, that she is holding back information he wants, information that would lead him to a career-year drug bust. He struggles with keeping his mind attached to the reason for his being there.

"Let me tell you point blank. I'll tell you what I know. You can bring Agent Leeds along for the ride but, for now, he has to honor my request for you to play out the scene alone with just me and the professor—a sort of ménage à trois," she says with a wink as she turns to face him.

She returns to the bottom cabinet briefly, enough to draw his attention again, then stretches to move the box of filters to a top shelf in the cabinet over the sink. "There! That's where they should be. Rick must have moved them."

JP now leans over the table. "You and I and Maddigan will share the mysterious numerical details of our findings and the specifics of the plan we have for sabotaging the drug delivery. But I will only fill you in if you promise to let us go with you to win back the *Here & Now*. That includes that no report would ever be made of the mob's blackmail threats that triggered Maddigan's involvement."

She turns to the coffeemaker buzzer and lifts the pot out to fill his mug slowly, deliberately, careful to make the slight brushes of her loose breasts against his arm seem like an innocent consequence of the small kitchen workspace.

Hartley appears to struggle with the decision but, in the end, succumbs to JP's allures. He acknowledges that she and the professor could actually prove valuable if any chance arose of their needing to operate or rig up their own boat.

"I am making this pact with you," he says, "but it's just because you and Maddigan are the only ones who know all the voices involved enough to identify Slam, Pulver, Eddie, Billy, and Heather."

He sips at his coffee, then adds, "And your boat and electronics skills might come in handy." But the truth is, that burned into his mind like the image left by a branding iron, the erotic views she'd just served up and that little brush on the arm...

"Most importantly, you two also have drug delivery and boat location information we need." Plus, from what little he could make of their plan to sink the boat that he and Leeds had learned was named the *Maltese*, it made more sense than the confrontational approach that the two agents had originally discussed. In fact, what she was proposing would probably risk fewer good guy injuries than the head-on collision course that the Narcs had originally been considering.

Hartley stands, takes a last gulp of coffee, and repeats his final warning: "You realize that what you're suggesting can be a major risk for both of you, and that you're asking me to violate standard DEA policies and procedures, and that I'll have to call in some valuable chips with my Coast Guard contacts? You realize you're putting me in a compromising position that could cost me my job?"

"Listen, Jake," said JP, fists on hips, "I understand all of that, and I'm not making light of it, but this is the only way that all of us get what we want out of this mess. You should also know that you and your Godzilla partner may think I'm just a dumb brunette-broad-Professor's-girlfriend-type, but reality is that I'm not. The bottom line here is that Rick and I have got what you need to make a king-size bust that will look mighty good on the front pages and in your personnel files. From our position, you have the ability to squelch a bad news blackmail situation and allow us a chance to recover our, his, boat that we need in order to get on with life. So how about you call your Coast Guard contacts and let's get going!"

"United States Coast Guard, Point Pleasant, Manasquan Inlet Station, Petty Officer Ken Poppele. How may I direct your call?"

"This is DEA Agent Hartley. Please connect me with Enforcement Chief Carl Pierce."

Chapter 34

LAVA on the WHARF

Into the wind, collar up, he heads toward the *Maltese*. Early shadows splice the chain-link fence line as he approaches the docks. His thoughts of escaping with Heather and Brianna are trying to punch their way out of his brain. He doesn't want the baby growing up with all this dangerous running and hiding lifestyle anymore than Heather does. But he is more trapped than she realizes. All he can do is keep alert for some kind of opening. Anything.

He sees the boat's outline. It's shrouded in fog, tied snugly to the bulkhead pilings, though not secured for the night. It's obviously not intentioned to be around for the next tide change.

No matter what plan he comes up with to gain freedom for his family, the roadblocks seem overwhelming. Is there no way out? If for no other reason than the baby—and Heather's steadily deteriorating sanity—he knows he has to do something, and it has to be soon.

The pinkie side of his hand bridges the smoked storefront glass with his forehead. He leans under the "Gilligan's" sign, and peers through the gull-dropping-splattered window. Half a dozen men, their backs to him, line the bar. Three others slump forlornly over a booth table in the corner, no doubt snoring. He pans to the opposite side. Simo's stool is unoccupied. As he steps back to get his bearings and get a closer look at the *Maltese*, he trips over a rotted railroad tie parking divider and stumbles forward into Lava's pick-up. The sleek, black muscle truck startles him. His hands slap against the hood breaking his fall. Absent-mindedly, he begins buffing away his handprints with a sleeved forearm.

He couldn't imagine what Lava would be doing here on the docks, Lava who rarely leaves the Boss's side.

Billy knows that tough-and-nasty Simo, tough-and-stupid Pulver, and tough-and-calculated Lava, are the three ogres in Apple's orchard that he would never go picking with. In fact he's made a practice of never getting between or too close to any of them. But now, the way things are going, with Apple and Slam dumping more on his plate, Billy may not be able to distance himself for long. He's been having to play along with, and up to, each of them more often.

Forever looming in the back of his mind is the conviction that none of these thugs would balk at cutting the hearts out of the other two, adding some bread and mustard, and then eating them for lunch.

Heather has succeeded in raising his consciousness, and guilt, about the fact that now he has a woman and daughter to think about. And his woman is an increasingly fearful and sensitive, almost hysterical woman. Heather's emotional state is definitely not improving, and she doesn't want to hear about his stress.

Daughter Brianna gets bounced around from babysitter to babysitter, and to Mayetta when they have to be at the Solamente Castle. The child has no friends her age, and lacks the emotional and geographical family stability to even have a dog. Things at home are not good at all, and Billy's not confident about keeping it all together long enough to get out of town. He needs Heather to hang on.

For all he can see—she's not in touch with the reality of their three lives being tied to his job performance. His unwavering, unquestioning willingness to follow orders, and at the same time maintain a calm, compliant façade is what's keeping them safe with food on the table. Somehow, though, in spite of her edginess, he's been able to persevere. And it's not like he can't get another job someplace. He just can't risk trying to sever these ties. Apple is not exactly a Mother Theresa model of forgiveness.

He looks past the truck and sees Lava climb aboard the *Maltese*, then notices him turn his head back and away, no doubt reacting to the stench of fish Billy knows to be deeply embedded in the gear and deck planking. Crewmen are tightening, winding, loading. Having only single bow and stern lines tied up would seem to confirm his initial impression that the boat is dock side just temporarily.

"Hey!" Billy hears the captain shout. "You ask permission to come aboard my boat?'

"Up yours!" the bodyguard thrusts a finger toward the wheelhouse.

"Listen, asshole, if it wasn't for the old man, I wouldn't have you even *step* on my boat. I sure as shit don't want your ugly face getting' in my way, and don't let me catch you botherin' any my crew, got it?"

Lava glares at Simo, "Don't push your luck, scumbag. I report to Apple and that's it. He wants me here, I'm here. Period. Now get your ass moving and make sure I don't need to kick your teeth down your freakin' throat to keep you and your boys on track."

Billy cringes in the shadows, expecting fists to fly. But Lava turns away and walks to the stern. Simo mutters something, but steps back into the shadows of the wheelhouse.

The next few minutes seem like hours to Billy as he crouches out of view alongside the truck. He watches as the two men exchange evil glances over their shoulders but remain apart, as distant as a fifty-six-foot fishing boat allows. He knows the two share the same killer instincts and believes they'll one day destroy everyone around them. He gulps hard at the thought, shivers convulsively, tugs his collar up another notch, then slithers away and returns to his SUV. He has re-signed to himself to report back to Slam that Simo is not to be found.

He sure as hell isn't interested in trying to buffer those two. He'd end up dead for sure, he thinks.

Openings in the fleeting night sky clouds, still laminated with layered white and gray swirls of fog, reveal bursts of swooping, glid-ing gulls that dot the horizon. Gulls pepper the frigid air above the parking lot and along the bulkhead. Lava smokes. He paces the deck with no regard for Simo's drone radio reports. Wheelhouse speakers call for off-shore winds and the probability of heavy rain moving in from the west.

Not much of a weather report believer, the captain decides to take the *Maltese* for a short run, through the inlet into the ocean and back, to see the seas firsthand. Besides, it will be fun to watch Lava throw up after the boat just happens to run into and around a couple of rogue waves. Simo smiles smugly as he orders the crew ready for a ride.

"I'm telling you, Pulver, I don't like Billyboy's news that Simo's some kinda incognito when he's supposed to be on the trawler. I'm going to ask Apple to try to raise Simo on the CB. You wait here while I call."

Apple, though, isn't responding to Slam's message. He knows Slam has no way of knowing that Lava is keeping Simo occupied, and he wants it to stay that way. Besides, Apple isn't about to contact the boat right now while Lava is there, just to get an earful of Simo's wrath. Conflict had been brewing between the two muscle-heads for a long time, and neither liked seeing the other get Apple's attentions. Apple also knows that the two henchmen would go for each other's throats in a heartbeat if he turned his back, but believes this drop will produce enough cash to quiet them both down. The next deal wasn't in the cards for Simo anyway. That one would take place in Belize, and Simo wasn't invited on the vacation trip.

The short run through the inlet gives Simo enough of the weather to know the latest reports are probably for real, plus he had his laugh at watching Lava turn green as they rolled up and down a few big waves. He heads the *Maltese* back to the wharf for a final once over, gas-up, and hose down—and to let the crew take a quick break to down a couple of shots at Gilligan's—before heading out for the big drop. In spite of some gouges in her steel hull, the *Maltese* is in good shape and the captain knows she can take a beating. But he also knows she's fifteen years-old, and her 300BHP Volvo engine is starting to show some wear and tear.

Simo wants to make sure there'll be no problems once the show starts. Given the unpredictability of March weather, and three recent storm sinkings, he also wants to top off the rust red vessel's diesel fuel at its 1450-gallon capacity. He wants to make sure they have plenty of gas to get through or around any storm or—in the event of any possible shortsightedness on Apple's part—be able to travel beyond any running distance that the existing plans call for.

Chapter 35

HOSTING COASTIES

He maneuvers her slowly back into her berth, with only a minor thunk and minimal grooshing as she rubs against the hanging tires and the nailed strips of firehose that drape the creaking wood pier pilings. The crew stands ready to tie her off—again with just two lines—and hopefully head for Gilligan's.

Well aware of their intended destination, Simo leaves the wheelhouse and positions himself at the boarding ramp.

Once the boat is secure, the crew heads for the exit. Simo takes a deliberate bullying step to the edge of the ramp in front of them, blocking their way. He bumps one of the men against the rail, and grabs a fistful of the first collar within reach. Eyeball to eyeball, he issues a threatening warning, "Remember what I said!" He didn't need to add "or else!"

His glare locks the others in their places. "Be back here onboard by midnight, and don't get fooked up!" he says to them as his hand snaps loose from the collar. They nod obediently to his sendoff warning and hop from the ramp to the wharf with considerably less than their usual carefree air.

Simo watches his crew head for the shadows. There is none of the usual clowning around or rowdy chatter. Their silence would have been unnerving had he not been the cause for it. A metallic clunk on the bow snaps him to attention. "Charlton? That you? You still here?"

"Yeah, Capt'n, I want to check out our winches and the bilge pumps. I thought I heard some grinding noises when we were coming in. You go ahead if you want. I'll give you a shout if anything comes up."

"Okay," Simo said, stepping off the boat. He sauntered toward the blue neon, "See you in awhile. Oh, and keep an eye on Lava. He's still in the head throwing up. Ha!"

No sooner did Simo leave than Lava emerged from below deck, looking grim, a little green, and wobbly. He grasped aimlessly at anything upright in his path, holding fast to each railing, hatchcover or fixture along the way until he could step to the next. Sweat was running freely across his drawn face. "I'll fix that bastard," he mumbled through clenched teeth. He stepped ashore and headed unsteadily toward his truck, where he'd sit until the boat was ready to go.

Half an hour later, the sounds of bulkhead-lined gravel shuffling underfoot usher an authoritative voice aimed through the open hatch, down into the engine room, "Yo! Anybody on board?"

The question is posed more like a statement. It comes from the smallest of a trio of dark blue shirts. Each shirt tops off matching dark blue pants, an open dark blue down jacket and dark blue baseball cap. Simple strips of white-embroidered block lettering on their left breast pockets, peaks of their hats, and backs of their jackets proclaimed U.S. COAST GUARD. Hands on holstered revolvers announced that the men in blue were there on business.

"Yeah, I'm down below. Who is it?" responds Charlton.

"United States Coast Guard," again, the big deep voice from the little guy.

"Just a minute. Be up in a minute."

Rising up the engine room steps through the turned-back hatchcover, Charlton appears. Head down, he is wiping oil from his hands onto a greasy rag that looks like it had spent six months in a Times Square gutter. Three hands ease off the holstered pistols. He looks up. "Hey! What's happenin' boys?"

"You the captain?" asks the little guy, who looks like a blue fire hydrant with legs. He is noticeably older than the other two.

"Nah, just a mate," Charlton answers, still wiping his hands, "What can I help you with?"

"I'm Officer Burchell," the Coast Guardsman continues, "This is Officer Abbott and Officer Infusino. We're going to conduct a safety inspection, and we'd like your captain to be here. Can you round him up?"

"Sure. Gimme three four minutes to get 'em. He's over at Gilligan's. Y'mind waiting?"

"No problem, Mate. We'll be right here."

Charlton jumps to the bulkhead and double-time steps into the shadows cast across the roadway.

The wharf-side activity and darting rays from the flashlight catch Lava's attention as he leans forward in the front seat of his truck. He sits up and watches, but—eyeing three hands on holsters—he decides against getting involved. Maybe they'll smash that asshole's head in me, he thinks. He sits back again. He watches.

Except for wheelhouse and engine room bulbs and one lamp-post about fifty feet away, the blue Pabst Blue Ribbon neon sign in the bar front window skims the only light along the wharf. Officer Infusino nudges his boxy looking boss, "Whadda ya think, Bruce? He doesn't seem unnerved or anything?"

"He's not the captain, Mike. Let's save our analytics until we meet Simo. Mr. Em, you okay with working this rust bucket?"

"Roger, Bruce. Piece-a-cake. I cut my teeth fishing on one of these babies. Practically lived in the engine room. Kept the damn thing going with Scotch Tape and rubber bands."

A voice intrudes from the shadows, "Well, *Em*, is it? You'd need mor'n that to get this baby cookin'."

The three turn to face Simo as he steps from the black into a sliver of blue light that dissects the parking lot.

"Say, ain't you boys a little outta your jurisdiction on the docks here and all?"

A glob of tobacco spit follows the question.

"United States Coast Guard. I'm Officer Bruce Burchell. This is Officer Em Abbott and Officer Mike Infusino. Are you Captain of the Maltese?"

A wooden match strikes some scrap iron next to the bulkhead where they stand as Simo lights and pulls on a cigar stub.

"That would be me, gentlemen. Captain Simo at your service," he says, waving the cigar like a baton–for a fleeting moment—conducting the New York Philharmonic in *Flight of the Bumble Bee.* "Now, what are you Coasties doing here at night bothering me from a couple a drinks, and not out at sea vigilantly protecting our hallowed shores from dastardly invasions and crime?'

"Sir, we..."

"My mate tells me you said you plan an inspection. Well, I'm not interested in inviting you aboard to do a dockside inspection at night, so you might as well move along and find some tourist boat to check out." He puffs his cigar again and waves it dismissively at the three officers as he begins to turn away.

"Captain Simo, I'm going to have to ask you to stand aside and cooperate." Simo stops abruptly and turns back to face the older Coastie.

Burchell continued, "Dockside boardings are permitted under law when a boat has been observed at sea, and our patrol personnel observed the *Maltese* under way—less than an hour ago, headed toward the inlet here. We're going to conduct a safety inspection using the checklist on this clipboard." The senior officer handed the clipboard to Simo.

"It will be in your best interest to cooperate, Sir. You should know that we are fully deputized and authorized by U.S. Coast Guard Enforcement Chief Carl Pierce to function as law enforcement agents. If you're not willing to show us around, then I'm going to have to order you to stand aside or risk being arrested."

Simo tossed the clipboard back, then crushed his cigar tip against a piling, dropping red sparks and ashes to the ground. He squeezed the tip between his fingers and put the still smoldering stub in his shirt pocket. He spit toward their feet, then again into the water.

"Okay, boys, okay. You win, but you don't have to be smart-asses about it. We have nothing to hide here, and the *Maltese* is fully equipped with all safety equipment operational. What do you want to see first?"

"We're glad to hear what you say about the boat, Sir, so if you're correct, you have nothing to worry about and we'll be done quickly. Officer Abbott will check the engine room while Officer Infusino will check your fire extinguishers, off-shore life jackets, ring buoys, signal flares, battery powered lights, flame arrester, life raft, signal devices, EPIRB, first aid equipment and radio transmission. It will save time if you or your Mate can show him where those items are stowed. Then I would like to review your emergency procedures with you while they're doing those inspections. We will board now and get started, Captain."

"What fooking happened to asking permission to board?"

Burchell smiled one of his "up yours" grins at Simo, "Sir, do we have permission to board?"

"That's better, Mister. Okay, let's get this over with." Simo spit again, closer to their feet than the first time, then led the trio across the ramp. "Engine room's there. I'll show you the other stuff, then you can ask me your questions."

Abbott headed below while Burchell and Infusino followed Simo up into the wheelhouse.

Lava recovered abruptly from the heaves and bout of seasickness when he saw the Coast Guardsmen board the boat. He leaned forward again, but he stayed put. He doubted that Apple would want him getting in the middle of whatever was going on. He'd just wait it out.

"So tell me somethin' Jake..." Agent Leeds spoke with the uncharacteristically soft steady tone of a golf match reporter, "You think this Bruce friend of yours and these other Coastie guys will be able to pull this off without tippin' our hand? I mean they haven't had the role-playing stuff we've had, and most of 'em are so young they can hardly keep their bullets in their belts, you know what I mean?"

Submerged in wharf-side shadows, the two DEA Narcs stood fifty yards away, watching through night binoculars, unaware of Lava parked halfway down their field of vision.

"And did you see the big guy spit? I'd like to pop him right now, that pig!"

"Yeah. Well, we'd never get the bust done that way, Rusty. Cool your duals. I've known Burchell for ten years, and he's a bull with brains. His boys are all in their twenties, you're right about that. But he's one tough boss. Reminds me of that football coach you had. Bruce's guys eat and sleep his commands. There're no screw-ups on his team. Remember we're talking Coast Guardsmen here, not traffic cops. Just sit tight. He'll call us when they're done."

"Yeah, I guess you're right. The Coasties I've known all seem plenty disciplined all right, and cops are, well, cops! Yeah, I guess you're right. Look! They're boarding."

Chapter 36

COPS 101

"You must be kidding!"

Palms out, eyebrows stunned, Maddigan gapes at his faculty department chairman, Dr. Charlie Stressen. The elderly academic, a balding recycled business failure with an irrelevant PhD from Moose Jaw University in Saskatchewan, is wearing pink horned rim glasses, white shirt, threadbare brown wool suit and a dark paisley thirty-five-cent necktie.

Stressen sits in one of the two chairs across the desk from Maddigan, and Dean Oliviero stands confidently next to the other empty chair. The dean—a handsome, rugged individualist who often reminds people how well his Maine upbringing serves his adventuresome spirit—puffs his unlighted pipe as he props one foot up on the contoured wood seat of the chair next to Stressen. He adjusts his sock, then his pants crease. He leans forward across Maddigan's desk, poking his pipe in a friendly way. "No, Rick," he says, clenching his jaw, a puzzling twinkle in his eye, "we're definitely serious about this."

"But, listen guys, I never..." Maddigan lowers his face to collect himself. Stalling for time, he takes his glasses off and pretends to clean the lenses on the bottom corner of his leather-elbow-patched tan corduroy sports jacket. He rubs his forehead briskly with his fingertips. Little counterclockwise circles. His hand goes to his beard as he looks up.

"I...I never taught *cops*! I don't know the first thing about law enforcement or how to deal with those people. What do cops—and troopers?—need to know about business management and marketing anyway? I mean if they're special agents who are chasing down embezzlers, maybe they should need to know some basic accounting or something, but we're talking about on-call, street fighter-types here. These guys like to rearrange faces, cuff wrists, and write tickets."

"You watch *Hill Street Blues* on TV, Professor Maddigan?" the dean asks without waiting for an answer. "I'm told it's a pretty realistic portrayal of police work."

Between the lines, Maddigan sees that the dean is attempting to launch into a major dissertation, and decides to cut him off at the pass.

"You think? Maybe it is, Dean, but this is little old Seaport County here that we're talking about. Cops here don't need to produce strategic business plans or write advertising copy. Isn't it more like: arrive at the scene, throw a punch or two, make the arrest, cuff 'em, read the rights, haul the bad guys off to jail, and go have a donut? Am I right?"

Tempted to crack a pair of smiles, the two older men instead exchange glances that confirm some earlier prediction of what they were encountering now.

"It's this way, Rick," the dean leads off, "we know from your faculty presentation—the 'Shrink Out' I believe you call it—that you have a certain expertise in helping people learn how to communicate better—a product no doubt of all your independent studies on human behavior. Anyway, we've been mandated by the State of New Jersey to provide our part-time law enforcement students who are full-time employed, with the basics in crisis intervention."

"Right," injects Stressen, "and the Faculty Chairman of the Law Enforcement Department—Harrison Murphy—you know Harrison, right? We got him last year from the Magen's Bay College of Correctional Studies?"

"Uh, I know who he is, Charlie, but..."

"Well Harrison cited statistics to me that more police officers are killed and injured in domestic calls than anything else—more than robberies, assaults, motor vehicle incidents, even high speed chases, more than anything." The Chairman checks a note card in his lap then continues, "Domestic calls, of course, are when police are called to the scene of a family dispute—husband/wife, brother/brother, father/son, that sort of thing."

The Dean chimes in, "Bottom line, Rick, is that these guys need to know how to deal with fights between relatives when they're called to a home. Oh, and work sites too: employee tangles, boss and worker arguments, irate customers—you know. Professor Murphy says no one in his department has this expertise. We're looking at some big-time financial subsidies from the State if we can provide a meaningful program. And we think that you are the answer!"

"Yes," the Chairman plows on, not allowing room for a response, "and we think with this base of information and training that you bring to the table, that you'll be able to pick up the specialized knowledge quickly—we'll set up meetings for you with area police chiefs—and we're sure you'll find some creative ways to design a curriculum that helps these people develop the skill sets that allow them to deal more effectively with these situations than their present methods. Right now, they simply bully disputing parties, intimidating and physically pushing them into settling down."

He stops to take a breath. "Right now, you see, these officers only know how to enter a home or business and—sort of like you described it—break arms and bash heads! They often end up accelerating the issues and provoking even more violence."

Maddigan's mind is drifting. *What a wonderful thing*, he thinks sarcastically, and not without some trepidation, about having to meet with a bunch of police chiefs. *Is that*, he wonders, *how someone would define "tempting fate"?*

His brain is suddenly back to butchering the dead turtle. He flashes to the answers he got to his two telephone questions. The exchange rewinds yet again:

"And what do you expect me to do with the leftover parts?"

"Eat 'em! Have a barbeque! Use 'em for fish bait! Make soup! Stick 'em in yer ear! What the hell do I care? Just don't get anything traced back to you, and keep yer mouth shut, got it?"

"Yeah, but what's on this chip of yours that's so important?"

"Curiosity kilt da cat!" Click.

"Jesus."

The image of the disconnected phone dangling from his hand lingered...

"Listen, Dean, and Charlie, I appreciate your confidence in me. Really. But..."

The faculty chairman overrides Maddigan's attempt at an objection. "Besides, you'll be doing the college a big-time favor because if we can demonstrate the ability to help our troopers and local cops handle confrontations like these with greater ease, with more understanding and skill, so that the injury rate declines, we will be in a better position to accommodate others who face crisis situations in their everyday careers. Plus, State assistance programs..."

Maddigan's thoughts fly to the comments he heard from Agent Leeds:

"Listen up! The two of you can calm down here and answer our questions, or keep up the hostile attitude, and we'll have to bring you in to our Newark office and question you there. If you're looking for a warrant, Missy, we can get one within the hour, and we're not going to be turning this place upside down looking for a boat. We'll start with the twelve-volt battery shoved under the table, the loose floorboard under the rug, the marijuana flakes on the kitchen counter, and the plastic bag of herbs sticking out of your apron pocket..." *Okay, so I've quit smoking dope, there's no pot around the house, and JP's succeeded so far at schmoozing Agent Hartley, but that doesn't mean they still can't file charges or come after me. What if they talk to a cop in one of these classes? That's like asking if I want to jump twenty floors onto concrete or steel!*

"Yes, Rick, Plus," thinking he could be more convincing than the department chairman, and certainly more even-paced, the Dean rushes to complete the sentence, "we'll be eligible for additional State funding. And you know what that means for a struggling little college like this, right?

"Additional funding will allow us to build that new student communications center you've been campaigning for, including, I imagine, a student radio station and improved student newspaper facility. And God knows our student newspaper needs a lobotomy."

Maddigan sits dumfounded. His two bosses are now adding "academic bribery victim" status to his secret marijuana blackmail status. Loud ticks fall from the big black-framed electric wall clock above their heads.

"I don't know, guys. I, well, I'm not sure. I would need some help with this. I..."

"We'll give you whatever you need," says the Dean between unlighted pipe puffs. "All you have to do is put a plan together and identify how you want to go about this. Tell us whatever it is you think you'll need to make it happen. We'll pull out all the stops for you. You have our promise to help with whatever you ask for. How about it, Professor?"

"I don't know what to say. I'm flattered that you think I could handle this, and I appreciate the opportunity to support this kind of effort, but..."

"Rick," Chairman Stressen is closing in for the kill, "just say yes. I'll get you Pam Kwasniki to start as your secretary. She's the best there is on the whole campus. And the dean and I will do the enrollment bit. You have a few days 'til the first class is scheduled. It'll be on Monday mornings, 8 to 11 a.m. with a twenty-minute break, Nursing Building, Room 6."

"Listen, Rick, when I did my Dean's Class Visit Evaluation for you this semester, I heard you tell your students that some action is always better than no action, right? Give it a chance. If this doesn't work out, we won't hold it against you for trying. Whadda you say?"

Maddigan smiles wryly. "Well, since it looks like you're obviously going to force the issue anyway—I mean you are blocking me from my office door." His grin widens. "I guess I can give it a shot, especially if I can get Pam's help. And I will want that student communications center and radio station idea committed to paper!" he adds.

"Great!" says the Dean, turning to the chairman, "Charlie,

let me know how you want to handle things, and I'll clear the way." Looking back at Maddigan, he adds, "Thanks, Rick. I knew we could count on you. Keep me and Charlie posted on your plans and what you think you need, I'll get you that communications center proposal in writing. Have a good day, Gentlemen." Oliviero straightens up, does a half stretch and smoothes his necktie.

Stressen stands. He gives Maddigan a little tip-toe pat on the shoulder, then steps in behind the dean. They remind Maddigan of a parade color guard passing the review stand. The two move toward the door, smile at Maddigan, and each other. The dean tips an imaginary hat. They leave the room.

"Good Grief!" Maddigan says out loud to himself, "This is all I need right now, teaching cops! What the hell am I supposed to do about the fact that I'm being badgered by two federal agents? What if any of these law enforcement students gets wind of what's going on? These guys do talk to each other."

He picks up the phone and dials, then tucks the phone into his shoulder as he packs his mailbag with quiz papers.

"Hi, Green Eyes. It's me. Listen, you'll probably get this message before I get back. I just wanted to give you a heads up that I need to talk with you when I get home. I'm canceling my office hours today. I'm anxious to hear how you made out with the little black jacket, and some things came up that I need to run through your genius brain. I hope you'll be around. Love you. Later."

Chapter 37

A LITTLE DAB'LL DO YA

Below deck, crouched into a cramped space that leaves little room for using or even reaching for tools--never mind stretching legs—Coast Guardsman Em Abbott is pretzeled up. Sweat is dripping freely down his forehead, face, and neck. He struggles to wrench free the rusted-shut drain plug. "Damn thing's probably not been pulled in ten years," he whispers and grunts between clenched teeth.

He can hear Burchell and Infusino in the forward cabin quizzing the captain and first mate. Abbott takes a small canister from his tool belt and gives the drain plug a couple of short bursts of WD-40. Hoping no one hears the spraying, he quickly replaces the canister, wriggles onto his side so he can swipe his sleeve across his forehead, then moves to the clamp that holds the bilge pump hose.

The clamp had apparently been changed recently. It's much easier to loosen than the plug. With the unscrewed clamp dangling from the hose, he moves double-speed to pull the connection apart. Heavy footsteps thump on the deck above him. He glances up at the open hatch. He knows his clock is running. He smears a dab of Vaseline on the edge of the exposed pipe and on the inside of the hose. "A little dab'll do ya," he sing-song whispers the old Bryl-Cream shaving jingle.

He replaces the hose—which now slides easily over the pipe—and pushes the clamp back to its proper location. He tightens it just enough to keep it from sliding around until after the engines are well heated.

Once the trawler is out at sea and throttled up, the combination of engine heat, loose clamp, vibrations, and the lubricated connection will cause the bilge pump hose to slide off. Without water running through the hose, the pump will burn itself out and there'd be no way to bail the engine room that would flood through the opening created by the dislodged drain plug.

"Shit! Almost forgot the drain plug!" he whispers. More footsteps above him. He can hear the captain asking where he is, and "what's he doing down there?" A panicky tightness pulls across Em's neck and shoulders that he's had to cram into a small opening against the ribs of the hull. He hears Burchell cover for him by asking the captain for a CB transmission check, and crawls back to the drain plug.

The spray did its job and he's now able to budge and loosen the plug enough so that it will tumble free from vibrations once the boat accelerates to wide open.

Maddigan had talked out his frustrations with JP. As always, she managed to see the bright side of the challenge. She pointed out to him that teaching law enforcement classes could turn out to be a big break for them. If he could do the sessions as effectively as he taught other courses, they might realize some benefit down the road that could help them out of the mess they were in, or at least serve to promote their "Anchor Out" ambitions. And, besides, she added, "It would be a 'positive life thing' to help police officers 'see better ways of doing things.'"

He studies the class enrollment list. All thirty-five students are active NJ State Troopers and local police officers. Most are based in Seaport County. Some are from the town where his boat is docked. Some are from where he and JP have their winter rental. Six are from nearby Seaport River, the county seat, where the college is located. *A bit close for comfort*, he thinks.

He reviews his class plans. He had taken crisis and anger management training a few times over the years and felt comfortable with knowing enough of the basics to be able to turn around and teach them to others, but he knew his beard and long hair might not go over too big with this audience. He pulled the silver five-leaf pin off his hat and pushed it into a corner of his desk drawer. JP had suggested what he already knew, that he would have to act like a tough guy from the first minute of the first class, or risk being trampled in the process. *Cops don't like wimps.*

The only ace he had up his sleeve was in knowing that he had an uncanny knack for delivering a commanding presence in the classroom, front-loaded by his determination, self-confidence and ability to always rise to the occasion. Besides, even though he wasn't a workout freak, neither was he a wussy in the muscle department, especially his runner's legs.

None of those assets, however, helped his churning stomach any when he thought about the intimidating setting of himself as the authority figure in a sea of hard-ass tough guys with guns and badges. Throwing up was not out of the question.

The night before his first session, Maddigan cornered the building custodian and recruited his help in moving all the classroom chairs and desks into an adjacent storage room. "The dean says it's okay. I need the floor space for a staging area," he told the older man who was not pleased with the extra work, "for a police class. And

I'll see that all of this furniture is returned and set up in time for the nursing group when they come back to use the room."

While Officer Burchell hands Simo the inspection approval paperwork, Coast Guardsman Infusino reaches to help Abbott up through the engine room hatch. "Looks okay down there," Abbott says as he lands both feet on the deck.

"See," scolds Simo, "I told you our shit was in order. Now supposin' you Coasties get your asses off my boat and go catch some criminals—or crabs—or some disease or something. We got work to do here and you're in the way!"

"Roger that, Captain. Here's your paperwork showing that your trawler's passed inspection. Sorry for the intrusion, but we gotta check everybody, you know? You're no exception. Let's go boys." The blue uniforms hopped to the bulkhead. Simo spit after them.

"Okay people, line up around the room against the wall!" a bit more command in his voice than usual. "I've removed the chairs and tables so you can practice sleeping while you stand. That, you will find, is a useful skill when listening to your superiors give speeches." Some nervous snickering and puzzled looks flashed cautiously around the room.

The students, half in uniform, shifted, shuffled, and settled against the walls. Maddigan stood in the center of the room, checking his note cards.

"All right, you guys," he said in his best assertiveness training octave, "my name is Rick Maddigan, not 'Serpico,' as I've heard whispered in the halls, and I don't pretend to be a law enforcement expert.

But—I am a business professor with specialized skills in communications and human development, which is what you're here for."

He paced, chin up and shoulders back. "We're going to be recreating some serious conflict situations in here and I don't want any accidents, so let's start by putting all your guns on the floor against the wall behind the door, and safeties ON. That way, they're out of play as we go forward, but easy to..."

"Listen, Professor," a gruff baritone voice bounced out of the far corner, "we're not putting our leg strap-ons on the floor. We're trained to always keep those on, no matter what, and..."

"I'll tell you what, Officer, you are..."

"Dixon, Sir, with an 'x' not a 'cks': Danny Dixon!"

"Yes, right. Well, Officer Dixon with an x, I'm here to tell you that this is not a 'no-matter-what' situation. This is a college classroom, and you are here to learn how to deal more effectively with stressful encounters like domestic calls without having to rely on your gun."

Maddigan allowed the silence to underscore his last seven words.

"So, okay, let's start by leaving your gun where I've designated. That's everybody, please. ALL guns over on the floor behind the door. NOW, please. If any of you have a problem with that, you'll have to explain the report I send to your commanding officer announcing your departure from this program."

It didn't take long to register that Maddigan was serious. There were some agreeable nods, a couple of startled whispers, but full compliance. More than fifty weapons lined the floor against the wall behind the door. He had made his stand and established himself as a tough guy. He was internally unnerved by the arsenal alongside him on the floor, but managed to hide it well and proceeded to assume control of the room.

"Okay, Gentlemen. Thank you. Now let's talk about some guidelines you'll need to follow in accepting the role-playing assignments I'm going to be giving each of you. You'll be taking turns acting out different parts, and alternately serving as factual observers..."

The call to Agent Leeds brings relieving news. "It looks like we might have broken some of this CB code that Jake gave us, Rusty. Like, *Now* means north and *Wednesday* means west. Anyway, you want to round him up and get your butts over here to headquarters so the lab guys can fill you in?"

"You got it, Captain. Be there as soon as I can pull him away from Mrs. Obco's Donut Stand."

"I thought you were Mr. Glazed Chocolate himself, Leeds. What, is it catching?"

"Nah. You don't have your signals straight. I'm only good for when they got the two-for-one special going Tuesday and Thursday nights. See you on the rebound." Click.

"SHIT!" Fast Eddie yelled across to Simo as the two vessels puttered shoulder-to-shoulder away from the bulkhead, the *Here & Now* literally dwarfed by the massive trawler.

"WHAT'S UP EDDIE?" Simo called.

"GOT NO RADIO. PULVER NEVER TOLD ME THAT SOMEBODY PULLED THE DAMN CB OFF THE PROFESSOR'S BOAT! I THOUGHT PULVY WAS TUNIN' IT UP IN THE CABIN WHEN WE DROVE UP HERE TO THE MARINA. NOW I FIND OUT IT'S BEEN YANKED!"

"TOO LATE FOR GOIN' BACK," Simo returns the shouts. "STAY CLOSE AND WATCH OUR LIGHTS. YOU GOT THE LOCATION. BLAST YOUR BOAT HORN IF YOU START TO LOSE US! YOU GOT THAT FRENCH JERK-OFF JACQUES WITH YOU?"

"YEAH!"

"HE CAN READ THE CHART, ASSUMING HE CAN FOOKIN' READ. AND YOU BE THE PILOT, EDDIE! MEET YOU AT THE TARGET!"

Chapter 38

ANOTHER SMOTHER

"Hi Heather. This is JP. I'm really sorry I didn't call you back the other night when you left your message. I've been so busy working two jobs and trying to keep up with class work, plus my Dad's not been too well, and..."

"Hey, no problem! I've been pretty busy too, between school and my little girl. Listen, I'm sorry about your Dad. Is he all right?"

"He'll be fine, just some arrhythmia thing with his heart that the doctors needed to test him for some stuff, but—listen—maybe we could set a time to get together and go over our study notes for the spring exams? Maybe, y'know, help each other out?"

"That'd be great? I could definitely use some help? It's a little tough for me though with my daughter? She's too young to leave at home? I mean, someone's here to watch her when I'm at school and all? But...uh, maybe we can meet at the library or something?"

"The library. That works. What's your schedule like?"

"I'll have to get back to you on an exact time 'cause I'm supposed to be taking a make-up class sometime this week? But it's not set yet? I'll know by tomorrow afternoon, though? Suppose I call you tomorrow night with a couple of choices?"

"Sure. What time did you have in mind?"

"Like ten?"

"Any chance of ten-thirty 'cause I don't get off 'til ten, and..."

"Yeah? Ten-thirty's fine? Talk to you then? Oh, and thanks for calling me back?"

"Hey, better late than never, right?"

"Hey, no kidding? Talk with you tomorrow night?"

"Ten-thirty! Gotcha!"

"Bye?" Click.

"Lissen, Boss, I need ta ask you a couple a questions."

Apple is busy polishing his eagle statue. Mayetta isn't allowed to touch it. Still bent over, he looks up over the tops of his reading glasses.

"Yes, Slam, what is it?"

"Well, I was thinkin' that Lava ain't been around, and you know what good work I do, me and Pulver, and that maybe we should be Lava's back-up, you know, like when he's away like this 'cause nobody's watchin' out for you. We don't need no more money or nothin'. I just was wondering, and..."

"That's very thoughtful of you, Slam." He raised an eyebrow in acknowledgement, but kept up with his polishing while he spoke, "and I appreciate your interest in formalizing an arrangement like that, but I expect you and Pulver to simply perform that function anyway without any special job descriptions. I would certainly turn to you if I needed anything in Lava's absence."

"Thanks, Apple." Slam watched the eagle's talons get shined up. "Hey, Boss, you know if any of the guys have been pokin' around my restaurant lately? Magee, who runs the kitchen says she seen a couple a weight-lifter types hanging out in the parking lot, eating donuts early in the morning."

"No idea, Slam. Maybe they're craps losers headed home from the tables in AC. Probably lucky they could afford donuts and the gas to get as far north as your place. I wouldn't worry about it, unless Magee sees them again. Tell her to keep alert."

"Right, Boss, I'll do that." Apple bent to huff on the bronze wingtips before buffing them.

"Aaah, Boss? Ev'ryting okay with the Simo deal? Anything I can help with?"

"Everything's on track, Slam, thank you."

Apple Solamente was about to extract himself from the conversation. He straightened up, stretched, put the buffer cloth on the table, and for the first time turned to face his visitor, "Now, I need some time alone with Benji. Would you please ask him to come in here on your way out? We'll be in touch."

"You got it, Apple. Later."

"Hi Benji. I see Slam found you."

"Yeah, whadja want, Dad?"

"I want you to do something for me, but I don't want anyone else to know about it, okay?"

"Sure, Dad, whatever you say. I mean that's why I'm here, right? To listen and learn and take care of whatever you need, right? Whassup?"

"Good. I want you to keep a close eye on Slam for me. He's beginning to make me nervous. He wants to know a little too much, lately. I don't like all his questions. And just now, he tells me a couple of goons have been nosing around his restaurant. I don't want any surprises. Tail him if you have to, but don't let him know. And watch out for Pulver too. He can be dangerous. The two of them have been acting about fifty percent too chummy these last few weeks. Keep a distance, but let me know what they're up to—you know: where they go, who they see, what you hear them say. Stuff like that, okay?"

"Yessir."

"Good boy, Benji. I knew I could count on you. Call me later. And stay alert!"

"Hey!"

"Hey, yourself! I did it, thanks to you! The cops were eating out of my hand by the time I finished up the class. I set up some brain-drain family fight scenarios with rubber knives and water guns, then had two guys role-play their arrival at the front door while the others took notes of what they observed. You should have seen them trying to separate the fighting family. Scary. Now I know why the college is getting grant money to train them. These guys don't have a clue about how to calm things down. Even worse, you'd have cracked up laughing at their feeble attempts to separate factual observations from opinions!"

"Sounds like a lot of separating! Like egg whites or something. And that's no yolk!" The last four words trailed off when she realized her humor missed its mark.

"Serious Rick, I knew you had it in you. Listen, I just talked with Heather and..."

"She called again?"

"No, I called her. I was feeling guilty for not answering her message the other night. Anyway, I'm going to meet her at the library in the next day or two. She'll call tonight after I'm home from work to set a time. Maybe after that, you and I could hook up to rock n' roll some Rolling Rocks at The Ark?"

"Sounds like a plan. What's with our favorite DEA Agent?"

"I got them, or the friendlier one, Jake, at least,coming here to-morrow night. Figure we can try to go scare up that microchip from your turtle friend while they're preoccupied with the drive over here and while they make themselves busy searching for us."

"Is that such a good idea? I mean them being here when we're not? What if they get inside and find stuff?"

"Good question, Professor, but first off, you've dumped all your pot and paraphernalia. Second, I don't think they'll break in, especially if we leave all the lights on and the blinds up so they can see we're not here."

"And, third? You always have a third."

"That's good, Rick. You keep up all this deductive reasoning junk and you might end up being a college teacher or something. Third, I'll leave them a note on the door saying we had to leave to take my Dad to the doctor's. I'll tell them that I'll call them when we get back, that we can see them instead first thing in the morning."

"You always have all the answers, Green Eyes."

"That's why I get the big bucks, Professor!"

"Okay. But let's at least get the battery back into the fishing shed, and where—by the way—do you think we're going to find the chip?"

"Apple's house. Where else? I've figured out the address."

"Whoa! Just a minute here! You some kinda whack job? Whadda you gonna do? Just blast through the front door like some one-woman SWAT team?"

"First off, Professor, I figured you would keep me company—the two heads are better than one deal, y'know?"

"But even with the two of us, the odds of success there are like paddling a canoe upstream with a tablespoon. You must be nuts! I'm not going to let you go prowling around some gangster chief's house in the dark, and neither am I! Look, you don't know these creeps like I do, Green Eyes. It's just not safe. Period. I can't let you do this, and I wouldn't go with you either...I..."

"Mmmmmph!"

She smothers him with kisses and reaches inside his shirt."Hey, Rick, you allowed me a tablespoon. I mean that beats a teaspoon, right?" Her hands are in cruise control across his chest.

"Well, okay...maybe. I mean maybe I'll consider something here, but you know we'll have to be really careful because..."

"Mmmmmph!" Another smother.

Chapter 39

THE WAIL

1:30 AM. Freezing sheets of surging salt-water spray wash across every square inch of deck. Storm intensity is increasing in measured clicks, like the accelerated churning that's triggered by ratcheting up a food blender dial. Winds whip the rain sideways. Waves crash and break over the bow. Leaning into the controls, Simo is smiling wryly at the sight of his crew clinging to the handrails on the deck below him. He lights a cigar and steps from the comfort of his wheelhouse to face the growing fury of weather that now engulfs his boat.

He pulls his yellow, duct-tape-patched, foul-weather gear hood and visor up to shield his cigar, opens the cabin door, lumbers a few strides cautiously along the rail and yells down to the galley for coffee. He sidesteps his way back into to his command center cocoon. Once inside and still shifting his weight to keep pace with the sea sliding vessel, he pushes back the dripping hood, and puffs to rekindle the glowing stub.

Like a giant vacuum, the roar outside finds its way into the wheelhouse.

Simo turns up the squawk box volume and gets louder static. His ears reach to pick through the crackle, straining for more information on the closing storm head that's now rocking his trawler, threatening the delivery plan. Like his feet are bolted to the floor and his legs are made of rubber, he sways to the rhythm of the waves. The door flies open ushering in a burst of wind and rain.

"Yer coffee, Capt'n," comes the muffled voice from under the drawstring-tightened rain parka.

"Ain't no fookin' body taught you to knock first?"

"Sorry, Capt'n, I didden want yer coffee gitten cold."

"Gimme that damn cup and get the hell outta here—and close that door—tight!"

The cook nods, turns and exits quickly with a second wind/rain blast, but without a word.

Simo sips from the steaming mug, then slips it into the console cup holder. The updraft of coffee steam fogs his windshield. He flips the toggle switch for the blower to clear the glass, but the rain is hitting the boat faster than the windshield wipers can clear it, so the blower isn't helping his view, or his agitation from having lost visual contact with Fast Eddie and the professor's boat.

Rocking in time to the erratic rise and fall of the waves, he sits up straight in his control seat trying to make sense of the staticky reports rattling in from the National Weather Service. The *Maltese* is now ten miles due East of Long Branch, New Jersey. They're headed directly into the raging onset of the nor'easter, which is expected to hit full force in the next two hours—almost exactly the time that delivery is scheduled.

He would have to ride out "the blow" or head straight into it in order to be sure they could keep the rendezvous. They could always drift back with the wind behind them, but treading water might deposit them too far from the delivery point. He decides to plow forward, full throttle. He knows he can handle the boat okay, but he's not sure how sea-legged his crew is. He hadn't seen them work through a storm before—all except Gator, a man he's sure can do the job.

Between Eddie dissolving away with the professor's boat into the onslaught of weather, and Simo's hunch that they'd be seeing a lot more storm before making it back to land, he knows he needs a contingency plan—insurance. He knows he can't screw around with Solamente. The man has too much power and too many dickheads that would be out for his ass. He puffs and sips as he stares at the water pelting across the windshield like it was being blasted from a fire hose.

He thinks of Lava. As much as he hates Lava's guts, the guy is an animal. And if things do happen to run amuck, the boss's bruiser is strong enough to haul on the entire shipment by himself. Simo files the muscleman on his mental back burner with a footnote that Lava can do the work of three men, and might have to. There may be no choice, Simo tells himself. But if the job gets done, that's all that matters. Getting his wallet fat is all that matters.

If he has to recruit the bodyguard's body, Simo would deal with any resistance later. Maybe even buy him a beer. Lava wouldn't walk away if the situation grew tight and his boss's mission appeared doomed. It's no secret to anyone that Lava would always do what had to be done. But just in case he didn't, Simo knew what had to be done to Lava.

As for losing Eddie in the back-up boat, he'll just have to make do with the *Maltese*. It's been through rough seas before. It'll make it this time.

Like a smack on the side of his head, Simo is jerked from his control seat as curlers pound the bow and wash over the decks. The boat lurches sideways, rolling and twisting, listing to starboard.

He grabs a handrail and pulls himself back to the controls. He punches the intercom button. "CHARLTON? YOU THERE?"

"Yessir, Capt'n!"

"I want those bilge pumps to earn their keep, y'understand? Check 'em every twenty minutes, y'hear?"

"Yessir."

"GATOR! YOU THERE?"

"Yeah, Simo. Whaddaya need?"

"Get your ass up here! NOW!"

"Aye aye, Capt'n!"

The seas give no hint of easing up. The trawler, now rocking and swirling, forges brazenly ahead into the tempestuous wind and rain. Struggling to cross the deck and clinging to the handrails as he works his way up the ladder steps to the wheelhouse, Gator takes minutes to make what is usually a ten-second trip. He knocks, turns the latch handle, and the door jerks violently out of his grip. It whips open, depositing a sheet of rain across the floor. Simo backs into the corner and pushes the door shut.

Gator throws back his hood, "Jesus, Capt'n, we got us little blow goin' here!"

"Yeah, well we got us a delivery to pick up too, and I don't think Ruiz's boys are gonna have the *Hombre* sit out there waitin' any if we're not at the right spot at the right time, so get with the game plan here." Simo gestures to the wheel and control panel, "And keep me posted while I try raisin' them on the radio!"

"Yessir!" Gator snaps forward to the controls.

"Looks like we're ridin' the crests and the current both right now, Capt'n, so we may catch a break and actually get there ahead of them."

Simo pays no attention to Gator's prediction as he flips channels through broadcast static set at a deafening volume level. He clicks on the microphone.

"Hombre, Hombre, entrar! Hombre, Hombre, entrar! Maltese aquí!"

Static.

"I'm having trouble holding her steady, Capt'n."

More *static.*

"Goddamn it, Gator, use some muscle! Can't you see I'm busy?"

More *static.*

Back to the microphone: "Hombre, Hombre, entrar! Hombre, Hombre, entrar! Maltese aquí!"

Static followed by "Hola Maltese! Hombre aquí. Dónde está?"

Static.

"Buenas noches, Capt'n Ruiz. Simo here. Qué passé? We're approaching mile marker eleven. Where are you?"

Static.

"Roger that Simo. We at mile marker twenty-six and closing rápido. This tormenta your idea?"

Static.

Simo laughs, "Nah, we thought you brought the storm up with you to add some emoción to our reunión. We should connect right about a la hora prevista, si? I give it thirty, maybe forty minutes for us. You should hit home in about twenty. Hold on!"

Static.

Simo taps Gator's shoulder, "Put your hood up and step outside a minute. I'll grab the wheel, and I'll wave for you to come back in. Got some personal stuff to tell the dude!" Another blast of wind and rain rush through the wheelhouse as Gator obliges.

Simo clicks the microphone, "Still there, Capt'n?"

Static.

"Does a bear mierda en the woods, Senior Simo?"

Static.

"Ha! Listen, Amigo, the boss wants to make sure you got the eighteen...dieciocho?"

Static.

"Sí, Capitán Simo. The dieciocho is—how you say?— oven-ready? You got the dinero?"

Static.

"Absolutamente! Veinte y cinco grande ones for your wallet!"

Static.

"Magnífico! Esta punto de partida! See you soon."

Static.

"Roger that, Capt'n. Over and out."

Static. Simo mutters to himself: *punto de partida? That means 'starting point' -- he must be talkin' about doing another deal soon.* He shuts down the radio, then waves Gator, who looks to be near drowning, back inside as he replaces the mike. Both men stagger and slip across the confined space of the wheelhouse floor, holding onto whatever rails and ledges they can grab. The trawler's hull is taking violent hits from rogue waves as the engine room alarm siren suddenly begins to wail.

Chapter 40

APPLE BITES

An air of agitated apprehension shrouds the gathering at Apple's library command center. Pulver, Slam, Billy and Heather all stand, hovering over Apple's highly-polished, uncluttered desk where Benjamin commandeers the static-squawking CB and ship-to-shore radios. Apple paces his trademark circles, alternatively tugging at his mustache and sweater, pushing back his steel wool-looking pad of hair, listening for a break in the crackling transmissions that fill every cubic inch of available audio space.

Mayetta breaks the concentration as she swings through the French doors with a tray of glasses and a bottle of sambuca. Still standing, everyone looks up but quickly returns to staring down at the top of Benjamin's head. The maid surveys the room in search of some acknowledgement between the frowns and snarly expressions. Hisses and muffled little snaps spew from the equipment everyone's huddled around at her boss's desk. She puts the tray down, uncaps the sambuca and makes a quick exit.

Apple picks up the bottle and, in a head sweep around the room, nods an offering to the others. No one accepts. He pours himself a hefty double and gulps it down, accompanied by a wheeze, shivering shoulders, and a wet dog headshake. He re-fills the glass, sniffs at it and, with slow steady counter-clockwise swirls, carries it at his side by the rim, with his fingertips, as he moves toward the desk. He stares at the radios as if his glare alone would magically evoke the voices he wants to hear.

JP had overheard Agent McGrath giving his partner telephone directions to Apple's waterfront island compound. She knew the road. It was only a few miles from where she worked. Maddigan wanted to "scope it out" first on his own, but she wouldn't hear of it—too much time wasted. He grudgingly agreed to her plan for them to just go there directly.

They take his Jeep and park, lights out, in the marshy weeds a quarter mile on the mainland side of the bridge to the compound.

Both wear matching head-to-toe black, topped with dark blue hooded rain slickers. Crouched in the fog by the stone pillar at the foot of the estate entrance bridge, they are virtually invisible. Her voice is lost in the wind and rain to all but her mate, who is inches to her right. Her tone is hushed yet filled with alarm, "Rick, I see someone moving around in that window over there on the left."

"Where?"

"Shhhh! Straight over the stone pillar at the other end of the bridge. It's hard to see through the fog and trees. First floor. Somebody cleaning or something. Maybe a maid?"

He cups his hand over his eyes and squints. "Right. Got it. Looks like a maid."

"I just said that!"

"Hey, I always repeat intelligent remarks. Okay, let's go, but stay alert and keep low as we cross the bridge. The guardhouse looks empty, and nobody's likely to notice us anyway, dressed like this, but let's try to stay out of that spotlight all the same. We need to stay in the shadows."

"Right. Like, what's that old radio thing? Who knows what evil lurks in the hearts of men? *The Shadow* knows. Mmm-ha-ha-ha-ha-ha-ha."

"JP! Chill, will y'uh?"

They jog hunched over, between shadows, headed for the main house, they slow to a tiptoe as they pass the unlighted six-foot square stone booth guardhouse at mid-bridge.

As soon as they pass the guardhouse, they break into a run. They scramble across the other side of the bridge and into the tree line of shrubs that surrounds the sprawling stone fortress of a house.

Approaching headlights poke over the rise in the bridge behind them sending them diving headlong into a jumble of dripping wet rhododendrons, shrub twigs snapping and wet mulch flying. The car lights go out as the car passes the guardhouse and settles at the edge of the driveway, but no doors open.

Breathing heavily, they crouch motionless, collecting themselves.

"Who the hell is that?" he whispers.

"How would I know? Maybe it's that bodyguard guy you told me about—that guy Smasher or something who was with Spam?"

"Pulver, yeah Pulverizer, the guy with Slam. Maybe. Let's wait a couple of minutes to make sure whoever it is stays in the car or goes in the house before we start through these trees."

"Okay. Can I have a kiss?"

"Green Eyes, you really pick the times, don't you? Jeeze. A kiss. Sure."

The rain slickers crinkle as they kiss, lose their balance, and roll

toward one another, then the thunk of a car door drives some panicky black furry creature scurrying past them at ninety miles an hour.
They both bolt to their hands and knees. Maddigan's left hand covering her right, their hearts pounding, they wait and watch. Through
the rain and haze, they can make out the outlined shadows of two
gangland-looking figures emerging from the car. JP and Maddigan
stare intently through the trees at the fog-smudged forms of the two
men, who station themselves under the eaves of the garage on each
side of the driveway.

Barely audible from where the two microchip hunters kneel in
the shrubs, the men's voices are just a murmur as they speak to one
another. The two men check their watches, and then seem to plant
themselves in the mulch that borders the driveway. One lights a cigarette.

"Look, Dad, put the gun away, will you please?" Benjamin urges
from his half-turned swivel chair at the desk. "Simo will call," he reasons. "They probably got caught in some rough water or something.
And Eddie's there with the backup boat, and you know Eddie, he's..."

"Shut up, Benjamin! You don't tell me what to do! Got that?"
Apple snaps, sounding melodramatic but brandishing a revolver he'd
pulled from the wall cabinet and had been absent-mindedly rubbing
with his bronze eagle polishing cloth. Everyone flinches as he thwats
the cloth against the French doors, and nervously twirls the .38 on
his stubby finger. He pours another double and gulps it with less ani-
mation than the first two rounds.

"Lissen, Apple, the kid didn't mean no harm. Simo's good to
call. We just need to keep cool, right Boss? I mean it is a little on the
stormy side out there, an' even though Simo's got a lotta experience
with..."

"AND YOU SHUT UP TOO, SLAM! I'LL SAY WHAT-
EVER I WANT TO SAY TO MY SON, AND IT'S NONE OF
YOUR GODDAMN BUSINESS, Y'HEAR? AND I DON'T
NEED YOU OF ALL PEOPLE TO TELL ME WHAT TO DO.
YOU UNDERSTAND?"

"Ye...ye...yeah, Boss. I understand. I...I'm sorry. Really. I...I
wasn't thinkin'"

"YOU'RE NEVER THINKING SLAM. THAT"S THE
TROUBLE WITH YOU. NOW SHUT UP!"

The gun is pointing to the floor as he walks up behind Benjamin and put his other hand on the boy's shoulder. His son shudders
and looks back up at his father pleadingly.

"It's only a couple of minutes after they were supposed to hook
up, Dad. Simo said it would take at least half an hour to unload. He'll
call."

Apple raises his bushy eyebrows, pats the boy's shoulder and
tucks the revolver into his belt.

"You're probably right, Benji. Sorry, I lost it there for a minute.
This weather thing has me nervous."

He turns to face the others who now seem to be huddled in
the corners, worried looks coming from each face. Slam looks like he
wants to crawl into a hole and throw up.

"Sorry, folks. There's a lot at stake here, that's all. Benji's right.
Let's all settle down here and have a drink. Mayetta!" he calls through
the doorway, "Get in here and fill some glasses for my management
team here!"

The maid appears and follows orders. Everyone sips, or pretends to, as Apple continues wearing out the floor. Ten minutes pass
without a sound. It seems like an hour.

"Pulver. Step outside with me a minute, will you? I want to have a word with you." Apple turns to the others, "The rest of you just stay here. I'll be right back."

"Sure, Boss, anything you say," the muscleman nods, as he heads for the door.

No one moves an inch while the two are out in the hall, but they could see Apple with his arm around Pulver's enormous shoulders, the two conversing quietly on the other side of the glass. They see Pulver's head snap back and a momentary look of fear flutters through his eyes. Apple seems to be reassuring him. The two shake hands and return to the library filled with books, maps, radio static, and worried-looking faces. A minute later, Pulver pulls Slam aside, whispers to him, and the two leave the room.

"What's up, Dad?" Benjamin asks.

"Nothing, son. Nothing. Pulver's filling Slam in on a new assignment, that's all. Slam's going to have to take off, but we'll catch up with him in Belize. What's the word here? Anything from Simo yet?"

"Nah, not yet. Will Slam..."

"Slam, son, is history right now! Stay tuned in to the radios!" Apple turns to face the others, "What's with the rest of you? What is this, a funeral or something? Did everyone get a drink? Let's lighten up a bit, people. We'll be heading for the surf and sand by the weekend. Heather, how's that little girl of yours doing?"

"Whaddaya talkin' about, Pulvy? Why'd the old man tell you to bring me to the basement? It's dark down here, you know..."

"I do what the boss says, Slam. He says to snap your neck and spine and dump you in the town incinerator."

"Aaaaaaaaaaaaaaaayacht!"

The deed is done even before Pulver can finish saying "incinerator."

Just as he is about to haul Slam's body up the storm cellar door steps, he hears glass break, a window hinge squeak, a thump, and whispering in the dark on the far side of the cellar. Remembering he'd just been promoted, he moves quickly to protect his boss's house.

Warning honks and sirens are blasting out of every speaker, piercing the din of howling winds and crashing waves. Blinking red lights hover above every control panel. Walls of water are now breaking over the bow whipping the slipping, sliding, yellow-slickered deck crew into a panic mode. Hands are groping and grabbing for every solid protrusion—rails, ledges, uprights, hatch cover frames.

Chapter 41

GATOR BAG

"GODDAMMIT, GATOR, WHAT THE HELL'S GOING ON DOWN THERE?"

"We got us a Code Blue, Capt'n. We're takin' on water through the engine room. Charlton's down here knee deep...need your help, and that Lava guy too...stat!"

Simo shuts off the bilge pump, then backs down the engine to an idle and locks the autopilot on "Steady." As he pulls up his hood and zips his parka, he thinks for a moment about Eddie and the professor's boat, which he hadn't seen in over half an hour. He barges through the wheelhouse door and catapults down the steps to the engine room hatch.

The boat is rocking like some wild amusement park ride, but the situation is far from amusing. There's no harness to keep from being literally swept off, and no one's at the controls. He's not mistaking this ride for some three-minute adventure that ends with popcorn and cotton candy. This is all about survival and money.

He shouts through the blistering roar of wind and rain, "WHAT'S HAPPENING?"

Gator yells back, "BILGE PUMP HOSE BROKE LOOSE AND THE DRAIN PLUG RATTLED OUT. ME AND CHARL-

TON CAN GET THE HOSE BACK ON BUT WE NEED YOU AND ANYBODY YOU CAN FIND WITH MUSCLE TO GET THE GODDAMN PLUG BACK IN THE HOLE...MAYBE HAMMER A WOOD PEG IN FOR A QUICK FIX!"

But for the heavy bibbed rubber waders they're all wearing, they'd be soaked and freezing in the near-knee-deep salt water that's swirling through the bilge and around the engine blocks. Gator and Charlton are wiping something off the pump connections. Simo grabs a hammer and three wood pegs from the deck box and heads for the engine room opening. He calls to Lava to get out of the head. Apple's unwelcome bodyguard had been there alternating between barfing up bile and the dry heaves ever since they left the wharf.

"GET DOWN HERE, YOU PANSY! IT'S TIME TO SHOW ME YOUR MUSCLES!"

"SHUT UP YOU JERK, OR MY MUSCLES WILL PUNCH YOUR LIGHTS OUT!"

Lava emerges looking queasy and unsteady, wishing he could have stayed in his truck. He grabs the ladder and hatch cover and lowers himself into the rising churn of oil slicked water. Even with the engine idling, the below-deck compartment seems quiet compared to the raging storm on the other side of the hull and decks.

Framed in bare bulb light from the engine room ceiling, Simo's creviced face and wild eyes are one short fuse away from total rage. Lava fights his instincts to simply shoot the bastard and be done with him. Instead, he remembers Apple's instructions and sloshes through the swaying compartment.

Simo shouts over his shoulder as he inches toward the drain plug hole where seawater is gushing in, "WATCH YOUR STEP THERE, STRONGMAN, AND—IF YOU WANT TO KEEP A FEW LAYERS OF SKIN—DON'T TOUCH ANY OF THOSE

PIPES OR THE ENGINE BLOCK. EDGE YOUR WAY ALONG THIS SIDE. GRAB THE RIBS AS YOU GO. WATCH YOUR HEAD. HERE, TAKE THIS PEG AND PUSH IT THROUGH THE WATER STREAM INTO THAT HOLE," Simo points, "THEN HOLD IT THERE WHILE I HAMMER."

Lava reaches for the peg then watches it slip through his fingers to splash and skitter away in the oil-slicked swirl of water that's approaching his knees.

"YOU DUMB SHIT! IT'S LUCKY I GOT AN EXTRA. HERE, YOU MEAT JERKY BRAIN! DON'T FOOKING LET THIS ONE GET AWAY!"

Minutes later after Lava forces the wood into the opening and Simo unleashes some fast and furious pounding, the peg is tightly secured. Simo sends Lava back up the ladder and turns to his two mates who are struggling with getting the hose re-clamped. "Here, gimme that," he says as he snatches the connectors from Charlton. "What the hell's on this hose?"

"Feels like Vaseline, Capt'n. You think one of those Coasties set this up?"

"Sonnavabitch! We sure as hell wouldn't grease up a bilge pump connection." He digs out a shirttail and swipes the outside of the pipe and the inside of the hose, gets the dried pieces back together and tightens the clamp screw.

"Let's hope the pump doesn't burn out from all those minutes with no water running through it. Right now, run a siphon hose down here and bail what you can. I gotta get back to the wheel. Never did trust those damn Coasties."

Simo starts up the ladder mumbling, "Their ass is grass when we get back. I'll personally drown the fookers in Gilligan's toilet." He turns to see Gator staring at him. "WHAT THE HELL YOU

THINK YOU DOING, GATOR, WATCHIN' TV? MAYBE YOU WANT SOME FOOKIN' BON-BONS? GET YOUR ASS MOVING! WE GOT NO TIME FOR SCREWIN' AROUND HERE!" Gator scurries away.

The storm continues to worsen, but the current seems to have leveled out somewhat as Simo gets back to the controls. He flips off the autopilot toggle switch, turns the bilge pump back on and revs the engine, pushing the throttle open to half-ahead. Gator yells up that the pump is working, the hose and peg are holding, and that they're clearing the water out.

The fifteen-minute breakdown left them blowing away from their target, but Simo knows he can make up the difference once most of the water is cleared out and he can go full ahead. He has no doubts though that they are going to be late getting to the *Maltese*.

He tries raising Ruiz on the CB, and gets an earful of static in return. Five minutes pass, then ten. Finally, a breakthrough, and he picks up the voice.

"HEY!" he shouts, "WE TOOK ON SOME AQUA, MI AMIGO, BUT WE'RE CLEAR NOW. IT'S GONNA ADD SOME, ER, AH, UN PEQUEÑO TIME, AMIGO, BUT WE'LL GET THERE PRONTO. JUST ESTAR COLGADO! HANG ON! YOU KNOW WHAT I MEAN?"

"Sí, Capitán Simo, we will hang on, but don't take too long or your boss will cut off your testículos and then hanging on will not to matter, si?"

"Roger that on the testículos, Capt'n! See you in a short."

Simo thinks again about Eddie, wondering if he was anywhere near. "Should never have done this without radio contact," he says to himself.

Pulver rushes at the two barely visible black images in the dark cellar that had just broken and crawled through the basement window. He knows he has the advantage of his eyes having already adjusted to the dark room, and he knows the element of surprise is on his side. He throws a lucky punch that staggers the bigger one backward to the floor, and grabs at the other, pulling off pieces of clothing before gaining control with a headlock. He hefts the one he stunned over his shoulder, tucks the other, screaming and kicking, under his other arm, and heads up the stairs.

Simo takes two quick slugs of whiskey and swipes the back of his hand across his mouth. By some miracle, the nor'easter is leveling off. It is still raining and the seas continue to heave but the current feels steady, and most of the fog is blowing off. Out of nowhere it seems, Fast Eddie pulls the professor's boat up sixty feet off Simo's starboard.

Enjoying a momentary sense of relief, Simo starts to take a deep breath—but then like being interrupted in the middle of a yawn—he is interrupted and equally relieved, fairly astonished in fact to see lights from the *Hombre* just 200 feet off his port side. He smirks as he re-establishes radio contact to arrange the delicate side-by-side maneuvering and tie-up of the two boats.

Eddie gestures he will keep the professor's cabin cruiser close but at a safe distance.

Simo takes another slug of whiskey—this one celebratory. His temperament transformed in a flash when he sighted the two other boats. Now, he realizes, he is close to pulling off the deal and that means putting on the pressure. He knows his crew is physically spent from battling the storm, but refuses to let up on them—especially knowing all the players are now in place. He starts dishing out orders over the PA system, and curses anyone he sees who looks to be slacking off. Lava stands on the bow, braced awkwardly against a rail, with one arm wrapped securely around a guy wire. He manages to light a cigarette without ever taking his eyes off Simo. The two men seem locked in a stare-down contest through the wheelhouse windshield.

Battling the wind and rain and mostly the waves, it takes almost an hour to hook up the huge freighter and the trawler. Both crews stand at the ready as Simo claws his way across the rigging to the *Hombre* deck and exchanges handshakes, shoulder squeezes, paperwork, and whiskey shots with Captain Ruiz. The two men light cigars and climb into the hold to inspect the goods, razor-cutting random boxes to check the neatly packed hashish balls and vials of hash oil.

When the two men emerge, Simo signals Gator to start loading, and yells to bring him one of two waterproof bags from the wheelhouse. The second bag, as Apple instructed, is to be handed over when the load is fully transferred and inventoried.

The two captains stand drinking and puffing in between dishing out orders. As the crews get into sync and figure out how to work around the storm's interruptions, Simo and Ruiz retreat to the *Hombre* wheelhouse. By their second drink, Gator appears briefly with the bag of cash, then leaves. Ruiz opens the bag and the two captains pick out and fan random bundles, laughing, clinking shot glasses, patting one another on the shoulders. "The resto," says Simo, "in a few minutos." But neither man is trusting the other long enough to turn his back.

The seas remain choppy and the waves at twelve - fifteen feet make the event less than smooth, but the transfer manages to move along without incident. The two captains continue to drink and smoke and chat up the next twenty minutes in broken English and Spanish, more laughing, knee-slapping. Yet another twenty minutes of partying follow.

Door knocks, and shouts from the *Maltese* interrupt them to let them know that the load is done, but that it's too heavy and the *Maltese* hull waterline is now below the surface. Simo, who is starting to feel the effects of his half-dozen whiskey shots, shrugs indifference and continues socializing.

When eventually the shouting starts to sound panicky, it rouses the two men. Simo asks Ruiz if eighteen thousand pounds was a lot for the *Hombre* to carry on the high seas. Ruiz blinks and suddenly sits up straight.

"Jesus Christo!" he says. He leans forward and shouts into Simo's face and says he has "eighteen thousand TONS for the *Maltese*, NOT POUNDS, YOU IMBÉÉCIL! That's why I say the cash you tell me is just a start point. It only pays HALF!"

By the time Simo realizes what's happening, deckhand shouts begin turning into screams. The two men scramble from the *Hombre* wheelhouse just in time to see *Hombre* deck crew cutting the tie lines between the two vessels and the *Maltese* starting to go down. Simo flings his glass and leaps across to his boat, almost missing the rail.

His crew is running in every direction, grabbing float rings, ropes, rafts, seat cushions, and lifejackets. He heads for the wheelhouse and the second bag with the other twelve and a half million, but runs into Lava's fist instead, and is sent sprawling across the stairway.

Lava reaches to grab Simo's neck and in return gets kicked in the groin. Lava yelps as he falls on top of Simo and the two clutch each other into a tangle of flailing arms and legs—punching and screaming angry curse words that no one could hear above the rough seas and pandemonium. They roll and slide across the deck and, choke-holding one another, break through the starboard railing, plunging, enraged, into the unforgiving blackness of the stormy Atlantic.

The *Maltese* suddenly begins to spark and ignite in flames as it rolls over and sucks the two wrestlers under with a huge gurgle. Shouts from frantic, dog-paddling *Maltese* crewmen are drowned out by the ocean roar and *Hombre*'s engines as Captain Ruiz Reyes decides to cut his losses. The Colombian freighter turns then pulls away.

Eddie and Jacques throw spare lines and use boat poles to board the men who swim to them onto the professor's Chris Craft. Gator makes it to the boat's *Here & Now* transom, and struggles to climb aboard with the second bag.

Chapter 42

TIME AND TIDE

The bedlam continues. Fifteen miles out at sea, the weather has turned once more for the worse. Gator, who saved himself from drowning by shedding his rubber bib overall waders when he hit the water, is now plastered to the *Here & Now* deck—aches, pains, cuts, bruises, and chills, but still alive. He crawls to a corner of the cockpit, nine feet to Eddie's left.

Gator grabs a passenger seat footrest that's bolted to the boat cabin bulkhead, and pulls himself away from the deck edge. He falls like a dead body dropped from some roof, and lands on top of the black nylon bag. His stinging left wrist is rope-burned and blood-reddened from the bag handle he had wrapped around it.

One heaving drenched body after another is dragged aboard and shoveled next to him, into a gasping, groaning heap of collapsed crewmen, who look like they'd been slammed against a brick wall by a crane-mounted wrecking ball. Grasping at anything within reach, including each other, they sputter and pant and moan.

Barely coherent, the surviving seamen claw and crawl over the deck, seeking to trade up to something more solid to hang on to than the first upright that came their way. They are, to a man, close to being overwhelmed by the forty-five-degree rocking, the tumult of whipping winds, torrential rain, and crashing waves cascading over their heads.

The safeboat isn't feeling so safe, but it's all there is. Its tons of weight and straining engines are being tossed between cresting waves like a block of Styrofoam, but somehow Eddie manages to keep them afloat. "Damn bullnose hull is what's keepin' us alive," he mutters between curses. Controlling the wheel exerts his every muscle. The stress of the ship's hickory captain's wheel, trying to hold the rudder steady, sometimes feels like it's about to snap off, like the jagged barrel of a broken baseball bat flying across the infield.

In attempting to beat her retreat from the calamitous event to what is now by comparison the relative sanity of the violent wind-swept sea, *Hombre's* wide open engines throw back a wall of exhaust fumes. The fumes whip themselves into the overbearing frenzy of the moment—something known and understood only by those who have battled and survived the odds. As the twin-masted Colombian freighter powers away into the coal darkness, the ship's fumes are now only barely discernible to those who lay heaped across the wave-swamping stern deck of the professor's escort boat.

Despite the evil intent of their mission, Eddie and Jacques are heroic in their response. They succeed at keeping control and pulling the cabin cruiser away from the blazing, then rapidly sinking trawler. They work furiously to continue hooking and dragging the panic-stricken drowning crewmen up and over the escort boat's rocking *Here & Now* transom—surfaced then submerged, surfaced then submerged—losing sight first of the *Here* and then of the *Now*—slapped senseless by relentless waves.

Gator watches trancelike as Simo's and Lava's grimaced faces are last seen in the *Here & Now* searchlights Eddie has thrown on them. Their four hands still choke each other while their illuminated entangled bodies are sucked mercilessly into the *Maltese* whirlpool, oblivious to shouts to save themselves.

Debris floats everywhere. Groceries, wood, plastic, tarps, splintered decking, sections of railing, papers, laminated charts, empty lifejackets, tie-lines, fishing nets, seat cushions, cardboard boxes, pieces of canvas and bedding, buckets, a sock, a shirt, hash oil vials, and thousands of balls of hash that burst from their water-logged boxes in the explosive sinking practically blanket the wave crests.

Some pieces of contraband ignite in the flaming surface slick oil and produce an eerie, drifting, intoxicating odor that hovers over the last swirls of the ocean hole. The red-hot glowing hash balls somehow withstand the vicious winds and pellets of rain as they ride the waves. And the smoke produced seems to mesmerize most of those who remain alive. The men who escaped being numbed by the trauma, are now entranced by the hash smoke. The cook is nowhere to be seen.

For a few long minutes, it appears that the professor's boat may also be doomed, about to be vacuumed down into the ominous swirls of the trawler's wake. Somehow, the *Here & Now* miraculously steadies herself between rollers, and is able to escape the pulling forces of the trawler's deep dive. But without the help of moonlight or a radio, and the storm still raging, the *Maltese* survivors all know that even the *Here & Now*'s survival may not be in the cards.

JP squints into the bright ceiling lights, trying to figure out where she is. CB radio static is still crackling in the background. She's groggy, battered, and bruised. It takes her half a dozen deep breaths to realize that she's looking up from Solamente's library floor into the barrel of a pistol and a ragged shaped ring of obscure, backlit faces.

Fresh from being pummeled by Pulver and dragged up the

basement steps, she and Maddigan lay sprawled there, surrounded by feet that belong to the mystery faces hovering in knots around and above them, faces that are two or three feet closer to the ceiling than the gun which holds their total attention.

In her mind, JP relives the last few minutes and flashes back to the basement window struggle. Only now, she remembers her rain jacket, pants and hat being torn away. She starts to reach for her leg, but her jacket is pulled down under her back holding her arms to her sides. Her shirt is torn down the front and her breasts are exposed. Except for her disheveled bikini panties, her sneakers, and one barely fastened, dangling shirt button, she is practically naked.

She suddenly realizes Maddigan is next to her, and turns her head to see him. He looks dazed. His face is bruised and bleeding. He groans as he reaches to hold his throbbing head. He opens his eyes one at a time and surveys the ceiling. Slowly he turns to see JP and tries futilely to smile. He turns back to face the ceiling and now notices the faces looking down on them. Then he sees the gun. It rockets him to consciousness. He tries to sit up, but gets Pulver's boot heel in his chest and collapses back down against JP.

"What the..."

"Never you mind, 'what the,' professor! I want to know what the hell you are doing breaking into my home, and why I shouldn't just shoot you both right now for breaking and entering. Speak up professor, and this better be good!"

"Can we sit up, Mr. Solamente? Can we at least sit up to talk, to answer your question?"

"Sure, professor, be my guest, but the broad stays where she is. I'm rather fond of the view. Besides, if I don't like your answer, you're not stupid enough to try a move with her spread-eagled like that."

A yardstick's distance apart, each of JP's ankles is now pinned down by Pulver's and Benjamin's boot-heels. Maddigan pulls himself up to lean shakily on one elbow.

"So let's hear it. Tell me what you two are doing here."

Before Maddigan can even string his words together, JP shouts, almost hysterical, "Heather! What are you doing here?"

Maddigan, one eye already half swollen shut, looks up to the top of the only skirt in the room, then turns to JP, "*This* is Heather?"

"Whh...yeah, Rick. Do you two know each other?"

Heather takes a step back and answers for him, "I was in one of his classes last year."

"Whoa," Maddigan still dizzy and sounding drunk, "and you're the face I saw in the arcade. Why were you watching me? Oh, I get it! You work for these thugs! So that's how they knew..."

"Wait a minute, Professor," Billy steps forward, "I'm the one works here. She's..."

"Billy! I knew you were in this up to your ears, but I never thought Heather here was..."

"Rick, shhh," JP whispers, "Billy is Heather's guy."

Apple is waving the revolver in Maddigan's face.

"Enough of this lovefest reunion shit, all of you. I'm waiting on answers from you, Professor, and I am very short on patience right this minute. Now speak, or my boy here kicks your teeth out of your mouth and we spread your woman's legs even farther apart!"

"No. I mean please. I...right, Mr. Solamente! Yes, Sir! I understand. No need for over-reacting here. I'm, we're, happy to cooperate. I mean, here's the story: JP here and I overheard this Captain Simo guy talking about you one night at Gilligan's Bar, and saying how smart you are and how you could make anything happen, and we thought we could sneak in here and talk with you about helping us get my boat back from two guys—Slam and Pulver—who work for you because JP and I really need it to get our group counseling sessions up and running, and we..."

Apple is crawling out of his skin. He moves his feet in little circles without turning his eyes away and without moving the gunpoint which remains fixed on Maddigan.

"FIRST of all, Professor, women don't go to Gilligan's! SECOND, Simo doesn't talk about me! THIRD, how did you get my name and find out where I live? FOURTH, how do you know Slam and Pulver work for me? And, FIFTH, I don't give a damn about your counseling sessions —so stop the bullshit! Give it to me straight, Professor, or you're going to have to watch your little honey here go through such torture that you are going to wish for me to shoot her! Do you know what kind of torture that is? DO YOU?"

"Wait, Mr. Solamente, Please...I..."

"Rick," JP interrupts, "he's not serious, he..." Pulver steps harder on her ankle. "Eyaaah, OOOOOOW! RICK, HELP! OWW-WW!"

Apple stands glaring at JP. He waves the gun at his son and Pulver like a guy on the runway directing passenger jets into their parking spaces.

"So we got us a smartass little broad here, huh? Pulver, Benji, let's open the target. Spread her legs out more! Billy, give me Mayetta's broom over there."

Maddigan connects the dots and throws his arms up. From the look on his face, the gun might as well be jammed into his mouth.

"NO! PLEASE, Mr. Solamente, please...PLEASE! DON'T. PLEASE DON'T. PLEASE. I'll tell you what you want to know, just please don't hurt her! I beg you! She didn't do anything wrong here! She just came along with me. Please, Mr. Solamente."

Benjamin leaned toward his father, "Dad, you know we can get him to talk. We don't need her here. Why don't we..."

"Shut up Benjamin! S H U T U P ! I told you before—I make the decisions here. Me! And turn that Goddamn radio static down. It's giving me a headache! Billy, give me the Goddamn broom, NOW!"

Before Billy can move, Heather runs three steps across the room and literally flies through the air at Apple, screeching and cursing at him as she hits him full force and staggers him backwards into his eagle statue, knocking him unconscious. As Apple goes down, the gun discharges, shooting Pulver in the elbow. Blood and bone fragments fly. Mayetta appears in the doorway, sees the uproar, then turns and runs screaming down the hall. Pulver crumbles into a yelping heap as Benjamin and Billy both dive to retrieve the pistol.

Maddigan gives JP a hand up from the floor and she promptly stomps on Pulver's bleeding, rearranged arm. Pulver lets out a deafening scream. Then Maddigan pulls Heather's choking hands off Apple's neck as the mobster starts regaining consciousness, and lets loose with a punch to Apple's stomach that leaves the gang leader in a fetal position, totally winded and gasping.

Benjamin comes up with the gun and starts yelling at everyone to stop where they are. He reaches to help his violently panting father to sit up.

Everyone backs away except Billy who steps toward Benjamin, aiming to play his one last roll of the dice.

"Listen, Benji," reasons Billy in a calm, quiet, reassuring voice just a notch above a whisper, "we need to chill here a little bit. Supposing you and me do some of your father's sambuca here and talk this through, just the two of us, huh?"

Billy continues his surreptitious banter like no one else was in the room, "I mean, Benji, you the man. You got the gun. So you're the boss, Ben. I mean you're really the man of the family now. I always liked you best anyway. I've been waiting for the day I could work for you instead of your old man. I mean, just look at him, cowering over there. He doesn't have the guts and brains you have, plus he's nowhere near as good-looking or strong as you, Ben."

Slowly, carefully, Billy reaches to give a gentle squeeze to Benjamin's unarmed arm.

"C'mon, Ben, whatta you say?" then a full-fledged whisper into Benjamin's ear: "Just you and me?"

"Gee, Billyboy, you mean all that stuff?"

Except for Pulver squirming and wailing, and Apple still sucking for air, everyone else remains perfectly still.

"Sure, Ben—you're the best, man! Like I said, I've waited a long time to be with you without Heather and your old man in the way. How about that sambuca shot while we talk this out, okay?"

As the two move toward the bottle, Billy grabs Benjamin in a choke hold and wrestles the pistol away. Apple is now standing, wild-eyed, holding the bronze eagle over his head and charging Billy from behind. Maddigan points to the eagle and yells at Billy. Billy turns and fires. He shoots Apple in the stomach. Apple staggers backward into and over the top of his desk, as the eagle dives beak first into the desk chair leather.

Benjamin runs for the wall cabinet trying to get to the other pistol and is tackled by JP and Heather together. Maddigan gets to the cabinet first and pulls the other pistol free. He takes aim at Pulver, who has now managed to lift himself up to within inches of crushing Benjamin with a mahogany captain's chair. He is starting to backswing it like a nine iron. Maddigan fires and hits them both with the same bullet.

McGrath and Leeds, guns drawn, appear in the doorway with Mayetta in tow, just in time to see Pulver and Benjamin collapse on top of Apple. Maddigan and Billy both drop the pistols to the floor.

Leeds calls in the Seaport County Police and EMT Squad,

while McGrath begins trying to piece together what's taken place since arriving in Solamente's driveway.

After a brief hug and each being wrapped up in EMT blankets, and handed a glass of water, JP and Maddigan are escorted to a hallway bench outside the library French doors. They sit and begin to recount the events of the past three hours.

Chapter 43

THE WAKE

The professor's boat bobs, rises, falls, shudders, shakes, and yaws. First one way, then the other, but there's no pattern or advance warning to the passengers. One minute the men are shooting forward, hanging on to each other and anything they can grab. The next, the boat seems to stand motionless, and they crawl to the sides to throw up.

In between, the hull planking feels like it's about to rattle loose from the ribs and deck. Eddie and Jacques white knuckle the wheel and manipulate the throttle to synchronize boat speed with the driving currents that carry them into the darkness. All they can do is try to stay afloat 'til daybreak and hope they can find landfall. Minutes are hours long. No one seems to notice Gator as he makes his way down into the forward cabin, to the v-berth, and tucks his bag beneath him under the starboard bunk mattress.

Sirens and pulsing red and blue lights blanket the Solamente island estate entrance bridge and guardhouse. Emergency vehicles spill out scores of police and busy EMTs who are running back and forth up the wet driveway under the glare of tripod-mounted spots and streaming tunnels of light that pour eerily through the drizzle and mist from the basement and first floor windows.

Inside, the library resembles a hospital ER with equipment and bodies scattered across the floor. Garage and driveway-generated wires and foot-traffic run back and forth through the halls and up and down the basement stairs.

Groaning, wheezing and sputtering, Apple Solamente commands the most attention. A physician kneels over him checking vitals as a medical tech works to stop the stomach bleeding. Detectives stand to the side looking for an opening to question the mob leader.

Two uniformed officers hold Pulver face down to the carpet as they handcuff him. They ask the doctor to have an EMT give the struggling muscleman a knock-out shot.

Mayetta sobs hysterically in the corner. Heather holds her by the shoulders while Billy, who is shaking uncontrollably, is cuffed and escorted to a seat on the couch by a yet another uniformed officer. The EMT shuts down Pulver with a needle jab in the arm.

Unconscious from shock, Benjamin is being tended to by two EMTs who are attempting to revive him and plug the bullet hole in his leg with gauze.

Maddigan sits sprawled on the hallway bench as if he'd been a giant beanbag tossed there by some Herculean Olympic shot-putter. He has one eye open and is holding an ice pack against his head. JP leans against him. A young first-aider with astonished blue eyes and hair that looks like a tan washcloth explosion, discreetly reaches under JP's blanket to blob gauze-pads full of quick-fix ointment on her dozen or so cuts and scrapes. JP yelps at each medicinal sting and Maddigan flinches at each response.

Even though it hurts to the touch, JP clutches and clings awkwardly to the blanket that covers her nakedness and abused skin. She sits there, across from the French doors, speaking with Agents Hartley and Leeds. Watching the surreal battlefield cleanup accentuates her disorientation.

Leeds had fetched extra blankets from a nearby room and stands to wrap one around JP's shoulders. He spreads the other across her lap. Maddigan pulls the EMT blanket up over his chilled neck. Someone finally shuts down the CB radio static as more distant and arriving sirens penetrate the stone walls. Mist-muted flashing red and blue lights streak through the window blinds and vibrate off the hallway ceilings.

Sunrise creeps tentatively through the thick hanging air and aftermath of the storm. The debris has disappeared, the rain has all but stopped, and the waves are bigger and higher but more rhythmic, and easier to navigate. A muffled distant horizon of shoreline tells Eddie that if the *Here & Now* can continue to hold together, they might be lucky enough to make it back to land in one piece in a couple of hours, though he's not sure yet exactly where they'll pull in.

They could be anywhere between The Highlands and Cape May right now. His best guess would put them south of Manasquan Inlet, maybe near Long Beach Island but nothing would indicate being near Atlantic City, usually visible from miles out at sea.

All Eddie can do at this point is continue to keep watch and hope the rapidly dwindling fuel supply holds out. The men seem to be recovering. Most are now sitting on the stern deck, backs against the bulkhead wall, or have retreated down into the cabin where they found waterproof matches, a dry pack of cigarettes, and a quart of Jamaican rum to pass around. Gator and Charlton are zonked out in the v-berth bunks. Jacques is trying to find odd pieces of charts and jigsaw puzzle them together to get a bearing.

Eddie is thinking about his last glimpse of Simo and Lava going down, a sight he thinks he that he alone witnessed, and wondering how Apple will take the news of what happened. Mostly, Eddie is just glad to be alive.

"Go ahead, Agent Hartley, Agent Leeds, you two can talk to him for a minute before we roll him out. I kept the two uniforms away when I heard this was your case," says Dr. Fries, the EMT physician who has been patching up Solamente.

"Thanks Doc," says Leeds. "How is he, I mean, will..."

"Will he live?"

"Yeah."

"Well, I don't think that he thinks so, but actually he should do just fine. Just between the three of us, you should know that the bullet missed his vitals and passed straight through. You'll probably find it in the couch, but I didn't tell him that in case you had some hard questions that he'd be more likely to answer thinking he's got a chance to get through the pearly gates, if you know what I mean?"

"Yeah, like a 'deathbed confession' thing," surmises Hartley. "Good thinking, Doctor Fries, thanks."

"Hey, every little bit helps when you're dealing with bastards like him. Good luck, guys! The EMTs will wait for your signal to pack him up."

The two black leather coats approach the gurney. Apple is still moaning and gurgling, coughing up some blood.

"Hey, you two dicks get that S.O.B. teacher who broke in here shooting up my house?"

"Listen, Solamente, here's the news fresh from the U.S. Coastguard," Hartley lowers his voice and talks at Apple's ear. "Your drug deal went belly up!" Hartley steps off to the side long enough to let that news sink in.

More coughs and growls. Hartley leans forward into Solamente's face, and continues, "Simo's boat sank because you dumb shits were trying to put 18 TONS of hash in a boat that only has an 18 thousand POUND capacity. And the hash is now floating in over boardwalk beaches all up and down the coast."

Hartley pauses again, and looks to Agent Leeds for a reading. Leeds nods.

"Your delivery ship, the *Hombre*, turned and ran back to Colombia with the money." Knowing nothing hurts a gangster more than losing money, he lets that sink in.

"Your lover boys Simo and Lava killed each other in the process and went down with the *Maltese*. The rest of Simo's crew was picked up by Eddie and Jacques, and they're all about to be arrested when their safeboat pulls into shore within the hour."

Solamente coughs up some more blood. Tears well up in his glazed-over eyes.

"Oh, yeah, there's more, Mr. Apple." Another pregnant pause. "We found your friend Slam dead in your basement. Pulver's condition is critical. And I'm sorry to have to tell you that it looks like your son, who probably deserved better, is, well, he's history. The bullet he took was fatal. The EMTs did all they could."

Apple's eyes are now streaming tears.

Hartley puts a firm hand on Solamente's shuddering shoulder. "Now YOU!" the agent says loud enough to command the man's attention, then turns his voice to a whisper as he lowers himself to within inches from the mob boss's ear. "We talked with the doctor here, and you may not have more than an hour, so this might be your last chance to fess up and meet your maker on good terms. Maybe you'll be lucky enough to be with your son again. Anyway, I heard that God favors those who depart life on earth by owning up to the errors of their ways. I think this may be your last time to speak."

The agent stands up straight, takes half a step back and resumes his normal voice, "So, I'm recording our discussion here right now. Okay with you, Mr. Solamente?"

Apple nods faintly and mumbles, "Yeah, it's okay."

He clears his throat. Hartley records the time, date, location, his name, Leeds' name as witness, and Apple's name.

Solamente talks to the ceiling, "My son. God, what a waste! What happened to him? No, never mind. I don't want to know. What a waste!"

There's a long pause as Apple appears to collect his thoughts. The two agents shift feet and exchange knowing looks.

"Listen, guys, I don't want to go this way." His tearful-sounding voice quavers as he holds back a muffled choking sound.

"I know I haven't exactly been Mr. Nice Guy all my life, but that's how the cookie crumbles, you know what I mean?" His face is filled with pained expression as he tries to twist his neck on the gurney pillow.

Then, almost to himself, Apple continues, "Too bad about Lava, but I'll probably meet up with him again someplace. Simo, I could care less. He was always an-eye-for-an-eye, live-by-the-sword kinda ogre-type, you know? Given enough time, he would have wasted everybody else anyway, so it's probably best he's gone. Him, I know I'll never meet up with again. He's the one killed Jocko and had Slam waste Jocko's old lady—or Mr. and Mrs. Rat, as Simo called the Jocko's. Ha! Actually, Slam had Pulver do the job, but Pulver, if he lives—go easy on Pulver, will you? He's okay, just dumb. Dumb's not a crime, right?" Apple's eyes looked pleadingly at the two men.

"That's not our call, Solamente," says Leeds.

"What else, Apple?" asks Hartley. "What about Slam?"

"Slam, yeah. Pulver did Slam too, but only because I told him to. Slam was getting in the way, couldn't be trusted anymore. Too bad, but he was even dumber than Pulver. What's going to happen to Heather and Billyboy? You know they have a baby? And what's with the other guys on the boat? I mean Eddie, for example. He didn't know anything. Just followed orders. And same with the others."

"We don't know. They'll all be arrested and then we'll sort things out. One more thing, how involved were the professor and his girlfriend?"

"Aaaah, shit! They didn't know from nothin'! Awfully stupid guy for a professor! Hey, she's a pretty good looker, y'know? Anyway, we just put the heat on them so we could get them to find out information from a microchip—which was in Benji's pocket. God! Poor Benjamin! We just wanted to use their boat for the drop, that's it. That's the whole story."

Solamente coughed up more blood. A look of panic seemed to crawl across his face and ignite a twitch under his right eye.

"So maybe that squares me with the big man in the sky. Maybe I'll see you in another life!"

"Right, Apple, another life. Sometime after you're on death row and we send flowers to your executioner!" replies Leeds.

"What do you mean? You said..."

"We said, we talked with the doctor," Hartley explains. "We said you may not have another hour. Who knows for sure? Agent Leeds and I might not have another hour either, Apple. And, by the way, the doctor says you'll recover just fine. So we hope you enjoy rough sex, and have a great rest of whatever life you might have—in jail."

Turning away from Apple's pained expression, the two agents

pocket the tape recorder, signal two uniform cops and the EMTs to strap the gang leader down and roll him out to the waiting ambulance. They return to the hallway to finish up their interview with Maddigan and JP.

Chapter 44

WHADDA

The undercurrent of whispering, paper shuffling, floor-scraping chairs, and chumpfing sounds of flopping media cable tangles come to an abrupt halt as six well-dressed individuals, three in uniform, plus two guys in black leather jackets file into the county courthouse briefing room.

The eight people parade across the platform and line up behind the podium in front of spotlights, flashing bulbs, and a battery of microphones. County muckity-muck John King steps forward, squinting, shielding his eyes from the thousand-watts of light.

"Ladies and gentlemen, good afternoon! Before clarifying the purpose of this press conference, please allow me to first introduce those who appear here before you. When I've completed the introductions, I will outline the circumstances leading up to today's session. Printed copies of the agenda and a two-page briefing backgrounder are being passed around as I speak. Please raise your hand if you do not receive these three pages.

"For those of you who don't know me, my name is John King. I am the Executive Director for Seaport County. On my immediate right is Captain Carl Pierce, Chief Enforcement Officer, U.S. Coast Guard Station at Seaport County Inlet. Next to Captain Pierce is

Seaport County Police Chief Bill Bowers, and to the right of Chief Bowers is Seaport River Mayor, Marian Marshall, and next to the Mayor is Seaport County Community College President, Dr. Andrew Moore Stafford. On my left is Drug Enforcement Administration Regional Director, Colonel Robert Wainwright Tuckerton. To the left of Colonel Tuckerton are DEA Special Agents Jake Hartley and Russell 'Rusty' Leeds."

Anticipation. The room is silent. Director King pauses dramatically to sip from the water glass on the podium shelf. He clears his throat and begins.

"Let me start by saying that all of the people you see up here—together with the behind-the-scenes support and hard work of dozens more to whom we are deeply indebted—are all identified by name and title and hometown in your take-home packets.

"In the last twnty-four hours, these dedicated public servants have successfully served our community and our country by joining forces to execute the biggest drug bust of 1981, and in fact, in the history of our nation."

The Executive Director continues, "As a consolidated force to be reckoned with, these people who stand before you and their support teams are responsible for aborting a long-term gangland plan and for intercepting delivery of eighteen tons of hashish and thousands of vials of hash oil with a combined street value of more than five hundred million dollars. That's over half a billion dollars worth of illegal drugs destined for our community streets, and other communities throughout the Northeast."

He pauses to take another sip of water. He looks around the crowded room of feverish note takers and anxious headset-wearers, camera-operators, and microphone-holders. He lets the information sink in.

"In addition to terminating this mind-boggling delivery," King continues, "in frigid, life-threatening stormy night seas fifteen miles off our coast this past Saturday night, they succeeded in apprehending a dozen suspects. Five others drowned in the process. The twelve perpetrators have been charged with drug trafficking and seven counts of first degree murder over the last six months.

"I am honored to tell you that Special Agents Hartley and Leeds, who stand before you here," he nods appreciatively at them, "were at the heart of the investigation leading up to these arrests and the aborted drug delivery."

Flashbulbs pop around the room. King goes on, "The incident also resulted in the sinking of a fifty-six-foot fishing trawler out of The Highlands, known as the *Maltese,* and the scuttling of the twin-masted Colombian freighter, *Hombre* which is being boarded right now, as I am speaking, by U.S. Coast Guardsmen, somewhere off the Florida coast.

"These two men, Agents Hartley and Leeds, risked their lives to break this case." More flash pictures. "In conjunction with their brave efforts, Colonel Wainwright Tuckerton has a special announcement to make. He will be followed by Captain Pierce who will file the Coast Guard report, and fill you in on the details. The others here will also make brief comments, and then we will take your questions, at which time you will be asked to raise your hand to be recognized, and then preface your question with your name and affiliation."

"Colonel Tuckerton?" The Colonel steps forward as the Director steps back.

"Thank you Director King. As a result of their years of dedicated service, personal sacrifices, and commitments above and beyond the call of duty..."

Tuckerton looks sideways to make sure the two agents are

tuned in. Both stand at parade rest with stern, game-face expressions.

The Colonel continues, "...in the foiling of this illegal drug exchange, and the apprehension of the Solamente Family Mob, including murderers and drug traffickers, I am pleased to announce that Agents Hartley and Leeds are promoted to the rank of detective with commensurate pay raises, effective immediately. Detectives? Is there anything you would like to add?"

Hartley steps forward and twists the goose-neck microphone toward him. "Yes, Colonel. On behalf of my partner Rusty and myself, we would like to thank you for your support and confidence. We would also like to extend our special appreciation to Professor Rick Maddigan of Seaport County Community College, and his associate, JP Haley, for their personal assistance with bringing these gangsters and drug-runners to justice. Without their help and guidance, at high risk to themselves, Agent Leeds and I could never have..."

"Well, Green Eyes, Whadda you think?"

"What do I think? Hmmm. I think that I'm so relieved that this nightmare is over, that we've come through it okay, and that we got your boat back. I think this weekend, we'd better get that CB radio re-installed, and make arrangements to tighten the rails and planking. Oh, and find another mechanic who can service the engines. I think we owe our lives to Heather and Billy. And I also think it's great that they'll have the chance to raise their daughter in a happy and peaceful environment. I think it's wonderful that you'll never have to lug another turtle through stormy night swampland—or do another 'autopsy.' You weren't much good at that anyway."

She winked.

"I also think the two agents turned out to be okay guys after all, and that their personal endorsement of us will serve to boost our Anchor Out session enrollments. I think that I am so proud of you for giving up pot, and for being my hero and sticking by me when the chips were down. Oh, yeah, and I think I want to jump your bones!"

"Wow! You do an awful lot of thinking, JP! But I do like your last thought!"

Twenty-Four Hours Later

And somewhere on the flowering vine-covered balcony of a palatial estate on a live pink flamingo-lined riverbank deep in the Central American jungles, two men sit sipping steaming coffee made from beans picked an hour earlier from the edge of a plantation field a hundred yards away.

"Well, Gator, Whadda you think?"

"Hey, Charlton. Truth? I think we are two lucky bastards to get away with the dough-re-me. If those jerks hadn't seen the handfuls of fifties and hundreds we tossed out the v-berth portholes, and stopped long enough on the way back in to scoop them up, which gave us chance to bust through the v-berth hatch and jump and swim to the edge of the marina, and no doubt everyone there thought that we drowned, we'd both be in jail with the rest of them by now."

"You can say that again!" Charlton tips his cup toward Gator and grins a toothy grin.

"Yup! And bottom line is that nobody knows we got away, or that we got the money. And from all reports, nobody ever will know. Wait 'til your wife and kids land and meet us tonight; they're gonna love it here." He takes another sip.

"This Costa Rica coast is like heaven—a rainforest on the ocean. Who could ask for more? And we can afford to pay housekeepers as well as buy us a couple of beautiful big boats and cruise around for the rest of our lives. You'll never have to worry again about feeding your kids, or those medical bills for your youngest. You can even donate all you want to other poor kids with medical problems. In fact, I'll chip in an equal share. How's that? And we'll still have more than we need to live on."

"Hey, Gator, I sure do like that 'no more worrying' thought of yours. Let's do it!"

"Well, Heather, whadda you think?"

"Are you kidding me, Billyboy? I never dreamed of being able to offer Brianna a life this good. I think you are the greatest, and I'm proud of you for taking control the way you did, though I must admit I was a little nervous about the act you pulled with Benjamin. Too bad about him, but he was never going to make it on his own in this world, and his old man deserves everything the cops and judges throw at him.

"And who would have thought with Ben gone, I'd be the jerk's only living relative? Having the legal rights to this Belize estate and getting Apple's hundred thousand in cash is like owning a little piece of heaven, plus having Mayetta along to help us raise Brianna, we'll be able to run the place like a real, honest-to-goodness bed and breakfast, and host—who knows?—all kinds of rich and famous visitors." Then, as a self-satisfying afterthought, she added, "And I won't have to end every sentence with a question mark again . . . unless, of course I actually decide to start a 'Valley Girl' thing in Belize? Y'know?" She giggled nervously.

"Y'know what, Heather? That's funny stuff, but what's most important is that I am proud of you! Nobody I've ever known was as brave as you when you flew at Apple like that! I couldn't believe it! Still don't. But, you know what? You couldn't be more right about Brianna, and about living in Belize together, and having Mayetta to help. We can run a water taxi service from the airport and book people for escape-to-nature trips, and in the meantime, we'll be living it full time. And, yeah, you won't have to be asking so many questions. Hahahaha! I love you, Babe. You always had my heart. Now you have my life!"

Chapter 45

THE LATE NEWS

Good evening. I'm Stephanie Matthews. In the news tonight, Seaport County Community College Professor Rick Maddigan and student associate, JP Haley, are being called heroes by police and county officials who say, all Americans can be proud . . .

This is the Evening News and I am Walter Bandurski. For roles they played this past weekend in facilitating the biggest drug bust in U.S. history, two area residents were awarded meritorious . . .

On the Late News tonight, a dozen crewmen were arrested on drug trafficking and first degree murder charges when the record offshore drug deal they were attempting went sour and b . . .

For more on this story, we take you to correspondent Walter Bandurski, broadcasting live from the front steps of Seaport County Courthouse where the twelve drug deal and murder suspects are being arraigned. Walter . . . ?

Eighteen tons of hashish and hash oil were to have been delivered by a Colombian freighter this past Saturday night to a New Jersey trawler contracted by the Apple Solamente crime family, fifteen stormy miles off the shore of Long Branch, New Jersey. The delivery was thwarted by . . .

Maddigan, JP, and the two agents were standing in the rental cottage kitchen watching the book-sized black and white TV screen on the counter.

"O h, m y G o d!!! OH MY GOD! RICK, DID YOU HEAR THAT? CAN YOU BELIEVE IT?" JP is jumping up and down. She dives at Maddigan's chest and bear-hugs him.

"And the money we end up getting out of this! They didn't even mention it on the news, which is a good thing. I really don't want the whole world to know. Even as it is, it will change our lives, you know? I don't mean like us, just that it will take away the stress.

"N-n-n-now we can get that new boat! You can help fund the student communications center and radio station you want, and get rid of that self-absorbed faculty advisor who's been destroying the student newspaper. I can get a top doctor for my Dad! We can start our Anchor Out sessions! And we can travel. We won't have to work summers! Oh, my God, Rick! Oh my God!"

"What if it doesn't work out, JP? What if..."

"It's true, Professor," Agent Hartley interjected. "Agent Leeds and I checked with our boss, Colonel Tuckerton, and also with Captain Pierce at the Coast Guard. Both said that the understood terms of any drug bust at sea are that the key informant source – and especially one who works cooperatively with law enforcement efforts – is entitled to ten percent of the recovered cash, tax free."

"Jake's right," said Agent Leeds. "The Coasties found $12.5 mil on the *Hombre* when they boarded her off of Jacksonville. That means, besides getting your boat back, you and your little lady here will get a cashier's check from the federal government for $1,250,000 —that's $625,000 each! So me and Jake here have only three requests to go along with that."

"Wow! It's just so hard to believe," Maddigan was clearly overwhelmed. "But, okay, what's your request number one?"

"You two take us both to a lobster and champagne dinner. We sometimes get a little tired of jelly donuts, and you made us hungry with that story about your boat deal dinner. Uh, but we don't want to go to Grand Slam Clams."

They all laughed.

"I think we can manage that. What's request number two?"

"Stay off the pot. We're glad to see you gave it up. Keep it that way."

"Absolutely! I appreciate that you would even think to include that on your list. And what's number three?"

"Request number three is that you promise us if you two ever split up, you'll talk JP into taking the DEA Admissions Exam. We'd like her for a partner."

"Okay, well you might have overstepped your bounds there on that one, guys. I mean you can definitely count on getting the first and second requests filled, and we'll do the dinner thing anytime you say. But JP and I are never going to split up. I need her dimple, and..."

"Ah, Rick?"

"Yeah."

"My dimple?"

"Hey! You know what I mean. Well. I...yeah, your dimple!"

"Um, Professor?"

"Yeah."

"What if I spackle it and sand it over?"

"Your dimple?"

"Yeah."

"I wouldn't like that at all."

"Then maybe you should remember that my dimple is the smallest of my assets."

"You are so right, Green Eyes!" He turns back to the leather jackets. "Y'see guys, it's like I said, we're never going to split up, and..."

"Um, Professor?"

"Yeah."

"Are you breathing?"

"Yeah. Sure. Of course. Why?"

"Well, suppose we change that and let me take your breath away by you giving me a kiss?"

"Aah, Babe, not right here right now...I mean these guys here don't want..."

"Mmmmmpf!"

"Thanks Walter. I don't suppose you've heard much about the spoils of this mission, but we're getting dozens of calls reporting 'cannonball-sized hunks' of hash surfing into boardwalk beaches on the high tide. Police are finding the hashballs in Point Pleasant, Bay Head, Mantoloking, Ortley Beach, Seaside Heights, Island Beach State Park, and as far south as Long Beach Island."

"Huh! Maybe I'll get my pipe and head over there when I leave the courthouse. Ha, ha, ha."

"That might not be in the best interests of your career, Walter. You should probably leave your pipe at home! Stay tuned, folks. We'll be bringing you more on this half a billion dollar drug bust."

ANCHOR OUT #1

6 Weeks Later

"Everyone settled? Good. JP and I want to welcome the twelve of you to our first Anchor Out session aboard the *Here & Now*. Help yourselves to the snacks and beverages over in the corner." He gestures.

With her back to the ship's wheel and controls, JP straddles the captain's seat so that her elbows lean over the back of it. Maddigan steps slowly and evenly along the transom ledge while he speaks. Being on opposite sides of the aft deck, and having participants seated on cushions along each side rail, allows the two of them to share cues and eye contact without being distracting.

"As you know by now," Maddigan continues, "the past couple of months have been—to say the least—difficult ones for us and, of course," he knocks his knuckles on a railing, "for this boat! My life and JP's have literally been turned upside down. So we decided that it might serve a purpose to share some of that with you because it kind of sets the stage for discussion with a group like this. But we all need to agree first that what's said on this boat stays on this boat, not even to be shared with family. Does that work for everyone here?"

Nodding heads all around.

"Good. Then we'll take it that we can accept all that head movement of yours as confirmation that you will respect our confidence as we will yours."

"Oh," JP chimes in, "and you needn't worry about not having enough time today to address everyone's concerns. We promise to not take too long with this. The point is," she adds after surveying each of the twelve faces in search of any signs of discontent, "if you think you have problems, give a listen to some of what we've been through here; it might help put your issues in a different perspective, right Professor?"

Maddigan nods and continues, "It's not easy to talk about some of it, but the greater good is that you may see that you're not alone. Even we, for example—who you might have thought have such an idyllic existence—actually face our own pile of life problems as well."

He paces slowly, looking above the group's heads, over the bow, at seagulls gliding low across the whitecaps of Gwyneth Bay. He clasps his hands together, as if in prayer, and shuts his eyes. To himself, he does an *Energy In, Tension Out* count of two, and then drops his arms to his sides.

"To begin, the news coverage of the drug bust JP and I were involved with thankfully omitted the fact that we would probably have never been part of this horrific incident if I had not had a serious personal problem with marijuana dependency. That's a nice way of saying that I was a pothead."

A couple of knowing nods are mixed among the mostly astonished facial expressions. Ten of the twelve participants lean forward; two pull their knees to their chests.

"For years," Maddigan continued, "I had been smoking pot, just a little at first, mistakenly convinced that smoking marijuana would demonstrate to my students that I could be seen as one of them, be more readily accepted. You know? Just a regular guy. I thought I needed this edge because I was feeling a pocketful or two of intimidation—most other faculty people came from academia, and I got into teaching from a business career."

"But, Rick." A voice floated over from the starboard side corner. "Why would that be intimidating? I mean you brought more experience to the table than most of those people who went straight through school and into teaching, right?"

"Thanks for the vote of confidence, Libby. I don't know why I chose to feel that way. It's just something that seems to come along with major career change. I saw colleagues who had planned to teach from the time they were in grade school, and who went straight through college, graduate school and doctoral programs with the specific intent of becoming professors. I felt like a 'Johnny-come-lately.'"

He rubs his hands together briskly as if he were a doctor scrubbing for surgery, then he unhooks his glasses to wipe the lenses with the tail of his golf shirt. He pulls thoughtfully on his beard.

"At any rate, I don't want to get too far astray." He smiles warmly, more naturally now.

"I started to believe that smoking dope actually made me a better, more creative teacher, that it was helping me stay calm while dealing with student's crises."

He looked down at the deck and shrugged haplessly. "I just never thought much more about it than that."

He turned to follow a swooping gull then remembered where he was and riveted back to the gathering around him. "I even wore that little marijuana pin on my hat that some of you might have noticed. I wasn't flaunting my habit. I just really convinced myself that pot was harmless and should be legalized. I didn't see it being any different than alcohol, or even cigarettes for that matter." He stared momentarily at Libby and took a deep breath. "It was simply a political statement."

Twenty-four mesmerized eyes followed Maddigan's every move as he stopped, gestured, ambled, stopped, gestured, ambled. JP watched the responses, prepared to jump in and signal him to cut it short, or lengthen it out, or just give him a quietly covert thumb's up.

"I knew it was illegal," he continues. "But I never thought of myself as breaking the law. I thought I just had to be cautious about buying it and using it. Then one night, it all kind of turned around. The federal agents you saw or heard about in the news approached me and JP to solicit our assistance because they found out that my boat—this boat we're on right now—was in the hands of ruthless mobsters, murderers, who turned out to be part of a drug lord's family."

He noticed some in the group start to squirm. "Aaaah, not to worry, we've had the entire boat fumigated and scrubbed down to get rid of all the germs and bad karma!"

Smiles—some no doubt of relief—worked their way around the deck like a football stadium "wave."

"Of course we had no way of knowing any of this, about the boat being illegally used, and we did try to answer the DEA Agents' questions, and provide them with whatever information we could, but in the process the two Narc's discovered my pot habit. Having these two DEA agents uncover my secret and berate me on my shortcomings, sent me a lightning bolt warning that threatened my very existence, and certainly my career and relationship with JP."

Maddigan and JP lock momentary eye contact. A sad look falls from his forehead like a stage curtain between acts.

"Anyway, I had the realization at that moment that I had taken things too far. The more I thought about it, the more I realized that escaping into drugs and making excuses for it was not a solution for me, but that it was in fact a problem, and a big one that I could suddenly see was only going to get worse. Have any of you experienced anything like that?"

Chapter 46

Mmmmmph

Epilogue
Same Time. Same Place.

JP un-straddles the captain's seat and, as she climbs down, swivels it around to face Maddigan, then leans back against it as she addresses the group.

Between thumb and forefinger, she absent-mindedly twists the hair that covers her left ear. "Rick even surprised me when he decided to give up pot. But, to put things in perspective, by the time he did that, we were already up to our ears in the whole boat/gangster mess, and knew we had to help the DEA Agents or risk facing public exposure of his addiction."

She pushes her hair behind her ears.

"And that would have cost him his teaching job, not to mention that the government would definitely have impounded the boat. So, none of this was what you might call a great heroic decision like the media made it out to be, but we did follow through -- we didn't back down from the challenge."

Like he had just taken the baton in a relay race handoff, Maddigan picked up the story. "JP's message here is an important one. I have to admit that it did feel good to have county officials and the media cast our roles as heroic, but we never thought it was justified. The truth is we did what we did because we were afraid." A distant look crossed his face; he lifted his glasses and rubbed his eyes.

"At the outset, we were afraid of losing my job and this boat. But as one of JP's favorite expressions—*like lickity-split*—those fears mushroomed into a something much scarier. Both of us cringed at the threats of being physically harmed, even killed."

Maddigan reaches to take a cup of water someone holds out to him, and sips.

"We acted out of necessity—maybe the same reason you're here with us right now? In other words, maybe you signed up for today's session because you felt a little bit desperate about trying to continue dealing with your own problems, on your own?"

He pauses and looks around. Sun reflections shimmer off the highly polished teak deck. The boat rises and falls gently within the bow-anchored circle of slightly choppy bay water that surrounds them. He stares vacantly out across the taut anchor line, past the precision-mounted boat equipment and perfectly looped lifesaving ropes. *One minute*, he thinks, *my brain feels like it hit a brick wall, and the next it's a scoop of ice cream oozing across a summer sun sidewalk in Sedona, Arizona.*

His mind drifts to turtle guts, classroom laughter, getting high, getting threatened, making love, and the Solamente Castle gun battle. But after an eternal half minute, he is jolted to reality, suddenly conscious of the surrounding group of seat cushion occupants looking up at him with wrinkled brows. He sees assorted hands covering mouths, holding back words. He continues.

"Whatever your reason is for being on this boat right this minute, it's the results you get from yourself that count! It's what you choose to make of your life from this point forward—not what you've done to get here, and not what you worry about on the way to where you're going."

Maddigan steps back as if on cue and JP slides off the seat and into an authoritative at rest, feet-apart-sea-legs stance. Embraced by the passing breezes, she steps out and seems to flow across the deck. She gestures with her hands, smiles with her eyes, and occasionally leans toward one person or another. She continues to stroll nonchalantly, her drawstring gauze pants billowing.

"You got that right, Rick!" She looks off to her left as if trying to remember details. "There was a moment when we were literally thrown on the floor at gunpoint in front of a roomful of gangsters. Rick had been head-bashed by one of their goons who caught us climbing through a basement window, which I'll explain in a minute. Our Professor here had one eye swollen shut and was a bloody, semi-conscious mess. I only had a few scrapes and scratches."

JP stops and turns away, as if afraid to continue. She unconsciously takes hold of the rolled canvas drop wall snapped to the custom roof that extends from the controls to the transom. She takes a deep breath and stares vacantly across the bow to a distant water-skier, then resumes, "They pushed back my jacket and shirt to hold my arms at my sides, and I had been stripped to my panties, then these creeps forced my legs apart while..." JP hesitates. Her face flushes. Tears build. She holds back a small choking sound, "...while the mob boss asked for a broom handle which he threatened to jam into me to force Rick to tell him why we'd broken into his home."

Gasps! More knees pull in. Two faces are buried in their knees. The rest now look horrified. JP is wiping tears away and catching her breath. Maddigan nods a gentle signal for to her to continue.

"I had one guy standing on each ankle and another on my shoulders...I...sorry...it's hard to not think about that, about how close we came to... we broke into the house to retrieve a microchip we knew they had. We knew it was there somewhere because they had earlier forced Rick to dig it out of a dead hundred pound Loggerhead turtle that they blackmailed him into finding in the swamp at night, in the middle of a raging storm.

"I mean they actually put a knife blade to his neck and threatened him unless he did this shitty (pardon me) disgusting job. These were the same animals that were connected to the person Rick bought pot from, and they threatened to expose his habit to the president of the college. So Rick agreed to go hunting for this turtle creature and then haul it back through all that muck off 7 Bridges Road; then he had to cut the thing up into hundreds of pieces to find the chip. Yuck! You can't even imagine how foul it all smelled."

Maddigan explains, "The chip they wanted me to find was coded with their drug deal plans that the DEA Agents needed. And we were the only ones who knew who the bastards were who were involved, because JP was able to intercept and copy their CB messages. We stayed up a couple of nights deciphering their names and codes."

"Right, and if it had not been for some quick thinking and action on Rick's part—and on the part of the mob-boss's niece who was there, who I had become friendly with—there's no chance on earth that we would even be here today."

"JP's not exaggerating about the niece. At the very last minute before we would surely have been tortured, she attacked her uncle. His gun went off as she knocked it away."

JP paused to take a deep breath. In the same way a yawn can be "catching," those who saw her followed suit. She drummed her fingers on the captain's chrome control panel, and then continued.

"Yeah, and the bullet hit the creep who tore off my clothes, the one who slugged Rick. He was the same muscle-head who dragged us up from the basement and threw us into the room. When the boss's son grabbed the gun, the niece's boyfriend soft-talked him, then snatched the gun away and shot both the son and the creep I told you about, who was already shot but was in the process of getting up to go after Rick.

"In all the commotion, Rick grabbed another gun that was in the room and nailed the mob boss in the stomach just as he was about to clock me and the niece. Whew! You know the rest from the news reports." She exhaled like a deflating balloon.

More gasps! "Holy shit!" Hands on heads. "Jesus!" Anguished looks. "Oh, my God! Sounds like a movie!" People are standing and group-hugging JP.

"Well," says Maddigan, "there's more, but at this point you need to hear the funny stuff too! Yes, there actually was some comedy that came out of this horror scene!"

The huggers start returning to their seats, hopeful looks are replacing the pained expressions.

"Really!" confirms JP. "Did you know that one end result of all this was that over thirty thousand cannonball-shaped hunks of hash and untold numbers of hash oil vials floated to the ocean's surface when the mob's boat sank?

"These vials and hash balls bobbed off into the night, and no one imagined ever seeing them again. But as some of you may have heard, over the next two days, those unbroken glass tubes and hunks of hash came surfing in on high tide to dozens of beaches all up and down the coast."

Smiles all around the deck.

"Ha!" exclaims Maddigan, "and did you know that every long-haired hippie within fifty miles stampeded over to the barrier island beaches with kayaks and surfboards?"

"And buckets and nets?" adds JP, now laughing. Everyone is now laughing.

Maddigan draws the biggest howls of all with his final report: "One guy told the police he was angry with them for keeping him off the beach because they ruined his one and only chance to find a stray ball of hash. He claimed just one of those one-pounders could have kept him and his whole family high for an entire year. When the cops got done laughing at that, this head-banded, long-haired, tie-dyed character started to cry. He whined that if they hadn't blocked him from romping through the sand, he might even have scored two or three hashballs, which would probably have enough to last a whole lifetime for himself and his mother!"

"So," JP wraps up as the laughter subsides, "there you have it dear Anchor Out friends: The 1981 HIGH Tide!"

"Okay," says Maddigan, "now let's spend the rest of this great day hearing each of your stories. And maybe we can begin by taking some deep breaths and focusing on the present here and now moment as we sit here rocking gently on the *Here & Now*.

Libby? Joe? How about the two of you start us off? What would you like most of all to change in your lives?"

"Hey, you already gave me more than enough incentive to stop drinking," says Joe, "and that was the main reason I came today, but I never thought I would want to quit booze just from hearing a story. I'm still shivering from JP's description of her ordeal."

And Joe's not alone," says Libby. "I thought I had big problems with my weight and eating too much junk food. What a joke! I mean you could have been killed, but you survived. No, actually, you flourished! I heard you have these sessions booked for six months in advance. That's wonderful! Anyway, I wasn't thinking I'd be talking about my eating problems here. The boat ride thing just seemed like a good way to get away from all that for the day. Now, I'm thinking I really can do something positive for myself. If you two can do all that in a few weeks, I should be able to get back to thin in a few months."

"Hey!" a voice from the cabin stairway, "you never told us what happened to the money. We heard you got some, but the newspapers also said that twelve and a half million bucks just disappeared. Is that true? Did it sink, or what? I mean should we be running up and down the coast looking for million-dollar-bills or whatever, to come skimming into our feet at high tide?"

"Not likely," responds JP. "All that cash floating in on the waves? Masses of humanity would invade the coast overnight. It would make the usual Jersey Shore Fourth of July beach crush look as sparse as a . . . one flea in a herd of elephants. And we wouldn't stand a chance of even getting near the water's edge."

She sips some water then continues, "Actually, Christopher, it's a good question that I'm surprised no one asked earlier. Rick and I get to split a percentage of what was recovered, so we each came away with about $600,000. That translates to a new boat so we have more living and group consulting space. It also affords us a major donation to the Seaport County College Building Fund to help pay construction costs for a new Student Communications Center, new radio station, and overhauled campus newspaper. I'll finally be able to fly my Dad to Arizona to see the famous cardiothoracic surgeon, Dr. Jeffrey Alpern. And, hmmm, Rick and I might even take a little vacation."

As she smiles and looks toward him, Maddigan nods approvingly.

"As for the rest of your question, Christopher," says Maddigan, "the missing $12.5 million? We hear indirectly that no one knows anything about it except that it appears to be being well-spent."

JP finishes with a broad grin: "The word is that plain, brown-paper-wrapped bundles of cash have been finding their way out of some remote jungles in South or Central America into the mailboxes of children's charity organizations around the world. Little handwritten notes are reportedly attached to each bundle, which say: *From 2 drowned fishermen.* These cash contributions have given giant financial boosts to Hale House in New York City, to St. Jude's Hospital for Children in Memphis, to Philadelphia's Shriner's Hospital and Children's Hospital of Philadelphia, and to Richmond Children's Center (now Richmond Community Services) up in Yonkers, New York. At least that's what we hear, so, hey! It's not buying drugs or weapons, right? And of course we're not sure of the source, but the anonymous notes certainly seem to point to the 1981 High Tide, y'think?"

Libby stood and swept her arm around the deck. "I bet everyone here would agree with me," she said, "that you two should take a deep breath yourselves, and..."

JP interrupts, laughing, "...and take up junkfood?"

The laughter was contagious.

JP stepped toward Maddigan, flashing her dimple.

"Hey," she says.

"Really JP! I can't believe you—a flea in a herd of elephants??"

"Well, okay. Hey, it might itch, but maybe a flea in a turtleneck sweater?

"Whoa! No more turtles in my life, fleeced or otherwise!"

"Fleas, not fleeced. You know what? You should just give me a kiss, Professor!"

"Here? Now? JP, honestly, I...Mmmmmph."

The applause could be heard halfway across the bay.
"Mmmmmph."

ACKNOWLEDGEMENTS AND VERY SPECIAL THANKS

To "JP" for the inspiration. To my astoundingly creative, talented, award-winning children—theatre teacher/producer/director Haley Murphy, and musician/composer/arranger and jazz recording artist Christopher Alpiar—for their endless love and support throughout and beyond that it took to complete this book.

To Richmond Community Services in Yonkers, New York, for the lifetime of love and dedicated caregiving to my special-needs daughter Melissa, enabling me to pursue my writing with greater freedom. To my brother Rick and his wife Ann, and my brother-in-law Tim for their friendship, trust, and kicks in the butt. To my NJ and DE softball buddies for their camaraderie and positive energy.

To my three sensational grandchildren Talley, Dylan, and Gwyn—and yes, my dear dogs, Zug, Olebollen, Captain, Sam, Maddigan, Tuckerton, Barnegat Girl, and now Breezy and Gracie—for all the unsolicited love and endless stress relief.

To my "California Girl," Jonena: You came to my doorstep at the most crushing time of my life, with arms full of love, guidance, encouragement and companionship. Thank you for helping me get back on the path of self-acceptance and well-being. I am a better writer and a better person because of you. To Donna, Pegi, Gail, David, Dave, Marie, Tennant, Sally, Jim, Sandy, Ed, Peggy, Terry,

Margi, Linda, Michael, John, Carol, Kevin, Danielle, Bill and Carl for all the extra pushes when I ran out of steam.

To the officers and staff personnel of the United States Coast Guard Station at Manasquan Inlet, Point Pleasant Beach, New Jersey, for your service to our country, and for allowing me full access to your facility, equipment, emergency systems and pursuit vessels—and for your unparalleled courtesy.

To the Newark, New Jersey-based DEA agents and New Jersey State Police Officers I befriended (gentlemen ALL, to the core) for your service and for your professional insights and hands-on help. To my friend Ken Motz for helping me figure out how to sabotage the trawler, *Maltese*.

To my publisher, editor, and friend, Valerie Connelly. She helped me rise above the political quagmire of literary agents and traditional publishing houses to make *HIGH TIDE* a reality. She made my story sing. Thank You!

ABOUT THE AUTHOR

HIGH TIDE is Hal Alpiar's first novel. An Amazon five-star author, Hal won a national book award for *DOCTOR SHOPPING... How to Choose the Right Doctor for You and Your Family* (HIP, 1996). He is also the author of *DOCTOR BUSINESS ...How to Boost Practice Growth and Strengthen Long-Term Relationships* (PMIC, 1995) a book for physicians. Both books were the products of his thirty years of personal, professional, and business development work.

Hal earned major small business and teaching honors along with national marketing awards. His short story "Dirt Floor Visit" was published in *THE ART OF GRANDPARENTING* (Nightengale Press, 2009). A commissioned 300-page memoir Hal wrote, *GOOD LUCK! Wisdom from a Life of Leadership in Turbulent Times* was published in 2010, and another, *HIGHWAY TO A HIGHER AUTHORITY. . . Driving Faith-Based Business through America's Trucking Industry,* is slated to be published in 2013. He is also a children's self-esteem development author and a published poet. As an educator, Hal custom-designed and delivered leadership seminars and webinars to more than 20,000 healthcare professionals, business owners and corporate management students. He contributed to two #1 New York Times and Wall Street Journal best-selling business books. As an entrepreneur, he created, edited, and published numerous business and healthcare magazines, and scripted and hosted more than two years' worth of his own daily radio show, *BUSI-NESSWORKS ON THE AIR*. Hal's entrepreneurial leadership blog www.BusinessWorks.US has been ongoing since April, 2008. A native New Yorker and thirty-year resident of New Jersey, he presently resides in coastal Delaware, where he is working on the sequel to *HIGH TIDE*.

Entrepreneurial Leadership Blog
www.BusinessWorks.US *(Ongoing since April 2008)*

Dedicated website for this book
www.HighTideNOW.com

Author Contact Welcome
Hal@TheWriterWorks.com

THANK YOU
FOR THE PERSONAL AND/OR FINANCIAL SUPPORT
THAT IT TOOK TO MAKE THIS BOOK A REALITY

Emily Abbott

Melanie Adair

John & Carol Allen

Dr. Jeffrey Alpern

Christopher Alpiar

Honey & Harry Alpiar

Rick & Ann Papa Alpiar

Lois Anderson

Bonnie & Clyde Austin

Walter & Stephanie Bandurski

Ed Banning

Jeff Banning

Tennant & Sally Barron

Sheila Birmingham

Marguerite Blattner

Barrie (Proctor) Bonacci

Kevin Bousquet

Ted & Rose Brown

Bruce Burchell

Charles & Marie Burton

Marjorie & Sal Corrallo

Gene Danneman

George Danneman Esq.

Ernst Dannemann

Petrice (Flipse) DiVanno

Dave & Marie Drayer

Susan & Gary Duchesneau

Jim Duffy

Dorothy Edmonds

Tony Emanueli

Frank Farrell

Barbara & Brian Favretto

Maribeth Fischer

Dennis Forney

Dr. Ian Fries

Richard Frome

Candi Frost

Joe Gahm

Bill & Rene Gilligan

Gregory & Donna Goings

Esther Groves

Jim & Tara Haines

Gail & David Hall

Jim & Sandy Hall

Linda Harp

Helen Harris

Rev. Gary Hayden

Roger Holowchak

Michael & Naomi Infusino

Dr. Arvind Jain

Jim & Annette Jordan

Rhodie Jorgenson

Karen Kavanagh
John J. King
Barbara Knoll
Suresh & Niva Kodolikar
Ken & Sara Kraft
Carol Kirsimägi
Andy Larrimore
Russ Lederman
Peter & Beatrice Leeds
Jenna Legnaioli
Robert Luzius
Patricia Magee
Charlotte Mari
Beverly Marsh
Cherry Marshall
Marian Marshall
Tim Marshall
Timothy Marshall
Dr. Andrew Moreland
Ken Motz
Bill & Danielle Dixon-Moyle
Haley & Harrison Murphy
John & Jan Oleson
Dr. Wilmot Oliver
Jim & Leslie Oliviero
Tammy Ordway
Ken Peach

Duncan & Joann Peek
Juris & Rosly Schlup Piece
Carl Pierce
Ken & Lois Poppele
Christopher Rausch
Rehoboth Beach Writer's Guild
Jerry Relth
Jonena Relth
Joe Rose
Ernie & Graceann Roy
Joe & June Santucci
Mike Slosberg
Ed & Peggy Smith
Ryan Smith
SonRise Church, Berlin MD
Tina Stafford
Lee Summerville
Pegi Taylor
Terry & Margi Thomas
Gail Tolpin
Richard & Karen Townsend
Kelly Trombino
Ken & Ginny Van Zile
Judy Vorfeld
Bob Wainwright
Heather Walker
Bo & Lois Wood

www.ingramcontent.com/pod-product-compliance
Lightning Source LLC
Chambersburg PA
CBHW051241260626
47162CB00002B/547